Praise for Vicious Rumer

'Brutal, stylish and relentless, *Vicious Rumer* is a blistering read' – **Chris Whitaker, author of** *All The Wicked Girls*

'This dark, twisting tale never does what you expect. Rumer is a strong, relentless heroine fighting the odds' – **CJ Daugherty, author of** *The Echo Killing*

'Razor sharp. A savage YA journey in the vein of Richard Kadrey's Sandman Slim series' – **Lucas Maxwell, UK Librarian of the Year 2017**

'Unpredictable, brutal, and utterly compelling' – **A Fantastical Librarian**

'A gripping and moody psychological thriller. It'll keep you up all night' – **Closer**

'A rare treat. Rumer is dark, demented and dangerous to know. I can guarantee you'll love her, just pray you never ever meet her' – **The Eloquent Page**

'One of the best YA thrillers I've read this year. You'll want to tell everybody about *Vicious Rumer*' – **Bookmark That**

'I loved *Vicious Rumer* so much! Impossible to put down and Rumer is one of the best female protagonists I've ever read. Think Jessica Jones meets Ellen Ripley!' – **Between The Pages**

'Clever and compelling... A must read' – **Set the Tape**

'If you're looking for a no-holds-barred thriller, look no further. *Vicious Rumer* boasts a Luther-ish kind of noir that makes for a loaded, dark story' – **The Roaring Bookworm**

About the Author

Joshua Winning is an author and film journalist who writes for *Total Film*, *SFX* and *Radio Times*. He has been on set with Kermit the Frog, devoured breakfast with zombies on *The Walking Dead* and sat on the Iron Throne while visiting the *Game Of Thrones* set in Dublin. Jeff Goldblum once told him he looks a bit like Paul Bettany.

A geek at heart, Joshua grew up watching *Labyrinth* and *The NeverEnding Story* on repeat, and was raised on a steady diet of Whedon, Cameron and Lucas. His literary heroes include Robin Jarvis, Stephen King and Daphne du Maurier. As a journalist, he has interviewed some of the most exciting names in the film industry, including Jodie Foster, Ryan Reynolds, Charlize Theron and Christopher Lee. He dreams of getting Sigourney Weaver to yell 'Goddammit!' at him one day. Joshua's dark fantasy series *The Sentinel Trilogy* is published by Peridot Press.

VICIOUS RUMER

VICIOUS RUMER

JOSHUA WINNING

Unbound Digital

This edition first published in 2018

Unbound

6th Floor Mutual House, 70 Conduit Street, London W1S 2GF

www.unbound.com

ISBN (eBook): 978-1-912618-01-9

ISBN (Paperback): 978-1-912618-00-2

Design by Mecob

Cover images:
© iStockphoto.com / bmchurch
© Shutterstock.com Openclipart.org

Printed in Great Britain by Clays Ltd, St Ives Plc

Dear Reader,

The book you are holding came about in a rather different way to most others. It was funded directly by readers through a new website: Unbound.

Unbound is the creation of three writers. We started the company because we believed there had to be a better deal for both writers and readers. On the Unbound website, authors share the ideas for the books they want to write directly with readers. If enough of you support the book by pledging for it in advance, we produce a beautifully bound special subscribers' edition and distribute a regular edition and e-book wherever books are sold, in shops and online.

This new way of publishing is actually a very old idea (Samuel Johnson funded his dictionary this way). We're just using the internet to build each writer a network of patrons. Here, at the back of this book, you'll find the names of all the people who made it happen.

Publishing in this way means readers are no longer just passive consumers of the books they buy, and authors are free to write the books they really want. They get a much fairer return too – half the profits their books generate, rather than a tiny percentage of the cover price.

If you're not yet a subscriber, we hope that you'll want to join our publishing revolution and have your name listed in one of our books in the future. To get you started, here is a £5 discount on your first pledge. Just visit unbound.com, make your pledge and type RUMER18 in the promo code box when you check out.

Thank you for your support,

Dan, Justin and John
Founders, Unbound

Super Patrons

Ginny Abell
Scott Anderson
Richard Bailey
Derren Ball
Caroline Banks
Steve Barnes
Jonathan Barnes
Thom Baylay
Samantha Billing
Charlotte Birch
David Blackburn-Clarke
Michelle Bornestad
Dave Bradley
Paul Bradshaw
Bobby Brook
Jay Brown
Jonny Bunyan
John Burns
Tanvir Bush
Victoria Butler
Christina Byford
Erin Callahan
Matt Chapman
Bonnie Clarke
Isabel Cooke
Katharine Corr
Sally Costa
Tracie Couper
Emily Ip & Steven Coyne
Sara Almira Cruz
Dad
Dan Dalton

Becca Day-Preston
Tinaz Denizmen
Emma Dibdin
Sarah Dobbs
Hannah Dolan
Rhian Drinkwater
Lisa Duley
Peter Duley
Mike Duley
Paul Duley
Phil Dunning
Jordan Farley
Kate Fitzpatrick
Rosie Fletcher
Troy H. Gardner
Robert Gershinson
Dianne Herrera Ghiringhelli
Suzy Gillett
Lydia Gittins
Philip Gittins
Matt Glasby
Alison Goody
Clare Gray
Michael Green
Stephen Green
John Hale
Kat Harvey
Jonathan Hatfull
Sam Haysom
Peter Heath
Kirsty Heath
Tom Hedley
Jamie Hewett
Torsten Højer
Susi Holliday
Richard Hollis

Kristian Hood
Kate Huff
Oli Jacobs
Clare Jarvis
Robert Jones
Richard Jordan
Tina Kendall
Michael Kennedy
Patrick Kincaid
Caroline Knell
Hugh Langley
Becky Lea
Alice Levick
Kate Lloyd
Matt Looker
Karl Ludvigsen
Shelley Marsden
Duncan Marshall
Marie Mathieson
Matthew Maytum
Scott Mckenzie
Sarah McMullan
Laurie McShea
Kirk Millis-Ward
Tim Mitchell
James Mottram
Darryl Nash
Roseanne Neal
Jayne Nelson
Kwaku Osei-Afrifa
Marka Palmer
Helle Patterson
Becca Philbin
Nev Pierce
Ellie Piercy
Steven Pomphrett

Abigail Potter
Mary Ramsden
Laura Reed
Matt Risley
Clare Robinson
Jorge García Rodríguez
Nate Roscoe
Lydia Ruffles
Sue Rylance
James Sambrook
Shaun Shaun
Sam Sheppard
Sam Sheppard
Krystal Sim
Rich Simmonds
Simon Simsav
Buffy Anne Summers
Natalie Taylor
Sophie Taylor
Jillian Tees
Joe Treherne
Meggie Treherne
Lisa Turner
Ali Upham
Graeme Vasey
Andrew Veal
Rose Walton
Shar Warner-Barnes
Gregory Winning
Ann Winning
Jeremy Woodhouse
Lynn Worton
Lois Wreathall
Delaney Zugelder

With grateful thanks to Mike Duley who helped to make this book happen.

CHAPTER ONE

I've killed more people than I can count but I never meant to. I'm not a murderer. Not in the way you're thinking, because I never *wanted* to kill anybody. Not really.

People have spat threats at me for years.

You're dead, Rumer!

You just bought a one-way ticket to hell!

I am SO going to kill you!

But they don't mean it. They can't know what it's like to end somebody's life, and when it's over, it's over. That's how it seems to me. No pearly gates. No chorus of angels. They put you in the ground, heap dirt on the box. Life goes on.

The people I killed, I couldn't help it.

Remember that when I tell you what comes next.

I'm holding a hammer. It's already bloody and the guy in the chair is screaming. When he's not screaming, he's sobbing like a baby. Like he needs his mummy, but mummy's not here and I figure if I shatter a few more bones, he'll remember that.

The sight of him makes my gut spasm.

No. Be angry. Angry because he should be talking by now. Not making me do this. I'm so exhausted I'd disintegrate if he threw a punch but he doesn't have that option with his hands bound up in masking tape.

'Rumer, enough. You don't want him to pass out.'

The voice comes from over my shoulder. Gruff and male. I barely register it. Everything has an unreal quality, like the cellar has no air and the floor's a bog of sucking cement.

Besides, I know what I'm doing. This is what it takes, right? I've been messed around, dragged halfway to hell and back, and all I need is for this guy to talk. Surrender a black pearl of information. Then I can drop the hammer and try to forget what I did to his face.

The guy's a mess. He's bound up in the chair, beaten beyond recognition, his shirt and jeans soaked with sweat and blood. Some of it's on my hoodie but I try to ignore it. Because none of this is real, right? I'm daydreaming, or night-dreaming, and soon I'll wake up with springs in my back and the leaky ceiling of my flat above me.

Except he's looking at me. One eye's puffy and closed up, like it can't bear to watch any more. I don't blame it. I probably look half mad. Sweat plasters my hair to my face and I'm shaking, static crackling in my ears.

I have to do this. I have to.

The growl rumbles up from my gut. 'Tell me what she wants and I'll stop.'

The thought that she's after me nearly sends me crazier than I already am. She's on her way now. I know it. Clutching cursed pendants and muttering hexes and seeking me out in the night, determined to undo me. Unmake me.

If I let that happen, none of this will matter.

'Tell me what she wants!' My voice is a shriek and he may be a mess on the outside, but he can tell I'm a mess on the inside.

The non-closed-up eye rolls in its socket, focuses on me. The guy spits blood at the floor. Some of it gets on my boot.

And for the first time I think I might kill somebody on purpose.

CHAPTER TWO

Two things about me:

1. I never looked for trouble a day in my life.
2. Trouble always, always finds me.

Part One
THE PIT

CHAPTER THREE

TWO DAYS BEFORE THE HAMMER

The back of the van is as cold as a meat locker and so dark I can't see. It wants to eat me. The dark. I've spent long enough in dark places to know. I'm slumped against the freezing metal and the van shakes me like it's trying to digest me, but I'm being stubborn and just sitting here, knees drawn up to my chest and trying to figure out how the hell I ended up in this pathetic state.

The dark's so complete that, when I first came to, I thought I was underground. Buried deep. Soil cramming into my mouth. The nightmare I've had since I was a kid. My first instinct was to choke it down, fight the clawing panic, surrender to the shadows, but that would have meant giving in, and Rumer Cross is no fucking coward.

I cough but there is no soil in my throat. I'm not in the ground. The back of the van's echoey and so cold my fingers are numb, and I'm here because of *him*.

The man in the street asked for a light then he knocked mine out. I was outside my place and I saw the fist coming, but I didn't move in time. He must have bundled me into the van I saw at the kerb. The engine grumbles somewhere behind me and, as annoyance hollows out my gut, I spy a hairline crack of light where the rear doors must be.

My head pounds and I go to scratch fingers through my hair, but they won't move. My wrists are bound behind me.

'Guy's a pro,' I mutter.

What does he want? And why the hell didn't I duck when he made a knuckle sandwich with his hand? That one I can answer; I didn't duck because nobody ever looks twice at me. I'm used to slithering around invisibly because I'm a shadow.

And I'm only half being dramatic. I've learnt to get by unnoticed – not that there's anything that noticeable about me anyway. I could be any twentysomething city chick, my jeans a little rattier, my home-cut black hair more tangled, always getting in my face, which is a sun-shy kind of pale. Kids at school called me 'Oddzilla' and 'Tumour' thinking it would hurt me. Fuck them.

That punch hurt, though. My mouth feels weird. Numb and... big. Swollen. The guy must have a serious collection of rings. I run my tongue over my teeth and taste metal. A jag of pain shoots through my gum. One of them is broken.

Forget the teeth.

I can't remember what the guy looks like. It was raining and my hood was up, so I didn't see him until he was right by me and, when he asked for a light, the rain got in my eyes.

He caught me at a bad time. I'd lost the guy I was shadowing and I was in a foul mood.

Is that why I'm in the van? Is this guy a disgruntled client? Somebody I followed?

Nobody's ever caught me following them, though. That's how good I am at melting into the background, like one of those artists who paint themselves as brick walls or bookcases.

I wish I could remember his face.

No. I need to get out. It feels like I'm in a coffin, the van shrinking around me and, if I think about that too much, it seems like the coffin has no air and the earth's weighing it down until I'm crushed.

The doors. If I can get to them, I'm home free.

As I try to push myself into a sitting position, I discover my feet are bound, too.

'Fanfriggintastic.'

Finally, I'm on my knees. I reach for my boot, but the knife I keep there is gone. I swear and bite my lip. Biting my swollen lip makes me want to curse even louder, but I catch the curse and swallow it and focus on getting out. Getting to the sliver of light.

I shuffle on my knees and wonder how filthy it is in here. The reek of oil sears my nostrils. I keep shuffling, inch by inch, wondering how big this goddamn van really is, until finally I'm at the doors. I wrestle with the bindings at my wrists, but they bite my flesh, refusing to let go.

'Up,' I order. 'Get up.'

It's crazy how difficult moving is when your feet are bound and your hands are behind your back. Even without the rocking van. I think of the driver and I suck in a lungful of stinking air, throwing myself against the doors, digging my boots into the floor.

I'm panting now and it's like I'm in a furnace. Sweat stings my eyes, but I'm up. I lean into the door and fumble for the handle.

There's no goddamn handle.

I release a mad laugh. I never was lucky.

The screech of tyres tears into my dark hole and the van jolts under my feet. I'm tossed through the darkness. My face smashes the floor. Everything's spinning and I'm not too proud to admit I might spew. I'm so busy trying not to heave my guts onto the van floor it takes me a moment to realise we've stopped.

Through the throbbing in my skull, I hear the driver getting out. Footsteps crunch and keys rattle. Grey light stabs the dark away.

'Wakey wakey.'

The voice is tarred with nicotine.

Lying on my front, I feel vulnerable and exposed. Fear pumps in my temples and, yeah, this is bad. I twist around, trying to get a look at the guy, but he's just a blurry outline, like he's drawn with chalk. He's carrying something. It goes over my head and I'm in the dark again.

'Out,' hacks the nicotine-tarred voice. Something drags at my wrists and I'm hauled into the rain. The guy's strong. He seems to have forgotten my feet are tied, though, and I roar as I bellyflop to the ground. The rain batters me. My jeans and jacket tighten around my skin.

'Are you a moron?' I shout.

'Quiet.' Hands yank at my ankles and the ropes slacken. I fight the relief as I kick them off.

'Up.'

I scramble to my feet, still blind with the bag over my head, the cuffs working at my wrists like razors.

'Go,' orders Nicotine Man. A hand slaps my backside and every nerve in my body erupts. I don't move. My jaw twitches with anger.

'Walk!' the man snaps. He's to my left. I can see his filthy boots kicking the tarmac. I'm betting he's armed, but that won't matter with the element of surprise.

'I said–' Nicotine Man begins, but I cut him off by snapping my head at him. Our skulls crack together and purple stars pop inside the blackness of the bag.

Nicotine Man shrieks and I bury my knee in what I hope is his groin. He shrieks again and I can't help smiling, shaking the bag from my head, savouring the rain as it runs down my face.

'Broke my goddamn nose.' He spits blood on the ground. He's wearing rain-flecked sunglasses and he's older than I thought. Mid-fifties, but lean with muscle, like a racehorse. Not a single hair on his head.

I hesitate when I see the gun holstered at his hip, but he's clutching his face, red dribbling between his fingers.

I run.

A derelict warehouse squats across a grey patch of tarmac. I run in the opposite direction, towards the forest. I can lose him there.

'Hey!'

Footsteps scrape the tarmac behind me. He won't shoot. He wouldn't go to all this trouble if somebody wanted me dead. Whoever his boss is, I'm betting he'd be angry if I turned up with a hole in my head. That's what I tell myself, but it doesn't stop my heart crashing against my ribs as if it's trying to outrace me.

I barely make it ten paces before I'm tackled to the ground. My hair's in my face and I can't see. He punches me in the kidneys and I coil up, the breath trapped in my throat.

'Stupid cow.' He jerks me upright and I get a twinge of satisfaction from seeing his bent nose.

'What the hell do you want?' I cough.

His hacking laugh starts again.

'Why don't you ask *them*?'

There's movement in the corner of my eye. The warehouse's battered doors are open and five figures in black suits and masks stand outside, each of them training a gun on me.

Nicotine Man's laughter fills my ears as the bag goes back over my head.

CHAPTER FOUR

I found out what my mother did when I was little.

They said that if you saw her, you started looking for a priest or a bottle of whisky. If you saw Celene Cross, you'd know you were finished. Everybody had heard about the places she'd been, the things she left behind. The way she set a place to rot, and no matter what you did, it'd keep rotting until it collapsed around you.

I've seen pictures online and in newspaper clippings. She looks like she grinds bullets for fun. Like nobody could ever hurt her, and she's hurt people, so she knows all about that.

There was one night, though, that changed everything.

She's pregnant but that doesn't make her soft. Her eyes are black cigarette burns, her hair dark and clinging to waxy skin. That's how I imagine her, anyway. She claws through the night, her cheekbones like jagged blades. The door damn near buckles under her hammering. When it finally opens, she staggers inside, almost crumples to the floor, only someone catches her. She's hauled to a bed, her teeth crunching together.

'No,' she grunts, batting hands away. 'Him. I need *him*.'

When the priest appears, he's carrying a wriggling lamb. Its tongue sticks out at her and my mother clutches between her legs, writhing in pain.

There are no comforting words. No reassuring caresses.

He tears her dress at her belly. Red splatters, still warm. Lamb's blood, spraying from its sliced throat, its head limp and dangling.

That's where I came in. Or out. My mother screamed and writhed and screamed some more and out I slithered. But I didn't scream. I didn't make a sound. I was purple and I didn't move, which is how she knew I was dead.

They say she didn't even stop to check. A woman gives birth, she's supposed to lie there and think about it. Not her. She took off like Beelzebub had her name and address, and she never looked back. She came out of the night and she went straight back into it.

Thing is, I didn't die.

The priest thumped my back and I coughed a breath, then kept on breathing.

They say the dead lamb started bleating then.

They say the house shook on its foundations and a shadow passed across the moon.

They say a lot of things.

The only truth I know: my mother was a terrible person. She killed and she didn't care. Sometimes they called her the Witch Assassin or the Red Widow. Other times The Ghost, maybe because people hardly ever saw her. She went into a place, did her thing, then left. Afterwards, it was like she'd never been there. The dead people had maybe done it to themselves. She was a whisper without an echo.

I'm pretty sure she wished I didn't exist, either, when she found out she was pregnant. It's not like I've seen her since. She died a few weeks later. Washed up in the Thames, pale and broken. The papers said she had it coming, she'd pissed off too many powerful people, but what do the papers know? They buried her in a cemetery in North London. Seeya, Celene. Nice knowing ya.

I shouldn't be alive.

Sometimes I wish I wasn't. I suppose some days, a lot of people wish they weren't. If you've got a crummy job or you hate the person you used to love.

If I had been dead a lot of things wouldn't have happened.

CHAPTER FIVE

Glass crunches under my boots. If I look down, I just about glimpse the grimy warehouse floor under the bag over my head. I hear rain again, the tinkling of chains – and something else. Scratchy music. The ghostly trill of a trumpet.

A hot stench floods my nostrils and I almost heave into the bag. It smells like rotting meat.

'It's worse than a morgue in here,' I mutter.

Something digs into my back. The barrel of a gun. I keep walking. I swear I can taste whatever's curdling the warehouse air. I'm actually grateful for the bag; it must be masking at least a little of the stench.

As I'm pushed on the music grows louder. A door opens and I'm shoved forward, presumably into another room, though it's hard to tell. Something solid knocks the backs of my knees and I land in what must be a chair. Pinching hands bind my feet to the chair legs. I clasp my tied hands together in my lap, rubbing my knuckles, reminding myself to breathe.

Feet scuff away and a door shuts. It's just me and the crackling record. I assume I'm alone. Reedy music warbles louder than ever and a smoky voice croons about how some guy did her wrong, how he was bad, bad, bad. The usual.

My head jerks to the side. There's another sound. Soft breathing. Somebody's nearby.

'So, here she is. The living Rumer.'

She hisses my name. There's a hint of an accent in her voice, but I can't tell where from. How does she know my name?

The bag's torn away.

My eyes are fuzzy after the darkness and I blink the room gradually into focus. Slatted blinds filter in a neon haze. Something brushes my cheek. The room's filled with strange ornaments and little shadows flutter everywhere. Butterflies. They cling to spider plants and caress the faces of Chinese dragons.

I thought we were in a warehouse, but this could be a seedy boudoir. There's even a chandelier. Across the room, a figure lounges on a sofa. In the gauzy light, she's little more than a shapely outline as she leans into embroidered pillows, dark hair tumbling, smoke curling up from a cigarette.

My stomach's alive with snakes. For a crazy moment I think it's my mother. Or the ghost of her. She's gouged her way out of the ground and, when the light breaks over her face, it'll be falling apart in chunks, her empty eye sockets like screaming mouths.

No. It can't be her. She's long dead, although that might explain the warehouse's stink.

'When a man loses something, he loses more than the object that is taken from him. Don't you agree?' The outline on the sofa speaks. 'He also loses a part of himself.'

I twist in the chair but the ropes chew my ankles. 'I don't know what you're talking about.'

The figure sits up. Yellow light breaks over a disarmingly pretty face. She wears a patterned kimono that forms a V over a muscular chest and I realise it's not a woman at all. The man's eyelids are painted pink. He puts a fresh cigarette to his lips. The flicker of orange from the lighter briefly illuminates his face and I see one of his eyes is milky white.

'No matter what a man loses when something is taken from him, the thief always comes off worse in the end.' His voice rasps like torn paper. It wavers between masculine and feminine. Soft then snarling. 'Jealousy is a dog's bark which attracts thieves. And you thought you could take from me without consequence.'

'Take…? I haven't taken anything from you.'

Something on his hand catches the light. A silver ring.

'I have little time for thieves and even less time for liars.'

Thief? Liar? I've been both, but I've never seen this man before. Whatever he thinks I've done, he's mistaken. He rises from the sofa and pads slowly towards me, muscle rippling, skin gleaming. I've seen drag queens. They're beautiful. Animated. This guy wears femininity the way a maggot wears an apple.

'Tell me where it is.' He pulls on the cigarette. Orange embers simmer in his eyes and the smoky one shifts as if it's sensed something mystical, something invisible to normal sight.

'I don't know what you're talking about,' I say. 'I haven't taken anything from you.'

He bares his teeth and there's a wink of gold. 'She lies with her mother's tongue.'

My stomach boils. He knew my mother?

I've forgotten about the rotting stench filling the warehouse. The butterflies. The scratchy music. Everything around him fades and it's just me and the man in the kimono. I chew my tongue, preventing the questions from erupting in a stinky spew.

He stubs the cigarette out in an ornate ashtray.

'You'll tell me,' he whispers. 'You'll tell me where the Crook Spear is.'

He's so close I smell his perfume. Cinnamon and something bitter. I'm certain I've never seen him before. I'd remember a face like that. I've shadowed plenty of people for Julian, followed them into alleys and grimy bars, but never this man. He's not like the others. They're petty criminals. This guy would eat them for brunch.

'I've never heard of any Crook Spear,' I say.

'Lies! I will not stand for them!'

He's trembling now, snarling, his pink fingernails contorted into claws.

'You've got the wrong person,' I say, desperation edging into my voice, because the look he's giving me is like needles and white fire. It makes me flush hot and cold and still the record singer croons about her rotten lover, her bad man.

'You'll never leave this place alive.' Again the accent, soft but implacable. The threat seems to calm him. He's back in control. When he speaks again, his voice is as thick as syrup. 'The Crook Spear. Where is it?'

'I've never heard of it.' My shoulders ache and I realise they're up by my ears.

'Your mother would be proud. The lie doesn't even sound like a lie.'

'What's she got to do with this?'

He strokes my cheek. 'In time. You will tell me where it is in time.' He looks past me. 'Take her to the pit.'

Nicotine Man has been standing behind me throughout the whole thing. He tugs my restraints and I kick my legs free. Before he can stop me, I'm on my feet, knotting my bound hands together and pounding them into his gut. He makes an 'oof' sound but grabs my hair and yanks. As my eyes stream, I thrash in his grip, but no matter how hard I resist, I can't stop him dragging me out of the boudoir and back into the warehouse.

Angry yells echo all around me, taunting me in waves, and I'm only half aware they're mine.

I'm hauled into a dirty grey square of a room. The smell's so awful bile bubbles up from the pit of my stomach. I see a rusted grate in the floor just as it's heaved up by a man in a black suit and a mask that covers his eyes.

'You've got to be kidding me–' I begin, but then I notice Nicotine Man's drawn a blade from his belt. His brows knit together and he's enjoying this, snatching my hands and running the blade through my restraints.

My hands snap free but then Nicotine Man tips me through the hole in the floor.

And I'm falling.

Falling.

Then *crunch*, cement breaks my fall. Angry fireworks fizz in my brain but, as I spit dust and grunt into the floor, something worse distracts me. I try to stop panting; try not to breathe the stinking air at all, because now I know where the stench is coming from.

I'm surrounded by dead bodies.

CHAPTER SIX

I'm ten and I've chopped all the hair off my foster sister's Barbie. I've used a black felt-tip pen to colour in her nails and I've smudged half moons under her eyes. Then I tell my foster sister that this isn't Barbie, it's Hormonal Harriet, who's addicted to sleeping pills. One night, Harriet took so many of them she didn't wake up for a week. She slept for so long her starving dog ate her left foot before she came to.

My foster sister runs screaming to her parents before I can close the scissors around Harriet's plastic foot.

(And yes, ten is young to know the word 'hormonal', but what can I say? I'm good at eavesdropping on my foster mother when she's bitching about her colleagues.)

I still have a few customised Barbies in my flat. I pinned one to my headboard like a voodoo doll. Not because I like Barbies. I'm not sure why I keep them around. I suppose they're a joke but at least they're in on it. Sometimes they feel more human than the people I shadow.

For a moment, I imagine I'm sinking into the worn mattress that came with the flat. The jar of bottle caps by the bed. A torn Stevie Nicks poster on the wall. Small touches, little things to make it mine instead of a cardboard box.

The mattress is solid cement, though, and I'm not in my flat.

I snap to, coughing into the floor. I must've passed out. A person can only take so many knocks before the shutters come down. My eyes scratch open and my lips peel over my teeth so I can draw a ragged breath, tracing a hand over my ribs. As I raise myself up off the floor, the memory of where I am is a fresh blow to the chest.

Indistinct shapes surround me, motionless and reeking.

Uneasiness skitters like a spider in my mind. It's been there for as long as I can remember, the spider, huddled in a dark corner, watching, listening, brooding on the things it sees.

The nearest corpse looks like it's laughing at me. It's lying directly under the grate in the ceiling and a net of grey light lies over it. I can't believe I didn't land on it when Nicotine Man threw me in here. The corpse seems to think that's funny, too.

She.

The corpse used to be a she. I can tell from the dress, which is dirty and ripped, but has flowers on it and probably used to be pretty.

I ease myself up from the floor, then scoot back into the shadows. The wall props me up and I hug my knees to my chest. Everything hurts. My wrists remember ropes and I caress the bruised skin, then stop because it stings too much. I grit my teeth and the jag of pain is a reminder that one of them is broken.

With faint relief, I realise the stink of bodies doesn't bother me as much as it did earlier. Funny how quickly you get used to something, though it might just be that the sight of them is worse.

I count ten. Ten bodies. There could be more beyond the light.

The nearest one is still laughing at me and I realise I'm the punchline. I follow people for a living but death follows me. Everybody I've ever been close to has died.

That's what my mother left me with. The curse.

It's so quiet I'm embarrassed to breathe. The shapes in the dark must think I'm mocking them.

How long did it take for her to die, the woman in the flower dress? She's lying on her front like she's sunbathing but her head's to the side and her dried-out eye sockets gawp at me.

Are they going to keep me in here until I'm like her?

No, they need me alive. They think I have the Crook Spear, whatever that is. Why does he think that? The guy in the kimono mentioned my mother – he talked like he knew her. I've never met anybody who knew my mother and curiosity nettles the spider in my mind. The stories I've read about her, it's not inconceivable that she knew somebody like him. The kind of person with a corpse pit.

Is she the reason I'm in here? Miles away from the cruddy flat I call home? All these years later, she's still fucking up my life.

My life feels so far away. I wonder if Julian knows I'm missing. Would he track me down? Or would he shrug, put his feet up on the desk and say he knew I'd do a runner one day? That's more likely. I'm just one of his paper cups attached to a piece of string. Who cares if one of the strings gets cut? He has a dozen more.

What about Bolt? My gut shrivels and I try not to think about him. I shouldn't be thinking about him anyway.

I breathe deeply and choke on the stench, pushing thoughts of Bolt and Julian and my mother away, drawing a curtain over them. Especially my mother.

It's going to be okay. They won't kill me until I tell them where the spear is.

Unless they decide I don't have it. Then what? I'm dead and funky like everybody else down here, smelling like the worst kind of meat you forgot was at the back of the fridge. Which is poetic justice, right? I've killed so many people in my nineteen years I was always going to end up somewhere like this. It was only a matter of time. I almost start laughing with the she-corpse.

A scuffling sound freezes me where I am. I wait, expecting a rat to dart across the floor. Or maybe there are bugs. A few of the bodies look like they've been here long enough to become maggot farms.

Another scuffle and this time I see where it's coming from. In the far corner, a slumped form. It's too dark for me to really see, but it's definitely a person. A male person, I think.

Somebody else is alive down here?

I fight the impulse to creep closer. He's down here, which means he did something to piss off Butterfly Man. He could be dangerous. I was thrown down here for something I didn't do, though. Perhaps Butterfly Man makes a habit out of imprisoning innocent people.

But... this guy could know something about him. He might even know who took the Crook Spear. He could be my ticket to freedom.

Yeah, that's a lot of *could*s.

'When did you get here?'

His voice is as weak as parched leaves.

'Just now,' I say.

'Lucky you.'

'How long you been down here?' Talking makes my head pound.

'Long enough to know it won't be for much longer.'

He winces. As my eyes get used to the dark, I see how skinny he is. I can't tell how old, but the voice is young. He sounds a bit like Troll.

He's not wearing any shoes and one of his grubby feet scuffs the floor, as if he wants to move, but it's too much and he gives up.

'What did you do?' I can't help asking.

'Nothing.'

'Who is that guy?'

His eyes are hazy dots in the gloom.

'Kimono? Butterflies? Bad case of cataracts?'

I nod.

'You don't know who that is?'

There's no answer to that. Should I know? I feel stupid, like somebody who's never heard of Pat Benatar or George Bush.

'Thought everyone knew about him,' Skinny says. He sounds more surprised than judgemental, as if he didn't realise there was another world outside of whatever crime ring he's part of. 'You really are lucky. Or, you were. Must've done something to get his goat. What did you do?'

'Nothing.'

His scrawny body convulses with laughter.

'What's his name?' I ask.

Skinny stares at me. Or, I think he does. I realise we're talking over the woman under the grate and I feel bad for her. I wonder if Skinny talked to her before she died.

'Reverend Mara.'

'Reverend? He didn't look like one.' I say it before I can stop myself. Of course he's not a goddamn reverend. It's probably a nickname or a title. If he's the boss of some crime syndicate, it stands to reason he answers to cardinals and – maybe somewhere – a pope.

'Might as well be one,' Skinny says. 'The way he thinks he's God's gift to London.'

'He's some kind of gangster?'

'Wow, you really don't know anything.'

I'd be angry if Skinny didn't look so messed up. If we weren't in this pit, I'd have smacked him. Of course, if we weren't in this pit, we wouldn't be having this conversation.

Mara's face flashes before my eyes. Beautiful and chiselled. When I first glimpsed his dark outline on the sofa, I thought it was her. My mother.

She lies with her mother's tongue, he'd said.

How did Mara know my mother? Did she work for him? Were they friends? Did she help him pick out kimonos? Mara's not how I ever pictured gangsters. I imagined guys in hats, smoking cigars, fingers hard with gold. What's Mara's story? You grow up in London, you see the different ways people live, none any better or worse than the other, mostly. Mara wears dresses, big whoop, but to do that in his world, a world run by angry men... That takes balls.

Despite myself, I shudder at the memory of his flashing nails. He had the deranged aura of a desperate man. Desperation makes people do crazy things. I should know.

Skinny's gone quiet in his corner.

'Hey,' I hiss.

No reply.

He might have passed out. Or died. I think I hear faint breathing on his side of the pit. Maybe he's playing dead. It doesn't make much difference to me.

'Hey, you still alive?' I ask.

No reply.

Fine. Be that way.

I just managed to get comfortable against the wall, but I have to move, even though my limbs feel so heavy it's like they're coated in lead. Grimacing, I prise myself up, my boots scratching the cement floor loudly. I peer up through the grate, but there's no movement. I don't know if we're being watched, but I've got a feeling Mara's guards are confident in my confinement. Nobody else down here escaped.

There has to be a way out. I just have to find the flaw in the pit. Something tiny, maybe. A mouse hole or an opening into the sewer. I'll Shawshank my way out of here somehow.

Moving must have disturbed the air down here because my nostrils are assaulted by a fresh wave of death-stench and I fight the bile, swallowing it down, trying not to think about the tiny molecules of dead skin and hair that must be floating around me in a putrid soup.

Breathing through my mouth, I trace the walls with my fingers, searching for anything that might give. The wall's knobbly and flaky, but rock solid. If I had a pickaxe, it'd take a week to bust through.

Stepping over bodies, I keep searching.

Nothing nothing nothing.

Wall wall wall.

Frustration sets my jaw ticking. I'm almost at Skinny's side when my fingers brush something different. Metal. My heart flutters and I don't want to get ahead of myself but, as I forage the surface, I realise it's a door. I tap it. *Thunk.* That's one heck of a door.

'It's locked.'

I nearly jump out of my skin.

Skinny blinks up at me from his corner. 'You don't think I already tried that?'

I ignore him, exploring the rusty contours. None of the bolts are loose. They're practically welded into the metal. What the hell was this cell used for before Mara and his mob moved in? Was it purpose-built by the Rev for his enemies?

My fingers find deep gouges in the door. Long, narrow furrows, like something tore at the metal, and I realise something probably did.

No way out through there. There must be something else. I eye Skinny as I go past. He's too weak to move. Besides, what would he get out of attacking me? We're in the same shitty predicament down here.

It's a good thing I like the dark or I'd have lost it by now. I try not to imagine what it'd be like spending weeks locked in Mara's pit. Slowly ripening, then rotting. My starving body eating its own flesh until I'm a withered skeleton, and then it's impossible to move, impossible to breathe, and just like that I've become the girl in the flower dress.

The dark's comforting. The shadows are an ally. I'm one of them and they embrace me like a sister.

My fingers discover something in the wall. I dab it, feeling something hard.

'What you doing?'

'*Quiet.*'

CHAPTER SIX

I work at the thing in the wall, cement crumbling around it. The object wobbles and I tease it out of the little hole it's nestling in. I turn and hold it to the grate's grey light.

A rusty nail twice as long as my index finger.

'Jesus,' Skinny breathes.

The girl in the flower dress grins.

So now I have a weapon.

CHAPTER SEVEN

FOUR YEARS BEFORE THE HAMMER

When I'm fifteen my best friend is Troll Mason. I can't remember why I call him that, and it's only partly because if you call him by his real name, Tashaun, he looks like he's stuck his hand in a bag full of broken glass. He's the only person who doesn't hiss behind his hand when I walk by at school. I've been living with my fifth foster family – the Trumans – for a year and it's pretty obvious they only take kids in for the benefits. They couldn't tell you my middle name if there was a cash prize. (I don't have one, actually, but they'd probably guess something insulting like 'Raven' or 'Inga'.) The one time they tried to discipline me for staying out late, I stared at the floor and nodded that I was sorry, then I snuck out the window to meet Troll in the park.

Their daughter, Pearl, is my age, and hated me on sight. I'm five months older and she's a pro at ignoring me. At school, her coven snicker and shoot me acid stares whenever I get within a hundred yards.

They're popular. I'm the weed crushed under their Converse. I wear black and purple and draw dark lines around my eyes. My ears are pierced in five places and my hair's an unruly black mane.

The five of them are like clones. (Pearl's the original; the others were grown in the lab. Probably from cells shaved off her arse.) They have blonde hair, jeans frayed at the knees, friendship bracelets from when they were kids. Lola's the only one who looks different. Her hair's copper red and she files her nails into talons. She always has a shoulder ready for me. Or a foot.

I can handle snake bitches like her now. Life's a bitch, now so am I. Deep down they just want their mummy. When I'm fifteen, though, I don't know better. I've bounced between foster homes and each move stripped away a piece of me until I'm not a whole person any more.

At least there's Troll. For a little while anyway. We're in a cemetery the day it happens. We look like the kind of kids who hang out in cemeteries, but it's the first time we've been here. I haven't told him why I wanted to come and I was too much of a coward to come alone.

When I stop by a grave, he clamps his mouth shut for once.

CELENE CROSS

The headstone holds my eye. Small, ragged like a chewed fingernail.

'Huh,' Troll says. He gets family shit. His mum's an alcoholic and his brother's a criminal, so his standards are pretty low when it comes to friends. Besides, I've always got on better with boys. They're easier to read and their secrets are generally stupider than girls' secrets, which can level cities if they detonate.

I stare at the grave, trying to imagine what's going on six feet under. It's been almost fifteen years since the Thames spat my mother out. Her remains have probably been digested already, picked clean by worms and insects and whatever else slithers around down there.

Everything I know about my mother floats to the surface of my mind like the scum on the Thames and I consider taking a piss on her grave. I ball the anger up in my fists, thinking about everybody who's died, the patchwork of holes in my life, all because of her.

Troll lights a cigarette and goes to lean against a tree. He talks too much, but for the first time he seems to get that talking won't achieve anything.

I retrieve a spray can from my jacket pocket and shake it, then I crouch down and add long black letters beneath my mother's name.

CELENE CROSS
BURNS IN HELL

Straightening, I don't look at Troll as we traipse out of the cemetery, not wanting to see the questioning eyebrows and, knowing that if I ignore him, he'll pretend this never happened. He's trustworthy like that.

We walk in silence but even Troll has his limits, finally launching into a sermon about how screwed we are, how it's all the government's fault; it's basically stuff he's heard old guys joke about on late-night TV, but he always adds a twist.

'We're the McGeneration!' he whoops as we head into a weird little park that's reserved for drunks, tramps and kids with nowhere else to go. 'We're getting rammed through a meat grinder until we all come out the same.'

'Sounds delicious.' My standard response.

The park's our private haven. We talk about what we're going to do when we fail our exams and end up taking jobs we hate. Troll's brother got banned from driving, so we take his Corsa out and Troll teaches me how to drive. I still don't have a licence, but I know how to get around without causing a pile-up. Hell, I'm positively restrained compared to most Londoners.

Troll introduced me to comics. *Tank Girl, Catwoman, Preacher, Umbrella Academy*. All the twisted stuff that, weirdly, I feel I've almost lived. He has cash to burn – something about his mum's conscience, though I'm pretty sure he steals from her when she's drunk – and he lets me read them when he's done.

'The best thing about *Preacher* is it just doesn't give a shit!' Troll's hopped up on energy drinks and nicotine. He leaps onto a low wall in the park, scattering pigeons. 'Religion? Fuck it. Firearms? Screw 'em. Old ladies in wheelchairs? They're worse than anybody! It's the most important piece of literature ever written.'

He does this sometimes. It's the day of the accident, but neither of us know that. If I'd known, I'd have made sure Troll was nowhere near the park. Or me.

He's giving one of his comic-book sermons while I sit rolling us cigarettes.

Neither of us notices Pearl and Lola and the others come into the park. It's only when Rufus, Pearl's scruffy, half blind Jack Russell, shoves a wet nose in my face that I spot them.

They line up by the gate, the saddest girl group you've ever seen. They never come in here and they eye the park with the same disgust they usually reserve for me. They must've seen us as they walked back home from the less interesting park down the road.

'Christ,' Troll says. 'What are they doing here?'

'Don't stop on our account.' Lola's got that dangerous look she gets when no adults are around.

'Rufus, get back here.' Pearl eyes me nervously, like I might do something to her precious pooch, but I never had anything against animals.

Rufus ignores her, snuffling around my pocket. I remember I have a Peperami in there.

'He doesn't know better.' Lola rakes her gaze up and down my body. 'Probably thinks she's another dog.'

'Nah, Rufus knows a lost cause when he sees one,' Pearl mutters.

That's actually a good one for her.

Troll jumps off the wall, his boots loud on the pavement. He's wearing a T-shirt with cut-off sleeves and his hair's spiked up like all the best rock stars. Before he can say anything, I'm on my feet and grabbing his arm.

'Come on, Troll.'

'Yeah, *Troll*, come on.' Lola's mouth twists.

Troll shoves my hand off. 'What's your problem, L-L-L-Lola?'

'Daddy probably said she couldn't have another pony,' I say under my breath. The dog's still trying to get into my pocket and I shove him away with my knee. Lola crosses her arms, flanked by the others, who snare me with their sneers.

'Look at those boots,' Lola says. 'Steal them off a tramp?'

'Yeah, 'cos you spent all that time on the street, right?' one of the others says. I think her name's Leah but they're so interchangeable I honestly don't know.

I don't say anything. It's true I spent a few weeks on the street. That was after foster home number four. I ran away, but social services found me and stuck me with the Trumans. The punishment doesn't fit the crime.

'It's rude not to answer when somebody asks you a question,' Lola says. She's the best at this. Probably had plenty of years picking on other kids before I turned up.

'Come on, she's not worth it,' Pearl says, finally grabbing Rufus' collar and dragging him away. Lola turns her back. 'She'll end up just like her mum.'

Red explodes in my vision and I'm not thinking as I throw myself on her. Lola makes a strangled sound as we crash to the ground. She tries to shake me off but I grab a fistful of her red hair and pull hard, the knuckles of my other hand blazing white.

I barely hear the others yelling. Rufus yapping.

'She's lost it!'

'Get her, Loo!'

Something cracks me in the ribs. Lola's fist, maybe. I release her and stagger back, unable to breathe. Troll gets between us, his hands raised.

'This is all really arousing but do you really think it's the best–'

Lola's fist cuffs his jaw. Troll staggers sideways and Lola goes for me, but Pearl seizes her arm.

'My mum'll flip if she comes home with a black eye.' Lola grinds her teeth and I imagine steam snorting from her nostrils.

'Yeah, Lola,' I hear myself saying. '*Some* parents don't like it when their kids come home with black eyes.'

So that was a mistake. Lola lunges for me, then trips. Troll's stuck his leg out and Lola lands on all fours.

'Let's get out of here,' I say, but the other girls are blocking the park exit. I tug Troll in the opposite direction and I'm pretty sure he knows what I'm thinking. We hurry for a knotted old tree by the wall. There's a dump on the other side; we just have to climb the tree and hop over. We've done it a hundred times. There's loads of cool stuff in the dump.

'You're dead, *Tumour!*'

I shove Troll up before me – it's not the time to be a gentleman, not that Troll ever was one. Rufus yaps hysterically behind us and I hear the girls all yelling at Lola to leave us freaks alone, but I can hear her panting close by and I clamber up after Troll. I always knew she had it in for me, but I had no idea she hates me *this* much. It's like she's been waiting for me to hand her a permission slip to beat the crap out of me and, now she has it, she's going to damn well use it. I sort of respect that kind of dedication.

'Rumer!'

Troll's made it onto the wall. He puts his hands out and drags me up just as Lola seizes my ankle and yanks. I manage to kick her away and scrabble up next to Troll, gasping for breath. My heart sinks as I peer down into the junkyard. They changed things around. Below us are thirty-foot containers filled with twisted metal, old bits of farming machinery. Spikes that used to be bed frames and warped pipes that used to be I-don't-know-what.

Lola's on the wall now.

'Run!' Troll yells.

'Wait!' I cry, but Troll's already taken off, running the length of the wall.

He trips.

He barely has time to cry out before he's gone over the edge.

A horrible, dull thunk rings out and his cry's broken off.

Lola's right beside me, but she's standing stock-still, her face pale, her hands clenching and unclenching.

'Troll!'

I hurry along the wall to where he fell. My insides are shuddering and, as the adrenaline washes away, I realise I'm going to cry. I can't stop it. I know this feeling. The shuddering's building towards an eruption and I collapse onto all fours, clinging to the wall.

I peer over the edge.

His breath rattles.

He's bent at an angle. The way he landed in the container has broken him. He's been impaled and he's looking at me, but he doesn't see me any more.

A screeching sound echoes across the park. I tear my eyes away from Troll's twisted body.

'RUFUS!'

For a second I don't know what's going on, then I see Pearl dashing out the park exit, running into the road.

'RUFUS!'

I think I hear a high-pitched whine. I feel the wall tipping beneath me and I dig my nails into the bricks. Straining, I make out a shape in the road, squashed under the car's wheel. There's blood and fur and

Pearl throwing herself onto the tarmac, shrieking and clawing at her hair.

When I get home later, it's dark. I stand shivering in the hall. The ambulance came and took Troll's body away. At least, I assume it did. They hadn't managed to get him out of the container before the police turned up and asked questions and we were all taken to the station. Lola didn't look at me. Pearl sobbed into her shoulder. Rufus must've got away from the girls while Lola was chasing after me. Idiot dog.

When the police were done with their questions, I left. The Trumans didn't try to stop me. Pearl was hysterical and I don't think they even noticed me slipping away from the station.

I hid in my secret place for a few hours.

From the hall, I hear Pearl crying in the lounge with her parents. They're cooing and pawing her on either side of the sofa. I watch from the lounge door.

Pearl sees me before they do and bolts to her feet. Her eyes are red raw and I've never seen her so ugly. It shocks me.

'Are you happy now?!' she yells. She's holding something in her hand. A dog collar. 'Now everybody's as miserable as you?!'

'Pearl,' her dad begins, getting to his feet.

'You always defend her,' Pearl shouts, her gaze fixed on me. 'But she's a psycho. She killed them! She pushed him off the wall! And if it hadn't been for her getting into that stupid fight, Rufus wouldn't have run off–'

'Pearl,' her dad says again. She shoves off his hand.

'Why don't you just leave? Everything you touch turns to shit!'

For once, she's right.

CHAPTER EIGHT

This is the truth I fear.

That I was born cursed.

I was born dead.

And if anybody gets too close to me, they'll die, too.

I know, melodrama is alive and well in Rumer Cross but, honestly, stick with me. You'll see why I'm right; why the curse has robbed me of every single person who ever meant anything to me; how they died screaming in a spray of agony.

But right now I'm in a pit full of bodies and it's time I start trying to piece together the broken fairground ride that is my life.

CHAPTER NINE

TWO DAYS BEFORE THE HAMMER

So it turns out the pit's impenetrable. The rest of the search is a bust. No more nails, no more doors. It's designed for one thing: death. But I'm damned if I'm going to die down here surrounded by half-rotting skeletons. I'm disgusted by them all over again. They gave up. They were weak. If they'd really wanted to get out, they would have.

Exhaustion drains my resolve and I sag against the wall, sliding to the floor. I turn the rusty nail over in my hand, over and over, imagining the kind of damage it would do.

I've never killed anybody, not on purpose, but if it's between them and me, I know who I'd choose.

A swift jab to the throat. Or the eye. Between the ribs. That'd hurt like hell.

The thought of sinking the nail into tough flesh turns my stomach and I wonder if I really could go through with it. Killing somebody. Ending their life in a gush of red. You corner a rat, though, it'll show you its teeth.

My gaze drifts to Skinny in his corner. I could threaten him. Drag him into the light below the grate and press the nail to his jugular, start screaming my head off, that I'll kill him unless I can talk to Mara. Tiny flaw in that plan: Skinny's been left here to die. I'd be doing him a favour. No way Mara would let me out for threatening to finish the job he started.

Shit.

Shit shit *shit*.

The girl in the flower dress. I'm drawn back to her toothy skull, the flesh hanging off in leathery pieces. The guards are used to seeing her lying there. She's been there at least a month, by the look of her; her flesh cementing into the concrete. Would they notice if I moved her? Put on her dress? Took her place? I could lie there, waiting patiently, and when somebody eventually came into the pit, I'd jump up and throw myself at the open door. I'd be out of here before they could do anything about it.

Ugh. I've watched *The Silence of the Lambs* too many times.

But... the bodies.

I jerk upright, my fist crushing the nail until I think it might snap in two.

There are ten bodies wasting away in the dark, including the grinning girl. I look from her to the grate directly above her, judging the distance, a germ of a plan splitting like a seed. It might work. The grate's a good fifteen feet above the pit floor, too far to jump, but close enough to reach with a little help. Skinny's too weak. He'd never make it. This is on me.

I'm sweating with excitement, the idea smouldering as it takes root. This could actually work, but I can't rush. If the guards catch me, it's over. They'll know what kind of rat I am and they'll put me somewhere even worse; somewhere I really can't escape, no matter how sharp my fangs.

Standing, I slide the nail into my boot and stare up at the grate, listening. I'm met with a wall of silence. No boots scuffing the floor. No hushed voices. It's as if the pit's floating through space. Do they even bother patrolling this place? Or are the guards on the other side of the door? Nobody would be stupid enough to try to crawl back out through the grate.

When I'm sure nobody's up there watching, I get to work. I grab the nearest body. I think it used to be a man, but it's pretty hard to tell by this point. I avoid the oozing flesh, seizing his boots and hauling him across the floor. He's light as a sack of hay, but the stink that comes with disturbing the body nearly makes me black out.

'What you doing?' Skinny asks. He sounds even more feeble. Maybe he's afraid I'll grab him next.

'Getting out of here.'

'You're nuts.'

Let's see if you think that when I'm out the grate and you're still down here.

I lay the body next to the grinning girl. My eyes water at the earthy reek of decay, but I have to keep going. If I stop for a second, I'll start thinking about how the bodies feel – wet and brittle – and I'll never do this. I grab the next carcass and throw it on top of the other two, then lay another beside it. Something oozes in my hands and vomit floods my mouth. I retch into my shoulder, swallow.

'Jesus,' Skinny mutters, curling up in his corner, throwing an arm over his face.

Four down, six to go.

The next body is little more than a skeleton and I'm glad. The one after that is the worst. Underneath, it's become a squelchy mess of goo and muck. It smells ten times worse than the others and I really do black out for a moment as I drag it over the floor and throw it onto the pile.

When I'm done, I lean against the wall, breathing through my mouth, my stomach foaming, threatening to empty itself. I stare at my masterpiece, a monstrous pile of limbs and heads and slippery wetness. It comes up to my waist. I won't know if it's high enough until I've climbed on top, a thought that makes me want to pull my hair out and scratch my skin to ribbons.

It's the only way. If I move quickly enough, I won't have to think about it. What I've done to these people. Would they be glad they helped me escape? Or would they curse my name? They wouldn't be the first.

I edge over to the pile, peering up at the grate. Beyond it, I glimpse the warehouse ceiling, but no guards. No Mara. Silence crashes down on me and I have to do this. Now or never.

Scowling at my creation, I clamber onto it, horror plucking at my nerves when I grab a stiff, wet hand. I release it with a grunt and seize something else, an arm maybe, I honestly don't look, heaving myself up, watching the grate, only the grate as it bobs closer.

At the top of the pile, I teeter and suddenly I'm afraid I'll slip and crash to the floor, but I regain my balance, crouching there like a spider.

'Shit,' Skinny whispers, and I swear there's admiration in his tone. Out of the corner of my eye, I see him struggle to his feet, his legs trembling at first, then not trembling any more.

The grate's so close I could touch it. Not yet. I listen, straining to hear anything above me. It's unnaturally quiet. Where are Mara's men? I'll just have to risk it. Gritting my teeth, I reach up and slip my fingers through the grate.

Blinking through the sweat trickling into my eyes, I push it up.

My belly somersaults. I keep waiting for a guard to appear and stamp down on the grate, but nobody comes. I ease the grate up even more, straining, the bodies shifting under my boots, pushing, pushing, until it swings up and creaks into its hinges, standing upright.

The square above my head feels huge. A window to freedom.

Drawing a few sharp breaths, I lunge for the hole, gripping the edge with both hands and flexing, trying to haul myself up. My shoulders feel like they're being torn from their sockets but I kick and scrabble and dig my nails into the hole, then I'm up, halfway into the warehouse, panting. One last heave and I roll onto the floor.

I want to lie there. My chest's on fire and I'm sweating so much my clothes stick to me.

Instead, I roll onto my feet, resting on one knee, drawing the nail from my boot and brandishing it in front of me.

The warehouse is empty. This room, anyway. A massive cement space with stained floors and chains swaying from the ceiling.

'Hey.'

I check all around, but I'm alone.

'Hey, my turn.'

Skinny. I peer down into the pit and he stares up at me, balancing on the body pile, reaching a hand up. He looks so small. Broken. Looks can be deceiving, though. If I help him, he could turn on me in an instant. It'd be easier to escape without him slowing me down.

I turn away and a spark spits up from the ground.

Across the room, a masked guard points his gun at me.

'Took you long enough,' I hiss.

The guard considers me for a moment, then three more appear, fanning out in front of me. Boots beat the floor behind me. I'm surrounded.

I feign a lunge in one direction and sparks erupt around me.

They're goddamn shooting at me.

Clenching the nail tight, I consider my options. Run. Bargain. Get caught. Die.

Great.

The guards don't give me a choice. They rush at me, popping bullets at the floor, making it impossible for me to move, so I do the last thing I want to do, the one thing I definitely *shouldn't* do.

I dive back into the pit.

Skinny's still on the pile of bodies and I crash into him. We tumble to the floor, grunting, limbs flailing. As I scrabble to my feet, I see Skinny's already up. He throws a bony arm around my neck and there's something else pressing against my throat. Something sharp. And I realise I'm a total idiot.

'HEY!' Skinny shouts. I struggle and the sharp thing digs into my skin. The nail. I dropped it when I jumped back into the pit.

I realise Skinny's yelling up at the grate. He stinks of sweat and dirt.

'Open the door, or Lucky here finds out what it's like to be a kebab. OPEN IT NOW!'

He's so scrawny but he's as tall as me. I had no idea he was this tall.

'Get that thing away from my throat,' I growl, but Skinny shakes me and hisses at me to shut up. His meaty breath stinks worse than the pit. I guess Mara doesn't let his prisoners use a toothbrush.

Agitated shapes swarm above our heads and their shadows flicker through the window in the pit's ceiling, making it seem like the dead girl is moving. There's the sound of metal, a lock, and then the door opens right next to us.

A figure charges inside and Skinny shoves me away. As I grab the wall a gargling scream echoes around the pit. My cellmate has thrust his weapon – *my* weapon – into the jaw of one of the masked guards.

Blood spurts all over the floor.

Skinny removes the nail and the guard collapses. More are behind him.

All I see is the open door.

A gun fires deafeningly and a voice screams at me to run, to use the confusion to my advantage. What happens next probably only takes a couple of seconds but, in my head, we're in slow motion, as if gravity's given our strings a yank.

Three figures tackle Skinny, wrestling with him and the nail-dagger.

I stare at the open door.

Nobody's guarding it. They're too busy trying to subdue Skinny, who slashes his weapon, gouging a red line across one guard's face.

I stick to the shadows. I slide along the wall, blood screaming in my ears.

Skinny shrieks as a guard seizes his wrist. The one with the nail-dagger.

The door's so close I want to scrabble for it, but I know if I do the guards will see me. I inch closer, expecting them to spot me any minute, but I'm good at being invisible. I imagine I'm painted grey as the walls. My breath's caught in my throat and I swear the roaring of blood in my ears will give me away.

Skinny bites the guard's hand and angry grunts roll around the pit.

The door. It's right there. All I have to do is—

'You, stop!'

One of the guards has seen me. We lock eyes. He begins to raise his gun and I know he'll shoot me. Maybe not a kill shot, but definitely one to stop me, and that bullet will hurt like hell.

I keep staring at him, willing him to see I shouldn't be here. This is all a mistake. He should just let me go. Nobody needs to know he was the one who let me escape.

The gun's still being raised and it's almost pointed at me.

I run.

A breeze block explodes somewhere by my legs, but I'm out.

Out of the pit.

I don't have time to think about where I am. I hurtle down the corridor, which is so dark it's like I'm in one of those funfair rides where monsters jump out at you, but they're just guys in costumes and the real monsters are right behind me. I pass other doors which must lead to other pits, and I'm damned if I'm going back in.

Bullets ricochet around my feet. The guard's a bad shot or it's too dark for him to aim properly. Either way, I'm not down yet. I crash through a door at the end of the corridor and collapse against a set of metal steps.

Footsteps pound the floor behind me and I'm on my feet again, sweaty, panting, clambering up the stairs, trying to be quiet, but pretty sure I sound like a stampeding elephant. A single word pumps through me.

Out.

Out, out, OUT!

If I don't get out, I'm done.

I really didn't think this through, but there wasn't time. The dead woman's grinning skull flashes in my mind and I don't have time to wait for them to figure out I'm the wrong man. I didn't steal from Reverend Mara and I don't deserve to be locked in a pit with a load of rotting corpses.

The stairs come to an end and I'm back in the warehouse. Empty windows hiss rain. I stop. I have to. My lungs are crushed. I cling to the rail and scan the huge space. Empty, but there's a door on the far side. It's too far. I wouldn't make it halfway before the guards put a bullet in me. The rail shakes as they rush up, shouting to one another in a foreign language.

I spot boxes in the corner behind the stairs. The guards will assume I ran for the door. Why wouldn't I? I'd be an idiot not to. If I've learnt anything, though, it's that sometimes the only way to outsmart someone is to do something stupid.

I rush for the corner and squeeze between the wooden boxes. One of them's covered with a tarp, which I draw over my head.

The guards burst into the warehouse. I watch beneath the tarp, not blinking, not breathing. If they check my corner, I'll be back in the pit in minutes, and who knows what they'll do to me as punishment. I could end up with an eye like Reverend Mara's. Maybe two.

The guards scan the area, then charge for the door, disappearing through it.

Quiet returns.

I sag against the nearest box.

My heartbeat slows and I'm able to think about what just happened without wanting to laugh like a maniac. Skinny had a makeshift dagger at my throat. My stomach rolls. Is he dead? He was damn near it anyway.

I realise the longer I spend hidden, the more time the guards have to sweep the area and close in on me. Within the hour, the warehouse will be crawling with them and then I really won't be able to escape.

Silencing the spider in my mind, which urges me to stay hidden, I draw the tarp aside and crawl out.

No guards. Nothing.

It's dark and wet beyond the busted windows and I'm grateful. There's no way I'd make it further than the car park in daylight. I have no idea which part of the warehouse I'm in, though. It looks different to Mara's neon-blushed boudoir.

I climb onto the boxes and peer out of a window.

The countryside's quiet under a crescent moon. The clouds have cleared and it's a starry evening. Lights bead the horizon. London? Or some far-flung suburb? It doesn't matter, as long as there's a working phone.

I examine the window, which is smashed like the others. It's a drop to the outside, but one more bruise won't hurt. Besides, the more beat up I am, the more Julian will believe my crazy story when I get back.

When. Not *if.*

I grip the frame and heave myself up, teetering on the ledge. Fresh air snarls my hair and I spot a figure below.

Shit.

This place is like a Korean prison. Those things are impossible to escape. If I can't get out through the window, I'll have to find another way. That means heading deeper into the warehouse. Great.

Hopping down, I scan the floor for something to use as a weapon and settle on a bent pipe. Better than nothing. I go to a door and listen, then head into another cavernous space. Skirting along the walls, I wonder what Tank Girl would do. Something kick-ass with a sassy pay-off.

I freeze.

Somebody's coming. Only one somebody, going by the echoing footsteps. The footsteps stop and I press myself into a door frame. Where'd the guy go?

The door opens behind me and a hand clamps over my mouth. The stench of cigarettes cooks my nostrils.

'Looky, looky,' Nicotine Man jeers in my ear. 'Somebody's broken their parole.'

CHAPTER TEN

The only thing worse than not escaping is *almost* escaping. I'm so close to getting away from this place I want to scream. Instead, I drive my elbows back and try to squirm free, but he punches me in the kidneys and I can't breathe.

'She's got fight, that's good,' Nicotine Man rasps.

His voice sends shivers through me and I'm so tired. Tired of fighting. Tired of struggling. All I want to do is lie down–

That's what she *did. The grinning corpse lay down, probably just for a moment–*

Defiance sparks inside me and I screw up the last scrap of energy I have left. I grab Nicotine Man's arm, the one he's got over my shoulder, and use my hip to spin him. He yells in surprise and his back crunches against the floor.

I'm free.

As he counts the tweety birds, I seize the pipe, which I dropped when his stinking fingers dug into me. I heft it, feeling the weight and clutching it like a baseball bat.

'Stay back,' I warn, my mouth dry, like I've been shovelling dirt into it.

He runs his tongue over his lip. He must've bitten it. Good, it'll match the busted nose, which he's stuck a plaster over.

'Girl, you wanna run? You run. Nowhere you can hide I won't find you.'

The steely glimmer in his eyes gives me chills.

'Come any closer and I'll bust that thing off your face for good.'

'My my, got your panties in a twist.' Nicotine Man's lounging against the wall now. A lazy jungle cat waiting for a moment to strike. I notice a bunch of keys attached to a loop in his jeans.

His van.

If I get the keys…

I swing the pipe. It crunches into the side of his head and he almost topples over. He quickly regains his balance and now his eyes are raging. He hurls himself at me and I don't have time to get out of the way.

The ground tilts and comes up to crack against the back of my skull.

I see every star in the universe. They swirl in front of me and when they pop and clear, Nicotine Man's rubbery mask of a face is pressing close to mine.

'Time we got you back in that pit,' he snarls, clasping my wrists.

The pain of him squeezing the rope burns jolts me to. I thrash against the floor, digging my heels in.

'Just – making – it – difficult – for – yourself,' Nicotine Man grunts, but I barely hear him.

Then he's got me by the throat.

'STOP!' He sprays spit in my face. 'Just like your goddamn mother.'

I stop thrashing, but he doesn't stop squeezing. I see the rage whirling in his eyes. Did everybody meet my mother but me? He's so angry he won't stop. He's going to crush my windpipe and then he's going to smoke a cigarette over my corpse.

Nicotine Man looks up suddenly. Has he heard something? The pressure at my throat lessens and I gasp a breath. Then, using the last of my strength, I bury my fist in his face. He makes an 'oof' sound, the way he did when I hit him earlier. I never get sick of that sound. I hit him again and grab the pipe, swinging it at him, bludgeoning the side of his head and he collapses on top of me. His sweaty cheek slides against mine and I grit my teeth, heaving him off me and struggling to my feet.

He's out cold.

A sound like creaking metal. I turn towards it and spot a spindly figure on the other side of the space.

Skinny. Blood's smeared across his face and his baggy T-shirt. He looks as knackered as I feel.

My gaze snaps immediately to his hands. They're empty. No rusty nail-dagger.

'Get the hell away from me,' I wheeze. It hurts to swallow, like I'm trying to gulp down the nail Skinny had pressed to my throat.

He ignores me, taking a step forward.

'Stay back!' I shout, then wince.

'You're welcome,' Skinny says.

'For what?' I sit up. I thought I ached before. My body feels like it's been put through a spin cycle. There's not a single spot that doesn't throb or ache or spike with pain.

'Got us out.'

'I got me out,' I snap. Nicotine Man isn't moving. I crouch by him and roll him over; a smelly sack of potatoes.

'You wouldn't have if it wasn't for me,' Skinny says.

'Just keep back.' I fumble with the keys at Nicotine Man's belt. I keep expecting him to jerk into life. He's still breathing, as far as I can tell. Assuming I didn't cause any permanent brain damage – or *more* brain damage than this guy already had – we don't have much time.

'What you doing?' Skinny asks.

I yank the keys free and get to my feet, limping a few steps before steadying myself against the wall. For a moment I feel delirious, as if I'm not really here. I swear I see Frances smiling at me and I don't know where I am, but I'm not here in the warehouse. I blink and Frances is gone.

'You got a ride?' Skinny asks, snapping me back to the present.

'No passengers.'

Straightening, I begin to make my way back through the warehouse, hoping I'm headed in a direction that leads to the van.

'Play fair!'

'This isn't a game!' I wince again, rubbing my throat.

'Jesus, you want them to hear?' Skinny's eyes are big as bottle caps. 'Look, just get me back to the city. That's all. Please.'

I realise he's right. The prank he pulled in the pit was idiotic, but it got us out. Would he have slashed my throat? Desperate people have done crazier things. If he thought it would get him out, would he have killed me? I still don't know what he did to piss off Reverend Mara. But if I leave him here, I'm condemning him to death, and then I'm no better.

Maybe I can save somebody for once.

'Fine. Just hurry.' Hesitantly, I add: 'You first.'

He traipses over to a doorless rectangle in the wall and I can tell he's badly hurt. He clutches his side and his movements are jolting, every step seeming to cause him pain. Sympathy tugs at me, but I'm aching enough myself without thinking of ways to make his life easier.

We go through the door frame into a garage. Black SUVs line up and Nicotine Man's ride must be here somewhere. But I don't see it anywhere.

I keep Skinny in my sight as we make our way between the cars. I listen out for Nicotine Man or his comrades, but it's quiet as the grave – or the pit – with only the shushing trees outside making a sound.

Skinny's stopped at the garage doors, which are open. Through them, I glimpse shapes moving across the tarmac. The place is swarming with guards.

Where are Nicotine Man's wheels?

I stop by Skinny and scan the area outside the warehouse. Then I spot it. The van's parked on the other side of the stretch of tarmac, by the trees. There's no cover between here and there, though. If we make a run for it, we'll be easy targets.

Skinny's probably thinking the same thing. He flashes a look at me and I remember him pressing the nail-dagger to my throat. The meaty stink of his breath. Would he give me up? Trade me in?

Whoever Reverend Mara is, I get the feeling he doesn't do trades.

'I'll distract them.' His expression is uncertain. 'You'll trust me then, right? I'll distract them, you get the van and pick me up. Then we get the fuck outta here.'

'You're crazier than I thought.'

'Only option,' Skinny says. He's still gripping his side, like he's stopping his guts from spilling out. This time, the sympathy's like stabbing glass. I can't let him do that. They'll shoot him on sight and I'll have to add another person to the list of people I've killed over the years.

At least one of us will get away. I hate myself for thinking it. He dies, it's on me, and I've lost count of how many people have died because they got too close to me.

Skinny seems to give up on me handing him permission. Before I can stop him, he slips awkwardly out of the garage doors.

'Hey! Ninja assassins! You want me?'

The guards spin towards him. There's shouting and the sound of boots on tarmac and, in an instant, they're after him. Skinny darts to the left, towards the dirt track that must lead out of this hellhole.

All eyes are on him.

I'm already panting, psyching myself up to run.

'Don't get shot,' I tell myself. 'Don't even *think* about getting shot.'

I hurtle forward, squeezing the keys in my hand until it hurts. It's impossible to be quiet when you're in that much pain and my panting echoes all around me.

A few of the guards swivel in my direction. Prickly heat causes me to start sweating again. Sparks spit up from the tarmac. They're shooting at me. *They're goddamn shooting at me.*

The van bobs up and down as I race towards it.

Something whistles past my ear and I try to ignore it. It's nothing. Definitely not a bullet. Definitely nowhere near my head.

I hurl myself at the van and the sound of boots is louder as the guards charge for me.

Psssewww! Psssewww!

Angry little hornets buzz through the air. Some of them hit the van with a tinny pop, but I'm already at the driver's door and wrenching it open. I clamber inside, slamming and locking it.

The keys shake in my hands and I shove one into the ignition. The rumble of the engine revving is sweet music to my ears.

Beside me, the window shatters and a gloved hand roves in.

I throw the van into reverse and rocket backwards, ignoring the thumps and bumps as guards get in the way.

'Screw you,' I say through clenched teeth.

There are guards everywhere. The van rocks as it's riddled with bullets. I shift into second gear and rev towards the dirt track Skinny was heading for, though he's either dead or captured by now. He can't be anything else.

But then I'm racing down the dirt track and I see a pale white shape, like a rag attached to a flagpole, and it's Skinny running. I reach over and throw the passenger door open. Skinny's wincing face appears and he struggles, can't lift his leg to get into the van.

I lean over the seat to grab his hand.

And I hear the bullet.

A second later, blood's all over the door and Skinny sags, dropping heavily onto the grass.

My face is wet with something warm and the sound of the bullet echoes around the cab, or maybe just in my ears.

It went straight through the side of his head.

Another bullet cracks against the van and I snap to, slamming the passenger door and pumping the engine. Then I'm racing down the track again, racing ahead with the sound of bullets receding into the distance.

Article from *Crystal Visions* magazine

The curse of Celene Cross

Britain's most famous mob assassin terrorised London for over a decade and, on the fifth anniversary of Celene Cross's death, *Crystal Visions* speaks to a reformed occult priest who reveals her disturbing legacy...

By FIONA WALLACE

She's renowned as one of the world's most violent criminals, having savagely murdered an estimated 150 people during her decade-long reign of terror, but horrifying new details about the depraved life of notorious mob assassin Celene Cross are still coming to light.

A cold-hearted killer whose legend thrives on the lack of hard facts about her life, Celene spent a year in Holloway Prison as a young woman after savagely blinding a man in a pub brawl. And while many details of her upbringing remain unconfirmed, it's clear she went on to work for a number of London's most dangerous gangsters.

On the fifth anniversary of Celene's death – her body was dragged from the Thames in 1998 – *Crystal Visions* spoke to reformed occultist Dominic Waters, who experienced Celene's demented behaviour first-hand.

'I've never met anybody so cold,' says Dominic, who encountered Celene through satanic cult The Divine Order. 'There were some nasty people involved in the Order, but Celene scared everybody. She'd mark her territory by stringing up skinned cats and nobody ever saw her sleeping. I was terrified of her.'

As a dark priest for The Divine Order, Waters led many of the cult's most disturbing practices during the 1980s. The Order, which is thought to have disbanded following the mysterious death of founder Takehiko Kobayashi, first attracted Celene in the late '80s.

Already rumoured to be working for Kobayashi, a renowned mobster, Celene was seemingly drawn to the cult's sordid rituals, which included satanic worship and animal sacrifice.

'She came to one of our meetings,' Dominic recalls. 'She knew Takehiko Kobayashi and stayed in the back as he talked. I remember her eyes. They were like a shark's. Dark and blank. I should have left then.'

Within a week, Celene had moved into the Order's squat, a building in a secret location Dominic is unable to reveal. 'It was a dive,' he says. 'The water was filthy and there were rats. As soon as Celene moved in, she began terrorising the other members. I tried to stay away from her, but it was impossible.

'One night I found her with a knife to her belly. She was pregnant but wanted to get rid of the baby. She pinned me to the wall and said she'd cut my throat if I told anybody. I still don't know why she didn't kill me.'

Things worsened for Dominic when Celene's behaviour grew even more erratic. 'A few months later, she was a mess,' he says. 'She ranted about the people she'd killed and how she was going to hell. She seemed to have grown a conscience. I told her about a ritual that could purge her of her past misdeeds – by transferring her bad karma into her unborn baby.'

Dominic continues: 'When she went into labour, we performed the ceremony. There was lamb's blood and candles. After the baby was born, Celene disappeared. The next thing I heard, she'd been dragged out of the Thames. I was relieved. She couldn't inflict any more pain.'

Dominic – who stresses he's a reformed occultist and now works at an animal sanctuary – claims to have no information on the whereabouts of Celene's child.

'I'm so ashamed of what we did,' he says. 'I just hope wherever Celene's daughter is, she's happy.'

The legend of Celene Cross continues to grow by the day – and has eclipsed even the sick crimes she committed. Unconfirmed reports had her working for select MPs, taking out their competitors, while one tabloid informant claimed she was responsible for the death of Tupac Shakur.

While the circumstances surrounding her death have been the subject of much debate – with some alleging Sebastian Grim himself was responsible for Celene's murder – the most troubling part of her legend is the supposed existence of a daughter. *Crystal Visions'* own investigation returned no results. If she does exist – and survives – she provides a truly tragic footnote to Celene's terrible story.

Part Two
THE DEAD ROOM

CHAPTER ELEVEN
TWO DAYS BEFORE THE HAMMER

I need to ditch Nicotine Man's van. Seems crazy after what I just went through to get it, but every second I'm in it, I'm traceable. It could be bugged. Reverend Mara and his dogs could be tracking me right now, tearing out of the warehouse and following a blip on their phones that says where I'm headed.

I shoot a glance in the rear-view mirror. Red tail lights stream away on the motorway like angry little fireflies.

So far, none of the other drivers have given me a second look. I'm a shadow, but I've never shadowed in a van. Any of the cars could be following me and I wouldn't know until I'm choking on their fumes.

I'm headed towards the city but I have no idea where to go. Nicotine Man grabbed me outside the hell pit masquerading as my flat. He knows where I live, who I am, who my mother was. And if he knows all that, he must also know who I work for. If Julian's involved, I'm screwed.

I peel my hands from the steering wheel one at a time. I've been gripping it so hard my knuckles are stiff. My fingers creak as I flex them.

The clock on the dashboard says: 00:34.

Skinny died roughly twenty minutes ago.

Time of death: 00:14.

I add him to the mental list of people I've killed. I don't know if there's a time limit attached to people who get too close to me. Does some kind of cosmic countdown start ticking the moment we meet? I can't be sure. Skinny scratched it and we'd only shared a few hours in Mara's pit.

With Frances, it took four months. Troll and Pearl's dog Rufus bit it after a year. The rules seem to change depending on the person.

But it's inevitable.

Everyone I meet will die, horribly and unexpectedly.

I wonder if Skinny had a family. He did something that twisted Reverend Mara's knickers, but that doesn't mean there isn't somebody out there who loved him.

My fingers ache again. I'm clenching the steering wheel too tightly. I force myself to take a deep breath. Focus on the road.

I still don't understand why the Reverend came after me. Why does he think I have the Crook Spear? And what the fuck is a Crook Spear, anyway? A weapon used by crooks? Spears seem pretty old school to me, though there was something sort of old school about Mara, too.

I run through a list of people who might have the intel I need. It's short, especially with Julian crossed off. I don't have any friends. I don't have a family. There's a guy who runs a Turkish supermarket across my street, but that's too risky. Bolt? It's an insane thought and I try to brush it off. But... the Reverend probably doesn't know about Bolt. How would he? He's not a friend, technically, and we're not related.

No. Not Bolt. Never Bolt. I must be desperate to even consider him.

I flip the radio on and crank up the music as Joan Jett thrashes out a ferocious anthem.

The traffic starts to bunch up as I get nearer to the city. I slow down, which sends a shock of irritation through me. I consider moving into another lane, but what if that one slows me down even more? The crawl back to London is a tedious kind of mental torture. Why do so many people want to cram into the city anyway? Seems to me the main reason they flock there is to get lost. Become nobody. Solidarity in anonymity. That I can sort of understand – it makes my job easier, anyway. But personal space? What the fuck's that?

Finally, I'm back in the city. I know North London well and steer off the motorway, entering a warren of smaller streets. I find a quiet street with no shops, just slumbering suburban houses. Parking the van, I get out. The rain's cleaned the air and I fill my lungs, suddenly grateful to be alive, to be back in the city, to be anywhere other than the place I just escaped.

I think about Skinny, the sound of the bullet and the hot gush of red, and shake it off.

Light floods the street and I stiffen, but it's just a car passing further down. The driver doesn't notice me, scooping the light away as he disappears round a corner.

'Quickly,' I tell myself.

I scan the parked cars and approach one. I've picked up a few tricks over the years. I work my magic on the car's lock and pop the door, getting in. My hands tremble as I reach under the steering wheel, yank the wires free and use them to start the engine.

The car eases away from the kerb. I keep checking the mirrors as I get back onto a main road, waiting for a black SUV to suddenly appear or a red dot to come through the window.

So far, so good. I feel better now I've dumped the van. I just need to get as far away from it as possible. It starts to rain again. Pretty soon it's pouring. The kind of rain that wants to beat you to the ground. I drive on and the windscreen swims, as if water's about to come rushing inside.

I glance at the rear-view mirror and my chest tightens.

An SUV is right behind me.

I try not to freak out, but there's no air in the car. I take the first right. The SUV follows me. Jerking the wheel, I take the next left, and the SUV's still behind me.

The rain pounds the windscreen and I imagine it flooding my mouth.

I pick up speed and turn onto a main road, but the SUV is right there, always in the mirror, its headlights filling the car.

I stomp hard on the accelerator and weave through the traffic. Red eyes blast through the rain, seeking me out, and I don't stop, tearing through the traffic lights. I think I hear a distant honking but I don't know what it is.

There's no SUV in the rear-view mirror now, but that doesn't mean I've lost it. I speed up, panic frothing up from the pit of my stomach, and I'm driving like a maniac, but maybe only maniacs escape gangsters, so I keep my boot wedged against the accelerator, the thrum of the windscreen wipers like a ticking clock.

Everything's so heavy. I can barely grip the wheel.

If I can just get to the house… But the car whines and we're crawling now. The world's slowing down. Straining against chains. Just a few more streets and I'll be there. Two more streets. One more.

Exhaustion sucks at my strength and it's so hard to keep my eyes open. Is this what happens when you've survived a near-death experience? Everything suddenly shuts down?

Crunch.

The car nudges the kerb and grinds to a halt. The headlights illuminate the house. It's like something from a horror movie. So run down it's forgotten what it's meant to be.

I should get out of the car. Into the house. The one place nobody will find me.

Frances, I think. *Frances, where are you?*

But Frances doesn't answer. It's just me and the rain and then even we don't exist any more because my eyes are so heavy that suddenly darkness swallows me whole and I'm a nobody who's nowhere with nothing.

CHAPTER TWELVE

FOUR YEARS BEFORE THE HAMMER

After the thing with Troll and the dog, I'm moved to another foster home. My sixth, but who's counting? It's only a few months until I turn sixteen and I plan on riding it out then hitting the road. No more social services. No more weirdo parents acting like your friend. No more skinny school bitches.

The weirdest thing is my new foster parents are actually decent human beings. Frances is Irish, in her late fifties, thin as a birch with silvering curly hair. George is a little older, paunchier and hasn't lost his Greek accent. He tells stories about how they met when Frances was on holiday in Greece and he moved all this way just for her. He never stops joking but he always fluffs the punchline and Frances' laughter trickles into every corner of the house.

She's the last person I killed, before Skinny.

We're driving. I've lived with them in their North London home (Victorian, creaky) for a month. Frances is behind the wheel and she's being mysterious about where we're going, which isn't like her. She usually lays things out plainly. Makes sure I know I'm not being tricked. She says we're going food shopping, but she's quiet and we're going the wrong way for the supermarket.

We drive into a run-down neighbourhood. The car draws up to a house with boarded-up windows and an overgrown garden. It looks like one of those houses you see in the paper; the ones where something awful happened, and I shiver despite the sun coming through the windscreen.

'Why are we stopping?' I ask.

Frances takes a moment to answer.

'Rumer, how much do you know about your mother?'

The question catches me off guard and I'm suddenly aware of the seatbelt cutting into my collarbone. I can't look at Frances.

'Some stuff… Enough to know I don't want to know more.'

That's not entirely true. I've read everything I could get my hands on. Newspapers. Magazine articles. They're all over the internet. Pearl's friend Lola brought a piece from some magazine called *Crystal Visions* to school one day; the article where Dominic Waters says my mother cursed me. Of course I read it. And of course Lola hung it over my head like an Acme anvil. You'd think she'd have been scared after finding out who my mother was. Shows how smart she was.

'It's understandable you'd only want to know so much,' Frances says in her soft Irish lilt. She's originally from Belfast, I think. 'Some of it is just too…'

'Fucked up?'

'Sad.' She doesn't tell me off for swearing. 'But it's important for a person to know where they come from.'

'Even if they come from the worst place possible.'

'Especially then.'

I don't want to be having this conversation. I thought Frances and George were nice, but they're just as fixated on my past as everybody else. Why is everybody so obsessed with my mother? All I want to do is forget she ever existed.

'You saying I come from *here*?' I eye the house again.

'It's the first place you lived, as far as anybody can tell. This is where you were found.'

'Found?'

I've been in The System since I was five. I know bits and pieces, but my workers loved stressing how important it was for me to live in the present, build a life with my foster families, yada-yada-yada. Like it's that easy.

The house stares back at me. This is where I lived before The System swallowed me up, but I have no memory of it.

'Social services found you here,' Frances says. 'You'd been living with a family; friends of your mother's, I think. Nobody's entirely sure who the family were, but one day they upped and moved and they left you behind. It's unclear how long you were here alone, but eventually somebody found you and that's when you were picked up and found a new home with your first foster family.'

The Carmichaels. I was with them for three years. They had five kids and I was the smallest. Mostly forgotten or used as a punch bag. My memories of that time are half glimpsed and confused, like they're projected onto water, only the ripples keep obscuring the stuff I want to see.

The dad, Liam Carmichael, died in a freak accident involving a power tool. The mum, Linda, couldn't cope and sent me back into The System.

(And do you really think it was a freak accident, knowing what you know about me?)

'How do you know this is where I was found?'

'I'm friends with Siobhan at the office. I assured her I thought it would be in your interest to be told certain things. You're almost a grown-up, you have the right to know.'

I don't want to know.

My past is a snapping mongrel at my heels, always catching up with me no matter how fast I run.

'Our past doesn't define us, Rumer,' Frances says. 'It's always a part of us, like a foreign accent or a wrinkle, but we can grow beyond it.'

The house is to my left.

Frances is sitting on my right.

I'm caught between them.

I want to believe her. Believe that, when we drive away from here, it'll sever some sort of invisible tie with my past. I can stay with Frances and George and be happy. Go back to school, maybe even university. Do normal things. Things people do when they're not cursed.

'Can we go?' I ask.

Frances starts the car and we leave the neighbourhood, but no matter how much better Frances tries to make me feel, it doesn't work. This is who I am. I am who I am to infinity and back again.

'Oh, would you look at that?' Frances tuts.

We're back from the shops and George is snoring in the lounge. She's not looking at him, though. She crosses to the window. A potted plant has shrivelled into a brown skeleton. 'Another one bites the dust.

My favourite, too.' She leaves the room. All the plants in the house seem to be dying, no matter how carefully Frances tends to them.

Later, George makes a Greek salad and some special bread that's almost like cake. He's so bubbly and Frances' laughter makes the living room glow gold. We eat with the dining room doors open so the summer air gusts in and the birds serenade us. I almost forget the broken-down house, but every time my mouth twitches into a smile, an image of the house kills it.

I notice Frances doesn't eat much, but she's never had a huge appetite.

We play poker all evening. It's one of the first things they taught me and I like the skill involved. The lies. My poker face is like a china mask. It's almost funny how easy it is to make them think they've got me figured out, then I swoop in with an ace and the expression on their faces is priceless.

My room's the best in the house. It's in the attic, hidden away. A porthole with coloured glass always catches the evening light, stamping a pink circle on the wonky floorboards. I like sitting and watching it roam about as the sun lowers.

Strings of bottle caps hang by my bed, decorations I make using things I find on the street, and I fall asleep listening to them.

I wake up to a strange sound.

Crying.

My stomach flips. It's Frances.

I go to my bedroom door. Frances and George are on the landing downstairs on their way to bed.

'She's a troubled girl,' George says softly.

'She's no trouble, none at all.'

'Then what's wrong?'

'I don't know. I just feel… different. Like something's wrong. I… My appetite's gone.'

I grip the door frame. I've never heard Frances talk like this. I feel sick.

'Perhaps you should go to the doctor.'

'I can't. I'd rather not know.'

'It could be stress. Or—'

'It's not stress! I've never been happier. Rumer's changed every-thing. I can't lose her.'

Lose me? Now I really do want to be sick. I don't understand what Frances is talking about. Why would she lose me?

'I just need sleep,' Frances says.

There's movement and I hurry back to bed.

When I hear Frances coming upstairs, I pretend to be asleep.

I don't know how long she stands at the door watching me, but I can tell she's still crying, softly, like she can't help it. And I can't help thinking it's my fault.

CHAPTER THIRTEEN

She's lying on the kitchen floor the next morning.

There was a crash that I heard all the way up in my attic room, and I stumbled out of bed, nearly tripping down the stairs, a hot, horrible certainty bristling through me.

'Frances? Frances? Speak to me.'

George is on his knees. Frances' hand is clasped between his, pressed to his cheek, but she doesn't move. Her chest doesn't move.

There's breakfast everywhere. She was cooking when it happened and a frying pan is tipped over beside her, baked beans splattered on the linoleum, the hob still burning. The heat's unbearable and I can't escape it. I'm rooted to the spot. I can see George's mouth moving but no sound reaches my ears.

All I see is her face. The trickle of blood on her top lip. Her eyes staring at me.

An aneurysm, we find out after the autopsy. It was only a matter of time.

They would say that. How do you explain the unexplainable?

I stay until she's buried. I owe her that much.

The next day, I pack my bag, leave George a note and spend my first night on the street.

In the nights that follow, when the summer heat starts to boil off and the autumn winds make it almost impossible to sleep, I sometimes feel Frances nearby. Like she's watching over me. Or judging me. Wishing I'd never come into her life, because if I hadn't, it would never have happened.

She was happy before me, and I was happy being miserable before I knew what it was like to be loved.

CHAPTER FOURTEEN

ONE DAY BEFORE THE HAMMER

A car horn jolts me awake. I grimace, rub my neck. I slept in the driver's seat. Why did I sleep in the driver's seat? And whose car is this? My mind tries to plug back into reality and, despite the knotted cables of my thoughts, I remember. All of it. The warehouse. The Reverend. Skinny. The SUV in the rear-view mirror and my panicked race through London.

I try to stretch but my body's bound in elastic bands. Everything hurts. I touch the broken tooth and shudder. For a moment, I feel like Frances is in the car with me, which is how I know I'm on the edge of delirium. I need food. Water. A soft bed and a dark room.

Cracking the door, I get out into drizzling rain and see where I am.

Across a gnarled lawn, the house creaks on its foundations, grotesque as a tomb. I'm parked at the kerb outside it.

This is where I escaped to. The only place that feels safe. I'm pretty sure nobody else knows about the house I was found in as a kid. Nobody ever comes here. It became my secret place after Frances died, and although my visits have become more frequent in the past year, I've only ever seen kids playing here once.

The wind whips my hair and I scan the deserted street, hurrying towards the house. I skirt around to the back garden and, crouching low, I pry open the basement window, slithering inside.

It's freezing down here. The stink of damp is comforting. Reassuring because it always smells like that. I hurry up the steps into the house. It's been gutted. A carcass of a home. The wallpaper peels away in raw-looking strips and the light's as fuzzy as my head.

I don't stop, going upstairs, my pulse quickening in anticipation. At the end of the landing rests a black door, the paint flaking as if gouged by claws. My legs tremble as I hurry for it, then I shove the door open and stagger into the Dead Room.

The walls are plastered with newspaper clippings. They form a tattered patchwork of headlines. My mother's yellowed face stares out from torn pages, distorted by ripples. There are other faces, too. Frances. Troll. Liam Carmichael.

These are the reports I cling to.

They tell the story of my curse. The people I've killed. Guilt twists a muscle I think might be my heart, but I don't fight it. Frances said I couldn't run from my past and she was right.

I sit cross-legged on the floor.

This is where I come to commune with the dead.

It's the only place I can be me. A few years ago, I went through a phase of hanging out in a nearby cemetery. Everybody there's already dead, but the Dead Room's different. I've read that a weirdly high percentage of criminals confess their crimes within hours of being arrested. Some are just boastful ingrates, but mostly I think the weight of whatever they've done is too much to bear.

I need this place more than anything else. I come here to confess and shift that weight, even just for a minute.

When I'm done with the Dead Room, I leave the way I came in. I feel more clear-headed but I can't hole up in there forever. I escaped Reverend Mara's pit and his troops will be after me. They won't stop until I tell them where to find the Crook Spear.

I'm in Enfield. My belly's so empty it's shrivelling inside me like one of those deep-sea rock plants. There's a row of shops not far away, but it's too quiet to go lifting. I'd be caught in seconds. The belly can wait until rush hour. Besides, if Mara finds me, hunger's the last thing I'll have to worry about.

Intel's what I'm after. Only way I'll even come close to getting the upper hand on that glorified lounge singer is to find out everything about him *and* what he's looking for. They say knowledge is power but I know better. Knowledge doesn't give you power, it gives you options, and right now my options are limited to run, die, hide. I don't plan on doing any of those things.

Ignoring the dull pang in my fractured tooth, I get into the car and drive. The fuel's running low, but it gets me close enough to where I'm headed. I park up a safe distance from the high school and check the dash. 11:39. Twenty minutes till lunch. I sit and watch the school, resisting the urge to pick at my nails, my knee bouncing like it's counting every snail-slow second.

A car shoots by so fast it rocks me in my seat.

'Get a fucking grip,' I tell the rear-view mirror.

Finally, the school bell rings and shapes jump behind the windows. Teenagers spill out into the front of the building, shoving, laughing. I'm out of the car in an instant and through a side door before you can say 'school sucks'.

Slipping between the students in the corridor, I keep my head down, hunching forward. In the countless times I've snuck in, nobody's ever guessed I don't go here. Never did, never will.

The library's at the back of the school and only the nerds use it. I push the door and go in, ignoring the librarian behind her desk; she's always too wrapped up in her phone to bother me. Scanning the dozen empty tables, I spot one that has a half-open rucksack. Inside, I see crisps, a can of Coke. My mouth fills with saliva and I can't resist.

Checking the library for whoever owns the bag, I only see a couple of students giggling over a German dictionary in the corner.

I pass the table and dip my hand in.

At the back of the room, five computers sit collecting dust. They're so ancient they should be knitting. The one in the corner is my favourite. It's tucked behind a shelf so nobody bothers me and I don't have to worry about anyone seeing crime scene snaps on my screen.

I slide into an uncomfortable plastic chair and boot up the relic, shoving crisps into my mouth and washing them down with Coke. I've never tasted anything so good, except maybe the liquorice they sell in the newsagent below my flat. That stuff could end wars.

The computer finally loads and I click open a browser. I type *Reverend Mara* and lean in, scanning the hits but, in ten pages, there are no matches. Plenty of reverends, plenty of Maras (including some actresses who look even more starved than me) but no Reverend Mara. I try adding *London* and *crime* but the search engine might as well shrug.

He has a different name and I don't know it.

My knee judders and I keep typing.

Reverend Mara Crook Spear.

Still no hits for the name, but a few pages contain the words 'Crook Spear'. Clutching the now-empty Coke can in my free hand, I scroll through, then frown. I scroll some more, chewing my lip.

As I read, my hand tightens around the can.

'You're fucking kidding me.'

It's a myth. The Crook Spear's a fucking myth. Every page I look at talks about some Arabian sorceress and a mystical weapon. It's like the Ark of the frickin' Covenant or something. An Eastern Excalibur.

I keep searching. This can't be right. This can't be *it*. I've stumbled across a load of occult nutters, that's all – there's enough of them online. But I keep looking and all I find are websites written by crackpots.

The can crumples in my fist.

One site has an excerpt from *World's Weirdest Wonders* by Damaris Harred.

While magic lamps and flying carpets are the most famous mystical arte-facts of Arabian myth, one little-known legend tells of the Crook Spear. Forged by a sorceress named Amira, it was used to murder a sultan and gifted the sorceress immortal powers. However, the spear was lost during a battle for the kingdom. Many scholars have debated the legend's validity, some arguing it is based on a real military coup – yet more have dismissed the story as a thinly veiled assault on patriarchy...

I'm practically chewing the can.

Just what is this? I've been kidnapped, pummelled like a side of beef, used as target practice and damn-near strangled all because some criminal wants to get his hands on the eighth wonder of the world?

This is a joke. Yeah, crazy shit happens in the world; I've seen first hand what curses are capable of. But a mystical Arabian weapon? I almost spit.

I've read enough. Tossing the can across the desk, I'm up and out of the library, knowing exactly where to go next.

Students keep getting in my way as I storm through the school, so I shove them, not caring if it breaks every rule of shadowing. Fuck it. Being invisible has done me okay most of my life, but sometimes it's a pain in the ass. I'm pretty sure somebody says 'Hey, who is that?' as I barrel past, but I don't stop to answer.

Back at the car, I slam the door and take off, tyres shrieking. Questions strobe in my mind, big and neon. How cracked is Mara if he believes in some ancient myth? And why does he think I have the spear?

That last one leads me to the only possible conclusion. Julian. Has to be. I don't know anybody else. He's stitched me up like a voodoo doll. Just thinking about it causes my foot to grow heavy on the accelerator and I tear down the road, aware I'm driving like a wild woman but not giving a crap. Screw the Highway Code. Julian owes me answers.

Twenty minutes later I'm outside his office. The sign says: HART DETECTIVE AGENCY. I've never been inside. Our relationship operates at one hundred yards and over. I've strolled by a few times out of curiosity, but he'd kill me if I broke his number-one rule. Time to test that.

Hot with irritation, I throw the door open and tear across the small office. Julian's behind a desk in the corner, feet up, phone to one ear. He barely has a second to register an emotion before I slam a hand down on the phone, cutting off the call.

'What do you know?' I demand.

He doesn't seem to be able to decide if he's angry or upset. He looks like a lawyer – big eared, rosy cheeked, navy suit – and his eyes are clear and blue. Honest eyes, the clients say, though I know he's anything but.

'Rumer,' he says calmly. 'You know the rules.'

'What. Do. You. Know?'

He grips the receiver, his gaze raking over my messy hair and clothes. Is he surprised? Was he expecting me to be dead by now?

I sense movement and see Rose on the other side of the room. Julian's assistant looks like a Japanese schoolgirl in her knee-skimming skirt and tight jumper. So sweet just looking at her gives you cavities. When she smiles at clients they become putty in her hands, but I know the smile masks a sneer.

'Stay there,' I growl, though I know she won't do anything stupid. It's not like she'd call the police.

I stare at Julian. 'Who the fuck is Reverend Mara and why does he think I've got some fictional weapon?'

71

'Mara? I've never heard of him.'

'Don't mess with me, posh boy.'

'Rumer, calm down–'

'That's the last thing you want to be saying,' I snarl.

Julian stiffens, then drags his feet off the desk. He eyes me a second longer and then drops the receiver back into its cradle.

'Rose, fetch us some coffee.'

His assistant keeps her gaze on me all the way into the kitchen out back. From here I can still see her and she knows it.

'Please, sit.' Julian gestures to the chair by his desk.

Warily, I drop into it, leaning forward to rest my elbows on my knees.

'Bad night?' He's trying to lighten the mood but he's only making me more irritable.

'Mara. Who is he?'

'I told you, I've never heard of him.'

He's messing with me. Julian knows everybody in London, or at least claims to. Unless he knows the Rev by another name. His real name.

'Accent? Messed-up eye? Likes kimonos?'

'Rumer, what's this all about?'

Rose sets a coffee in front of him. I notice the one she's made for me is in a chipped mug. Why break out the good china for a tramp? She goes back to her desk and sips what looks like hot water and lemon. Skinny bitch.

'You look like hell, kid,' Julian says.

'You would, too, if you'd had the couple of days I have.'

'Do I want to know?'

Rose's pen dances over a pad and I wonder if she's writing down everything we say.

'Stop whatever you're doing,' I tell her.

Julian waves dismissively. 'Rumer, Rose can do what she likes. She's at every meeting now. Had too many that ended, uh, unfavourably.'

He's delusional if he thinks this is a meeting.

Rose keeps writing. Is she noting down our conversation? Why bother? Insurance? Is Julian's memory going? He can't be more than thirty-five. Is she recording the conversation, too?

I've not seen him in months and he does look older, though I can't think why. I don't know anything about him and he doesn't know anything about me. When he wants me to carry out a job, he leaves a file in an old phone box on the canal. It contains a name, an address, cash. I've lost count of the number of people I've shadowed in the past two years. I don't ask questions. I wouldn't want to know anyway. The people I shadow, they've got it coming to them, and I'll take the money. The places I've had to go for it, I should be paid triple what Julian lays out.

Usually I shadow a target for seven days. Suss out their routine. Note where they go. Who they talk to. What they wear. When I'm done, I leave a file in the phone box with my report. My English teacher would be so proud.

'I was following Blake,' I say. That's the job I was on when Nicotine Man jumped me. 'Next thing I know, I'm in a warehouse and this Mara guy's telling me I took something of his.'

Rose's pen hovers in mid-air for a moment, then she continues writing.

'You stole from him?' Julian asks.

'You really don't know him?'

'Whatever this is, it's nothing to do with me. Sounds like you did something to piss him off.'

I bang the table with my fist.

'This isn't a joke! This guy was serious. He had an army with guns and a bunker full of dead people. I nearly... They're after me, I know it, and I don't have whatever it is they think I have! Somebody's setting me up.'

Julian's blue eyes sparkle and I hate him. He may be my sort-of boss, but he doesn't owe me anything, and it's clear he doesn't think I should be coming to him with my problems.

'The spear,' I say. 'Crook Spear. That's what Mara thinks I have.'

Julian sighs and sips his coffee.

'Rumer, you're just going to have to accept it when I say I have no idea about any of this. This Mara fellow, the spear. Either he's new in town or he's small fry. Either way, it's over. Take a few days, then get back to work.'

'You have contacts. Put the word out. Get the 411 on Mara.'

Julian's gaze is steady. 'Rumer, what did we agree when you started working for me?'

I pick my nails. I painted them dark purple a few days ago, but they're chipped to hell. I think of Mara's manicured talons. The kimono. He should be hosting luncheons, not throwing people into pits.

Julian continues to stare at me. I should've known this was how it would play out. I've survived this far on my own, why did I even bother coming here?

Because I've never been in this deep and I'd rather make a fool of myself with Julian than end up back in that pit. The work I do for him, it's never landed me in trouble. Mostly it's kept me out of it. The past two years have been the quietest of my life. I shadow. I don't fight. I don't bargain. I don't care.

This is different. The bog's sucking me down and I can't stop it.

'Rose?' Julian says.

Her gaze is heavy on me. Long lashes unblinking.

'The Hart Detective Agency is not and never will be liable for any damages or costs incurred, nor will it be held accountable for any–'

'I know the deal,' I growl.

Rose falls silent. Goes back to her notes.

Julian sighs again. He takes out his wallet and slides a load of notes across his desk to me. He puts the wallet away and sets something beside the cash. A cheap mobile phone.

'Clean up,' he says. 'Lay low for a few days. It'll blow over. Call me when you're ready.'

Yeah, thanks for nothing. They both stare at me and I'm out of options. I stand, consider the money then grab it, screwing it up in my fist.

'The phone, too,' Julian says and I take it, shoving it into my pocket.

'Don't let the door hit me on the way out, right?' I say.

CHAPTER FOURTEEN

Julian just looks at me, so I go to the door and walk out without closing it.

CHAPTER FIFTEEN

The cafe's warm with the smell of fried breakfast. I followed my nose to the first place with food and this place is just grimy enough to be safe. A few guys in dusty boots and bright jackets sit at rickety tables, but otherwise it's quiet. The radio plays out back. Some headache-y pop crap.

I order a coffee and a bagel and grab the stack of free papers from the counter, going to sit against the wall so I can keep an eye on the door.

Flipping through the papers, I hunt for anything that might be Mara-related. There's no mention of warehouses or Skinny or ninja gangs. No missing person reports that could be his work. Nothing on the Crook Spear, either, because wouldn't that have been nice? For a moment I'm hopeful the spear's touring with some museum exhibit and Mara got confused, but there's nothing. The spear's a myth and Mara's a maniac.

The spider in my mind draws its legs up under its belly. I chew the bagel on one side of my mouth, the broken tooth radiating pain that almost seizes up my jaw.

I finish my coffee and start getting antsy, wondering if I was followed. I should keep moving. Change my clothes. Maybe even shave my head. Anything that throws the Reverend off. I feel him watching me now with that milky eye. He sees me sitting in the cafe and he pities how easy I'm making it for him to track me down.

And the more I think about it, there really is only one person who would have the intel I need, and it's not Julian.

There are people I've met over the years who've freaked me the hell out. You live in my world, you don't exactly socialise with suburban housewives. When I lived on the streets, I met the kind of crazies who made me look like Mandy Moore. There was Gia, who claimed she was raised by a circus elephant and spoke to the dead in her sleep. She overdosed a few years ago. There was Hack, who wore a string of cats' teeth around his neck and was always adding more. I don't know what happened to him.

And then there was Bolt. He was the worst. Sly Bolt, who knew London's shadier corners so well it was like they were part of his anatomy. Angry Bolt, whose temper was like spitting coals. Wily Bolt, who won every argument.

I can't put it off any more. I should have gone to him in the first place. Sometimes you're your own worst enemy.

My gaze drops to the phone resting on the table; the one Julian gave me. It's so basic it doesn't even have the internet and I'm trying to figure out what to do with it. Julian's never given me a phone before. I poke it like it bites, then tear the back cover off.

I remember the way Rose reacted when I mentioned Reverend Mara. Her expression was as blank as the paper in her pad, but her eyes betrayed something.

Has Julian set me up? He flicked me off the way he'd remove a bug from his sleeve. Guilty conscience? Am I a scapegoat? The kind of people Julian does business with, I wouldn't be surprised if he'd pissed a dozen people off in the past week alone. And blaming me would be an easy out.

Perhaps Julian has the Crook Spear.

No, there's no such thing! This is all so messed up I can't keep it straight in my head.

The contents of the phone stare up at me. They look normal enough, but what do I know? Julian could have bugged it. He could track me, listen in on calls, tell when I'm taking a dump, and I'd be the idiot who trusted him. Meanwhile, he's scheming to hand me back over to Mara. This time, the Rev'll chain me up in the pit personally, assuming I survive that long.

I dash into the cafe's grotty toilet, dump the phone in the sink and turn the water on. When the phone's floating, I shut the water off and stare at my exhausted reflection. My hands are in my hair and I realise I have to calm down. First thing a rat does when it's trapped in a box is panic, then it starts chewing.

After splashing water on my face, I hurry out of the cafe.

Bolt lives in Hackney. I could drive but the car's out of juice. I inspect the crumpled bank notes Julian left me. Over a hundred big ones. He must be feeling really guilty.

Tube? The thought of being trapped underground constricts my chest.

Taxi it is.

I catch a ride with a black cab. The driver tries to make conversation but she gives up when I stop replying. The rumble of the car threatens to rock me to sleep and I resist, though my eyelids scratch like sandpaper. I wonder if I'm concussed. In all the comics I've read, that's a big deal. I hit my head when Nicotine Man tipped me into the pit. Am I awake or am I dreaming all of this?

Am I still in the pit?

The taxi drops me off on a small street near Brick Lane.

'You be careful, love, lots of weirdos out there,' she says as I slam the door. Everybody's suddenly so worried about me.

'I am the weirdo,' I mutter.

The rain's eased off but the sky's swollen with black clouds. I check the street and I'm pretty sure I'm not being followed. By Reverend Mara. By Julian. Two days ago, I had no enemies. Now I have enough to start a rock band.

Shivering into the wind, I approach a run-down row of shops. Most of them are boarded up. Sandwiched between two windows is Bolt's place. Assuming he's still here. I eye the displays behind smudged glass. Mildew clings to the mannequins and the clothes wear furry green coats. It looks condemned, but aside from a fresh outbreak of black mould, it's not much different to how I remember.

The sign on the door says CLOSED. I knock.

I count to thirty. Then another thirty. I knock again.

Part of me hopes Bolt won't answer. Then I'll have to find another way. That would be easier than dealing with him.

Another minute passes and there's no sign of Bolt.

I turn to leave and an arm locks around my throat. I grab it, beating against sinewy forearms and the body pressing behind me, but then I'm hoisted back through the shop door and thrown against a wall.

A face looms towards mine. One side is burnt and waxy, a flinty eye shining at me. His nostrils flare.

'Bolt,' I gasp, his forearm crushing my throat.

'How you know my name?' His whisky-soured breath blasts my face.

'It's… Rumer… you idiot…'

'What are you doing here? Who sent you?'

'Nobody. Bolt… Get the… fuck off me…'

He shakes me and my lungs are on fire.

I knee him in the groin and he drops me. We both gasp for air. Bolt throws his weight against the shop door, double-locking it.

'It's good to see you, too.' My throat's dented and sore.

'Can't bang on a man's door like that.' He's wearing a stained white T-shirt that shows hard muscle and his hair's long enough to cover the burnt side of his face. It's hard to tell how old he is. Mid-twenties, but his paranoia ages him.

'I'm guessing you don't get many visitors these days,' I say.

'Nobody polite enough to knock.'

'That why the place looks like a neat-freak's nightmare?'

'What do you want, Rumer?'

Maybe I hurt him more than I realised. He's even more of a mess than he was a year ago.

'I need intel.'

His eyes are dark under his brow.

'Nobody ever comes with flowers,' he mutters, going past me to the back of the shop. Warily, I follow, trudging up a narrow stair-case into the flat above the shop. It's as creaky as the rest of the place. The lounge walls are cracked, revealing gap-toothed slats beneath the plaster.

Bolt leans by the window, which is barely covered by a rag of a curtain. Arms crossed, expression as grim as I always remember it.

'Well?'

That's the pleasantries out the way, then.

I don't know where to start. The past few days have been a chaotic jumble of places and people and faces. Now I'm in a room with Bolt and all I can think about is the fire, the upturned cars, dragging him across the road. Running. Leaving him to bleed into the tarmac.

I stay by the door and start with the part where Nicotine Man kid-napped me. I don't stop until I get to the bit where Bolt's strangling me. I try to read his expression but it remains blank throughout. He always was good at poker. When I finish, his expression's gloomy.

'And so you decided to involve me,' he grunts. 'Should've kept strangling you.'

'I figured if anybody knew anything about this, it'd be you.'

'Because everybody knows Bolt's always caught up in somebody's messy business.'

'Because you're a miserable bastard and I knew you'd get some sick pleasure out of seeing somebody else is miserable, too.'

His laugh cuts the air between us. 'You're right, there.'

We stare at each other. His green eyes are sharp as cut stone and I can tell he's trying to figure out how he can benefit from this.

'What's it been, a year?'

I nod.

A year since we argued in the car and you were so angry I thought you'd open the door and toss me out into the road.

Instead, something equally awful happened and Bolt quit his police job, handed his badge in, retreating into the shop his father left him. I watched him for a while, when I had plucked up the courage. He barely came out of the shop for the first six months, even when the bandages weren't plastered to his face any more. It got too painful, though, and I got busy working for Julian.

'You're in quite a pickle,' Bolt says finally.

'I wish I was pickled.'

He roams the room, his arms still crossed.

'If Reverend Mara wants you, you're in deep shit.'

'You know who he is?' My pulse quickens.

Bolt nods. Chews a fingernail. 'He's been throwing his weight around ever since Takehiko Kobayashi died.'

Everybody in London knows that name. Kobayashi was a Japanese businessman whose roots were tangled in the city's criminal underworld. Every deal he made, he sealed with blood. He had allies everywhere. The law couldn't touch him. Twenty years ago he was at the corrupt heart of the City. Then his skull made friends with a bullet.

'Mara?' I ask.

'Mara worked for Kobayashi. When Kobayashi died, various factions fought for his crown. Mara's spent almost two decades taking out the competition and now he's got a foothold, he's going in for the kill. Wants to become king of the underworld, and he's got some pretty radical ideas about how to do that.'

'Radical why?'

'The Crook Spear,' Bolt says.

'But it doesn't exist. He's chasing some kind of Holy Grail.'

'Doesn't matter. If he has this great, mythical weapon, nobody would dare challenge him.'

'Assuming they believe it has magical powers, too,' I say.

'I'm not saying it's not a flawed plan...'

'So it's a spear.'

'A pointy one, I'm guessing.'

My mind somersaults. 'If Mara thinks I have a spear, I can find a spear from somewhere, hand it over, job done. We'd be shot of each other.'

Bolt's grin doesn't inspire confidence. 'Some people say it's not a spear.'

'Of course they do. What do they say it is?'

'Hell if I know. It's all bullshit, Rumer. The guy's crazier than a flea-bitten cat.'

Stands to reason.

'Look, if he's after you, the best you can do is get out of town. If he thinks you have the spear, he won't give up.'

'I'm not hiding.'

Bolt comes closer. He's almost a foot taller than me. His hair hangs over his face and remorse leeches at me as I glimpse the waxy burns.

'Rumer, this guy's bad. When Kobayashi died, there was talk Mara did it. He killed his own father to take his throne.'

'Wait, Kobayashi was Mara's dad?'

Bolt nods. 'He's a pit bull. Worse, a Dobermann. He'll tear you to pieces.'

I stare up into his shadowy face, then frown. Kobayashi is famous as a mobster, but I know his name from somewhere else. For some reason, I'm thinking about my mother. She knew Kobayashi.

The curse of Celene Cross.

I remember the article I read as a teenager. Kobayashi was the monster who formed The Divine Order, the cult my mother joined before she fell pregnant. She worked for him.

It all comes back to my mother. A snake eating its tail.

Is that why Mara thinks I have the spear? Something to do with her?

'I should go.'

'What you going to do?'

'Find out who's setting me up, for a start.' I descend the stairs back into the shop. Bolt follows.

'You changed,' he says.

For a moment he almost looks sane. I forget the guilt and all I want is to forget everything else. Forgetting would be bliss. But I can never forget. Every time I've relaxed, somebody's died.

'You look good.' Bolt half lingers in shadow. 'I–' Before he can say something we'll both regret, I'm out of the shop and back on the street. I turn into the wind and stop suddenly.

Further up the street, a figure hurries round a corner and vanishes. I chase after it, but when I reach the corner, there's nobody in sight. I could swear somebody was watching me.

It looked like Julian's assistant, Rose.

CHAPTER SIXTEEN

So Rose is after me. I'm sure of it. I only caught a brief glimpse of somebody watching as I left Bolt's shop, but I could swear it was her. It's too much of a coincidence, and I've never really believed in those. Why is she shadowing me? Did Julian put her up to it? Or is she following me on somebody else's orders?

It's time I set a trap of my own.

I wander back towards Brick Lane. I shouldn't go far. If Rose is following me, there's no point setting a trap if I lose her.

I size up a hotel and go in. It's nothing fancy; a chain that probably looks the same no matter which part of the country you're in. The walls are sunshine yellow. A smiley celebrity probably paid a fortune for her face grins from every leaflet. A fake potted plant sits on the desk. The man behind it is just as genuine, grimacing through fake tan at my bedraggled clothes and hair. I'm surprised he doesn't shoo me away. Turns out beggars can be choosers.

'Will that be a twin or single room?' he asks.

I really want to say 'twin' and feed his sordid imagination, but I'm too tired and, honestly, he's easy prey.

'Single,' I say, pulling out the bank notes.

'Fill this out.' He nudges a form across the desk. I use the standard bullshit details I've perfected over years of filling out forms – my fake name, *Cherry Gently*, is too good to retire now – then pay him from my dwindling stock of cash. He hands me a key card. I ride the lift to the fifth floor and wander down a corridor that stinks of cigarettes and cleaning chemicals, then use the key to get into my room.

The bed looks so fluffy I almost collapse into it at once, but I resist with all my willpower. At the window, I peer through the net curtains. The street seems a long way down, cars honking as they line up. The building across the street is typical London – a fried chicken shop on the ground floor, and everything above it is flats. There's a flat roof the chicken shop guys probably use to smoke weed. It's perfect for what I've got planned.

I glance at the digital clock by the bed.

14:30.

How long will it take? I'm not sure. If Rose followed me to Bolt's it stands to reason she's followed me here, too. I wonder if she saw me check in. Maybe she's standing outside the door with a gun in her hand. Killing me won't achieve anything, though. If I'm a scapegoat, she needs me alive.

I go to the door and press an eye to the peephole.

The corridor's clear.

My feet take me back to the bed, but that would be the end of me. Maybe it's the exhaustion but for a moment I wonder if an end – ending it all – would be a good thing. I'm a deadly contagion. Spend too much time with me and I'm in your bloodstream, spreading sickness, setting you up for a messy fall.

On the bureau sits a pot of shiny cutlery. The knife looks blunt, but if I grit my teeth, I should be able to get the job done. That'd rob Rose and Julian and whoever else of the victory. I'd claim it for myself.

My fingers reach for the knife.

No. That wouldn't be a victory. It'd be giving in for good. I imagine the look on my mother's face, a kind of snarling disappointment, and I reach past the knife, grab the kettle. I fill it with water from the bathroom and make myself a strong cup of instant coffee. It tastes like dirt but I cram biscuits into my mouth, too, and I begin to feel better. Not as cold. My fingers tingle.

Turning the radio on, I clamber onto the bed and jump up and down on it, stuffing more biscuits into my mouth. I'm fizzing with nervous energy and I can't stay still.

Let's not make it easy for them. Whoever's setting me up obviously wants me floating in dirty water the way my mother was. Imagine how surprised they'll be when they discover my backbone's adamantium like Wolverine's. All the people I've killed, all the guilt and hatred and confusion, it hardens a person. I know what Bolt meant when he said I'd changed.

I'm not going down without a fight.

When I look at the clock again, it's 15:50. The world's darkening and I should probably get moving before it's too dark to see properly.

The bed looks suitably messy and I leave the bathroom light on, the shower running. If somebody listens at the door, they'll think I'm in here.

There's an umbrella in the wardrobe. I grab it.

Checking through the peephole, I see the corridor's clear and crack open the door. Peer out. Still nobody. The door clicks behind me and I hurry for the fire exit, shoving it open, relieved it's not alarmed. I peer down the metal staircase, checking nobody's lying in wait, then hurry down it, the stairs clanging in the enclosed space no matter how quietly I step.

I shove the emergency exit open and hurry into the cold autumn air. At the end of the alley, I glimpse the street and move swiftly towards it, scanning the alley for movement. I'm the only one here.

At the street, I huddle against the wall, watching. I don't see Rose. Or Reverend Mara. Or black-masked ninjas with guns. They could be anywhere. I'll just have to risk it. Better to risk it than get caught in this alley. They could do whatever they liked to me then and nobody would notice.

The umbrella clicks open and I clutch it low enough to obscure my face. Taking a breath, I hurry across the road, my heart thrashing in my chest. Reaching the other side, I hop into another alley.

It's almost identical to the one I just left. Filled with bins and tumbling newspaper rags. I feel beady eyes watching me from under the bins and hope it's only rats.

A wooden fence runs along the side of the alley. Over it is the space behind the fried chicken shop and a rickety set of stairs is fixed to the back wall. Another fire escape, just where I'd hoped it would be.

I listen. Hear voices. But they're coming through a window. Workers in the chicken shop's kitchen. Tossing the umbrella aside, I grab the fence and heave myself up. Splinters skewer my palms and I grit my teeth, throwing a leg over the fence and rolling to the other side, only just getting my boots under me in time to land.

Shooting a glance at the back of the chicken shop, I'm relieved the kitchen windows are steamed up. Nobody can see me. If I move quickly, they'll never know I was there.

Ignoring my stinging palms I rush for the fire escape, holding my breath the whole way up. I count five windows as I go. At the top, I clamber onto the grey square of roof, weak with relief.

It's spitting rain. I stare out across the network of rooftops. Broccoli-like treetops sprout between the buildings and, in the distance, a twinkle of light comes from the skyscrapers in Canary Wharf.

I'm suddenly aware of how exposed I am. The wind whips my hair into my eyes. Quickly, I cross the roof and crouch by the waist-high ledge, shielded from the road below.

The hotel rests across the street. Peeking over the edge, I count the windows until I reach a room with a dim glow behind net curtains. The bathroom light I left on. The room's still empty, as far as I can tell.

My pulse begins to slow and I slump against a chimney pot.

Now the waiting begins.

It's pitch dark before I'm even aware of the fading light, and with the dark comes a nipping wind. I wrap my coat tighter and put my hood up, but it doesn't help. The cold's in my bones. An icy certainty that this is all going to end with me dead and nobody even caring enough to put me in the ground. Which is fine. What have I ever done for anybody?

I glance periodically over at my hotel room, sure that whoever's set me up will break in at any moment. At least then I'll know who I'm really up against. I'll be pissed if it's Julian. He's provided the only income I've ever had. If he's using me as a scapegoat, I can kiss goodbye to the flat. The mattress on the floor. The odds and ends I put in there to make it into a home.

I have no idea what the time is. The traffic becomes a rushing torrent of fumes and angry engines, then finally subsides. I watch the commuter army cram into the nearest Tube station, then the street quietens.

It has to be around 8pm.

Huddling against the chimney, my mind wanders back to Bolt's place. He said I'd changed, but he was different, too. Calmer, when he wasn't trying to crush my throat. Maybe he's grown up. Unless he's in on this, too. He'd nearly choked me when I turned up, which I'd half expected. Was it just an act? Had he been calm after that because he'd been waiting for me to turn up?

I tear my nails with my teeth. I'm so paranoid I almost don't even trust myself.

Would you trust somebody who could kill you just by sitting next to you?

I catch movement out of the corner of my eye. A shadow passes through my hotel room. I tense against the roof ledge, craning as far forward as I dare, squinting at the hotel.

Somebody's broken into my room. Somebody's been following me.

Instead of feeling relief that I'm not completely paranoid, I chew the inside of my cheek. The shape in the hotel room moves stealthily behind the net curtain and I can't tell who it is. Rose? Julian?

The shadow goes into the bathroom, then comes out again and approaches the bed. Something goes flying. Must be the duvet. The figure's at the window. It looks out, searching. Then it stops moving. I crouch lower, but it's too late. It's seen me.

The figure draws the netting aside and I glimpse long, ghostly white hair. It frames a narrow, bony face. Dark eyes blaze across the space between us.

And I've gone mad.

I cease to exist. I'm blank and inside out and dead and alive all at once.

Because I know that face.

It belongs to my mother.

Article from *The Sunday Times*

Police hunt businessman's killer

By JAMES WALLACE
Reporter
Police are hunting a 30-year-old woman in connection with the murder of a prominent businessman.

The woman, believed to be Celene Cross, was captured on CCTV footage near Waterloo Bridge the night Takehiko Kobayashi, 45, was killed almost two weeks ago.

Mr Kobayashi was an influential tradesman who came to London in the '70s and quickly established a profitable empire. He was shot dead in his offices at Silver Tower on 20 May and found by his son, Chouko Kobayashi.

Ms Cross, who is reported to be pregnant, is also wanted for multiple murder charges and bank raids, including the raid on an HSBC branch in South Kensington, in which 13 hostages were killed.

Detective Chief Inspector Harriet Wilson said: 'I would urge anyone who thinks they have seen Ms Cross to contact the police as soon as possible. Anyone who sees her should not approach her.'

CHAPTER SEVENTEEN

I'm frozen. I've seen her face a hundred times staring hollowly out from the front pages of newspapers. The face of a killer. A sharp nose like a blade, bloodless lips, hair the colour of crows. The same as mine.

But she's dead. That's what they say. What everybody says. So why is she staring at me now from across the street? She looks like a dead version of the woman who murdered all those people in the '90s. A parody of Celene Cross. Everything that was sleek and vital about her has become ashen. Her hair's so white, like it's been drained of life, and her skin is a hard marble so pale it's almost blue.

Maybe she looks dead because she is. She's clawed her way out of the earth. Come for me. I've killed so many people, she's going to even the score. Make me feel the pain of every death, including hers.

She lingers in the window and I can't read her expression. Her white lips don't move. Her dark eyes are riddles, seeing me. *Seeing me.* My mother's looking at me for the first time and I'm looking back and neither of us can move.

A spark flashes on the roof next to me.

I jump, unsure what caused it.

Another spark and I lurch backwards, away from the ledge. My gaze roves up to the hotel roof and I see a shape crouched there. Hunched over a gun that's pointed right at me.

She's not alone.

She's gone from the window. The hotel room's empty.

She's coming for me.

It's raining bullets. Another spray narrowly misses me and I stumble back towards the fire escape. A lasso of pain lashes my calf. I hurl myself at the steps, surrounded by the tinny pop of bullets striking the metal above my head as I descend.

Urged on by some primitive instinct, I clatter down the fire escape. I push all thoughts of my mother from my mind, hurtling away from the roof. As I reach the bottom, dark shapes spill into the cement space at the back of the chicken shop.

Reverend Mara's dogs.

'You lie with your mother's tongue.'

It all becomes clear. She's working with Mara. She worked for his father and now she's moving down the family tree. That's how he knew who I was. Are we similar? Does she lie the way I do?

Something whooshes through the air and a knife strikes the bricks, missing my ear by centimetres.

I take the only route open to me, bowling into the chicken shop's kitchen. A couple of shocked workers stare as I crash through, knocking over pans and blundering on into the shop. I squeeze under the counter, ignoring the yells of the shop workers, and hurtle out onto the street.

The window shatters behind me. The sniper on the roof? Or Mara's ninjas?

Not wasting another breath, I turn and pound the pavement, shouts erupting behind me as the Reverend's men shove people out of the way to give chase.

This is bad. This is it. No way I can outrun all of them.

I see a corner up ahead. If I can just get around it, I'll at least be out of range. Maybe find a car. Maybe not get killed.

Even as I will myself to speed up, a figure in a baseball cap turns the corner and strolls towards me. He sneers and his teeth are stained, his nose fixed with a white plaster. Nicotine Man.

'Still running!' he crows, raising a gun at me.

I skid to a halt.

Time slows down.

The barrel of the gun is a black hole, a sucking vacuum.

The sound of screeching tyres fills my ears and I hear a voice shouting.

'Rumer! Rumer, get in!'

A vehicle mounts the pavement between me and Nicotine Man. A beaten-up van. The passenger door swings open and Bolt's at the wheel, calling, his hand outstretched.

In a daze, I clamber into the van. I hear Nicotine Man shrieking but then we're reversing and we're back on the road and traffic's whizzing by, but all I can think is *she's alive*. My mother's alive and she wants me dead.

Part Three
THE GHOST

CHAPTER EIGHTEEN

Everything I know about Bolt:

1. He was a police officer.

2. His mother died when he was a baby so his dad raised him.

3. Coffee makes him paranoid.

4. He's the only person who could see the shadow.

CHAPTER NINETEEN

ONE DAY BEFORE THE HAMMER

Bolt's talking, but I'm not listening. My hands are numb, my ears ringing. The windscreen wipers flip back and forth but all I see is the rain. It lashes the road and I want to get out and soak in it. Feel anything other than the sensation that my mind's splitting apart.

Her hair was so white. Her eyes so dark. It's like I've fallen into those black pits. Now I'm stuck in the filth at the bottom and, no matter how much I struggle, I'll never be free. She'll never let me be free, because I'm part of her, and she's part of me. Always.

'Rumer!'

I blink, look at Bolt.

'Are you hurt?'

'No,' I murmur. 'I'm fine.'

'You're bleeding.'

He's looking down at my leg. My jeans are torn at the back, blood leaking from my calf onto the car floor.

'It's nothing.'

'You've been shot. We need to get that seen to.'

'It's nothing. What were you doing there?'

'Doing where?'

'Following me! Are you with her?'

Bolt shoots me a glance and the spider in my mind practically goes belly up.

'Who's her?' he asks.

I can't say it. Even thinking it makes me feel like I've lost it. My mind's attached itself to a balloon and floated into the sky.

'I was worried about you,' Bolt grunts. 'Reverend Mara is nasty business.'

We screech around a corner. I have no idea where we're going. If he drove into the Thames, I wouldn't stop him. His gaze skips between the rear-view mirror and the road. Back and forth, like the wipers. Are we being followed? Is my mother still chasing me?

'Faster.' I can't breathe. 'Faster. You have to go faster!'

'Stop it!' Bolt pries my hands away from the wheel. 'Are you crazy? What's wrong with you?'

I collapse against the seat, trembling.

We don't talk for a while.

Bolt drives into an underground car park and stops the van. I get out and limp back to the street. It's still raining heavily. I stand on the pavement, staring up at the sky, soaking it up. I can breathe again. I'm Rumer Cross and the rain's washing everything away. All the dirty laundry. I can start afresh. Forget it all.

Bolt steers me down the street. I'm aware I'm limping, but I can't feel the pain.

'Where we going?'

'A friend's.'

Red and yellow lanterns bob above our heads, strung up between shop fronts and colourful signs and I know we're in Chinatown, though I can't think why. The smell of fried food squeezes my stomach tight.

Bolt leads me to a door beside a restaurant and we go up a narrow flight of stairs, away from the smell of food. At the top, somebody opens another door. A small Chinese man with a few wisps of grey hair on his head and a pale blue shirt. He's barefoot.

'Welcome.' The man bows. 'In. Come in.'

I'm in a daze as I go into a neat flat. Snaking dragons snarl in frames on the wall and rugs cover the bare floorboards. Colourful masks scream from their perches on a bookcase. More dragons and demons and things with snakes for hair. A low table in the centre of the room is surrounded by silk cushions.

'Peng, this is Rumer,' Bolt says. 'Rumer, Peng.'

'You are most welcome,' Peng says, clasping his small hands together in front of him. His eyes twinkle warmly in his lined face.

I nod and try to smile, but the signal gets lost on the way to my mouth.

How can she be alive? What's she been doing all these years? Whoever washed up on the banks of the Thames that day wasn't my mother. Was it all a set-up? Play dead and the cops'll dig a grave?

We all believed the lie. Everybody.

'Do you have dressing?' Bolt asks. 'Rumer's hurt.'

Peng nods. 'Dressing, yes.' He beckons us into the kitchen, the cupboards a green that makes me think of the ocean, plants spilling over the top.

'Sit, sit,' Peng insists. I do as he asks and he pads about, taking things from drawers and placing them on the table. Bandages and cotton wool and ointments. I examine my calf. It's bloody but I can't find the wound.

'I'll do it,' Bolt says.

'I'm fine.'

Anything to take my mind off the woman I just saw in my hotel room. I hitch up my trouser leg, sucking air through my teeth as the fabric grazes my calf. I swab the blood with the cotton wool, exposing a gleaming wound where the bullet sank its teeth in. Not too deep. I clean it with the ointment and wrap a bandage around it.

'You've done that before,' Bolt says.

Peng's joined us at the table. He pours sweet-smelling tea into handleless cups.

'Drink,' he insists, pushing a cup closer. 'Good for you.'

'Thanks.' I take a sip. It tingles all the way down, soothing my insides.

'Peng has a cure for everything,' Bolt says, slurping his tea. 'He owns the medicine place downstairs. They call him a miracle man.'

'How do you know each other?' I ask.

'Let's just say Peng's helped me out of a spot or two.'

Peng winks at me. 'Busy boy. Always in trouble.'

'He definitely knows you,' I say.

'You in trouble, too,' Peng says, his gaze fixed on me. '*Shen* no good.'

'*Shen?*'

'Energy.' Peng taps his heart. 'Here.'

'How do you–' I begin.

'Miracle man,' Bolt interrupts. '*Shen* is a person's spiritual energy. Been sleeping well lately?'

The black bags under my eyes answer for me.

'I treat,' Peng insists. 'Fix you up good.'

Laughter erupts from my mouth and I slap a hand over it. I hadn't meant to laugh, but the thought of somebody fixing me seems ridiculous after all this time. After all the people on my list.

'Sorry,' I say. 'That's... I don't need fixing.'

I can't be fixed.

'I try.' Peng nods energetically. 'I try. Come.'

He gets up from the table and holds out a wrinkled hand. Rising slowly, I take it and he leads me to a small room just off the lounge. It's bare apart from a bed with white sheets and a cart in the corner that's crammed with oils and a little machine puffing smoke.

'Lie down,' Peng instructs.

Bolt's at the door, but Peng shoos him away, shutting us in.

'You're in quite a predicament,' he says as he turns from the door. 'Quite a predicament indeed.'

I can't help staring at him. Peng's accent has vanished, replaced with a soft London lilt. He doesn't seem to notice my surprise, checking the ointments on the cart in the corner.

'Your friend's a good boy, but he has a tendency to land himself in trouble. Your *shen* is in far worse shape than his, though.'

'I'm sorry–' I begin, still staring in disbelief.

'Oh, the accent. Habit, I'm afraid. Some people expect the Chinese medicine man routine. I don't mind it, to be honest, but it can be quite tiring. I've a feeling you're not that way inclined.'

For what feels like the first time in ages, I smile.

'Please, lie down.' Peng gestures to the bed.

I can't refuse. I climb onto the firm mattress and stare at the ceiling, my hands resting on my stomach. Peng pads around me.

'Relax, take a deep breath,' he tells me. 'Close your eyes.'

I breathe deeply but my body's tense. I don't like it. I don't want Peng to get hurt.

'Close your eyes.'

For once, I do as I'm told and Peng's hands are warm on my forehead. Firm but soothing. Then they're gone and I hear Peng shuffling to the cart in the corner.

'Stone,' he says, and I feel a sudden weight against my throat, another on my chest. Finally, he balances a stone on my forehead.

'Still. Calm.' Peng begins humming.

I feel part-way between stupid and desperate. I can't be fixed. I've inherited every bad thing my mother ever did and it's been stewing inside me since birth, marinating as it condenses into poison.

As Peng hums, I realise my muscles aren't rigid any more. The tension's left them and it's as if my body's levitating. I'm floating up into the white ceiling.

White.

Like her hair.

The ceiling becomes a writhing mass of white strands. They snake around me, binding my limbs and I can't move.

Peng's stopped humming. I hear a gurgling sound and a drop of something warm lands on my cheek. My eyes snap open just as Peng collapses to the floor. In seconds, I'm on my feet and standing over him, though I'm too afraid to touch him.

Peng pulls himself up. Blood dribbles from one of his nostrils and he's muttering something in Mandarin. He won't look at me. Instead, he goes to the door and disappears into the kitchen.

I was expecting something like this. It's happened before. Gia, the girl who said she was raised by a circus elephant, tried to read my palm once. At first it was fun, but then she started saying some really messed-up stuff, and then she stopped talking altogether. She went and sat by herself in a corner and didn't speak to me for days. I never found out why.

Wiping the drop of blood from my cheek, I go into the lounge.

Bolt's by the window, peering down at the street. Peng's muttering in the kitchen and it sounds like he's throwing things around. Bolt casts me a worried glance.

'Everything okay?'

'Ask him.'

We go to the kitchen. Peng's plucking strange substances from little jars and tossing them into a pestle and mortar on the counter, always muttering in Mandarin, like he's praying. He grinds the ingredients into a paste.

'Peng?' Bolt ventures.

The miracle man ignores him, shuffling across the kitchen and snatching a large leaf from a plant. He uses it to scoop the paste from the bowl and hurries to me, gesturing for me to take it from him.

'Eat, now.'

He's back playing the Chinese old man card, but I think I catch a glint in his eye that wasn't there before.

'What is it?' I ask, staring down at the leaf in my hand. The paste is thick and grainy, a mustard yellow.

'You in more trouble than Bolt ever was,' Peng says. His gaze has hardened and I can't tell if he's afraid or angry. Did he see what I saw? My mother lying on the ceiling, her white hair snaking towards me?

'What kind of trouble?' Bolt asks.

'Curse.' Peng's sweating and I tremble, eyeing the paste.

How does he know?

'Take.' He pushes the leaf up to my mouth. 'Cleanse. Good for you. Very good.'

Unable to refuse him, I scrape the paste into my mouth. It tastes like he fished it out of the sewer and I fight the urge to spit it out.

'Finish,' Peng urges.

Eyes burning, I swallow. It oozes down my throat and I retch, but it stays down. My tongue sticks to the roof of my mouth and the aftertaste is almost worse than the paste itself.

Bolt wanders back into the lounge, sits at the window. I stand in the door and Peng sits on the floor in the middle of the living room, his legs crossed. He closes his eyes. He's meditating? Now?

Bolt looks at me but doesn't say anything. We have a sort of unspoken agreement that we don't talk about our pasts. When he found me, I was seventeen and living rough, barely eating, not speaking. The last person I wanted to speak to was a police officer, so we didn't talk. We'd play poker and sometimes I'd let him win.

I have no idea what Bolt made of the whole *shen* thing, but there's a flicker of something when he turns to face me. Concern maybe. Confusion definitely. He must have no idea what to think of Reverend

Mara suddenly tailing me, or my crazy behaviour in the van when he saved me from... her.

Even if he wants to ask me about it, he doesn't.

I remain in the doorway and my gaze slides to Peng.

'Do you know anything about the Crook Spear?' I ask. Bolt said it's a mythical object, and Peng seems to move in those circles. It's a stab in the dark, but it's still a stab.

Peng's eyes open slowly and he considers the table before him for a moment.

'Never heard of spear,' he says, and I wish he'd drop the medicine man act, but maybe he thinks Bolt likes it. Maybe he's been pretending around Bolt for so long, he forgets how to stop pretending. I sort of get that.

'I told you, it doesn't exist,' Bolt grunts, staring out the window. Paper lanterns bob on wires.

Peng gets up from the floor. 'You stay. Meditate. Make better.'

'If I stay any longer—' We've been here for at least an hour; I need to move on.

'You should rest,' Bolt says. 'Sleep.'

'Come,' Peng says, going to the room with the white bed. Hesitating, I follow. The need for sleep is almost overpowering. My eyelids feel heavy and just the thought of curling up somewhere eats away at my resistance. If Peng's done something to me, maybe it'll last a while. I can sleep for a few hours then leave. Figure out my next move.

'What about you?' I ask Bolt.

'Floor,' he says. 'Looks comfy enough.'

'You're not going back to yours?'

'Can't.' Bolt avoids my gaze.

'Why?'

He doesn't answer.

'Why can't you go back?' I ask.

'It's not there any more.'

'What do you mean? Bolt?'

'After you left, somebody torched the place. I couldn't stop it.'

My chest tightens. It can't be true. The shop was all Bolt had in the world. His father left it to him. It can't be gone. Bolt's body language tells me otherwise.

'I'm sorry.'

'Not your fault.'

We both know that's not true. It's too much of a coincidence not to be my fault. Somebody wants me to know I can't hide. And whoever tries to help me will receive the same treatment.

'Night,' he says, turning to peer out the window again.

'Yeah.'

I go into the room.

'You sleep, replenish,' Peng says. He smiles at me and shuts the door.

> **curse**
> [*kurs*]
> *noun*
> 1. the desire for a calamity, misadventure or evil to occur to the detriment of an individual or group.
> 2. a vulgar vow or curse word.
> 3. an evil that has been conjured against an individual or group.
> 4. an object that is accursed.

I read the article on Dominic Waters, *The Curse of Celene Cross*, when I was fourteen. It tipped me into an obsessive free fall. I killed hours in the school library tearing apart old books, hunting for anything on curses and how to break them.

Most of the stuff I read was bogus. You'd have to be cracked to believe it. The internet was no better. Everybody thinks curses are a joke.

Are you cursed? Top 10 signs to look out for!

A beginner's guide to breaking a curse!

How to hex your frenemies!

People are morons. Try living a curse, that'll sober you up. That's the weirdest thing. Cursed objects outnumber cursed people a thousand to one. There was a guy called Rasputin who did something really fucked up to the Russian imperial family, but the 'cursed' objects I found online looked like things from a scrapheap. The Dybbuk box, the Basano vase, a '70s painting called 'The Hands Resist Him'.

There was also something called the *Superman curse*, which is where I drew the line.

Whatever Dominic Waters did to my mother as she pushed me out, it was so dark you couldn't find a *How to…* online. It was some occult shit that only he can undo. And he won't be undoing it in a hurry. I couldn't find him anywhere. He'd either changed his name, moved or died. Probably all three. Either way, he was a guy who didn't want to be found and he did a great job of burrowing deep enough that people forgot he ever existed.

Nobody's going to save me.

It's just me, myself and Rumer.

I stopped researching curses.

Words lashed me in my sleep.

'Rumer! Tumour! Rumer! Tumour!'

And I dreamed the curse was a thing buried under my skin, growing skeletal fingers, hauling itself up my throat and out of my mouth.

And when it was out, its black eyes were my mother's, its hair was her black hair and it hissed and came for me, but there was no way of escaping because this thing is me and I'm it.

CHAPTER TWENTY

THE DAY OF THE HAMMER

I wake up surrounded by plants. They fill the floor around the bed, leaves everywhere, all different shapes and sizes. Peng must have brought them in while I slept. Weird, I usually wake up at the slightest sound. What was in that brew he gave me? Stretching and unsettled, I ease myself up, every muscle twanging, and scrutinise the plants. The ones closest to the bed have all withered into brown husks, but those against the wall are green and thriving.

Whatever Peng did, it seems to have bought me some time.

Time. I have no idea what time it is. Faint light's nudging through the blinds but it can't be morning already. That'd mean I slept all night. Fear thuds in my chest and I slide off the bed, gritting my teeth at the pain in my calf, which is even worse than the pain in my broken tooth. Hobbling between the pots, I open the door, scared of what I'll find.

Bolt jerks upright on the floor. When he sees it's me, he relaxes and rubs his eyes.

'Sleeping beauty,' he grunts, pushing his hand through his hair, briefly exposing the burns along the right-hand side of his face.

'What's the time?'

He looks at his watch. 'Seven.'

'Are you... okay?'

'Never.'

I release a breath. 'Can't argue with that. Where's Peng?'

'Shop. He starts early. Left you some of that stuff from last night, though. In the kitchen.' I can tell he wants to ask me about it. Maybe unzip me and see what's inside. If I really am carrying a curse, like an unborn child. Or a parasite.

I'm not in the mood to talk about it. There's a little orange pot on the kitchen table. I lift the lid and the stench of the paste forces my throat closed. Why does it have to taste so awful?

'He said it'll help.' Bolt's behind me and I jump. My nerves are frayed from the past few days. If he noticed my skittishness, he doesn't say anything, and I'm grateful. I feel like enough of an idiot as it is.

I scoop the paste out with my fingers and force it into my mouth, glad Bolt can't see my face. My eyes water and my nostrils burn, but I manage to swallow. I'd hoped it wouldn't be as bad the second time. It's worse. I can feel it stripping layers off my insides and my stomach's on fire. I cough and grip the table.

Bolt lights the gas hob and slams a tin kettle onto it.

'You done?'

I nod, don't look at him. 'I should go.'

'Gee, you're welcome.'

I flash him a look. I don't have time for his ego. I feel rested after the sleep, but I've stayed still too long. I need to figure all of this out. Reverend Mara's still after me, and so is my mother. If they're working together...

'I didn't ask for your help,' I tell Bolt.

'Except when you did. And then my place got set on fire.'

'I said I'm sorry about that.'

'And then there were a load of people who seemed to be enjoying using you as target practice. Pretty sure I rescued you but, even if I hadn't, you'd have been fine, right? You've got it all covered.'

My bad tooth throbs and the kettle whistles. Bolt stands staring at me, steam filling the kitchen. I won't blink. I won't let him intimidate me. The kettle shrieks. When Bolt doesn't back down, I drag a chair out and slump into it.

'Fine. You want in? You asked for it.'

A flicker of a smile crosses his face and Bolt turns and lifts the kettle from the hob. The shrieking subsides. Why does he want to help me? Paranoia pricks me again, a thorn in my palm. Bolt could be working with the Reverend or my mother. What do they all want from me? It seems everybody wants a piece. I went almost twenty years without anybody caring either way. Apart from Frances. Why now?

Bolt sets a steaming cup in front of me. He seems to notice my distrustful look and sets his own cup down, randomly switching them on the tabletop until I can't tell which is which.

'Better?' he asks, raising one of them to his lips. I can't tell if he's pleased when I sip my own. The tea settles the burning in my gut left by the paste and my temper cools.

'It's probably time you told me what made you flip your lid in the van yesterday,' he says. 'The way you grabbed the wheel... You almost tipped the whole thing.'

I peer into my mug, knowing he's right, but not wanting to face it. Face her. If I tell him, that makes it real. Everything I've ever heard about my mother crams into my mind, a sea of howling voices, all screaming something worse than the one beside it. She's a merciless killer. An occultist. A witch. If I mention her name, she'll come bursting into Peng's home, blade drawn, ready to make sure I really am dead this time.

'Rumer—'

'It was my mother.'

'Celene?'

My head snaps up. 'How did you—'

'It used to be my job to know these things.' Of course he knows about Celene Cross. What policeman wouldn't? She's like one of the Kray twins. Bolt probably profiled her. Tried to figure out what made her tick.

He's looking at me in a way I don't like.

'But... she's not... since the nineties...' he ventures. 'Rumer, she's dead.'

'Not any more.'

'I read about this. They pulled her out of the Thames.' Bolt's voice is softer than usual and I realise this is Bolt being kind. It's an odd thing to witness.

'It was her,' I say.

'Maybe somebody who looked like her or—'

'IT WAS HER, OKAY? I saw her. You don't think I know what she looks like for Christ's sake?' I want to scream at him. *Don't you think I've studied that face like I was going for a frickin' PhD in Celene*

Cross? Like I haven't held her photo up to the mirror and searched every inch of my face for the bit of me that's her?

'Okay, okay…' He must see something in my expression because the look he'd been wearing is gone, replaced with a blank sort of acceptance. 'Shit,' he breathes.

'Yeah.'

'So. You think your mother's working with the Rev?'

Hearing him say it somehow makes it worse. I nod.

'Makes sense. They're both evil bitches.'

If he was talking about Frances, I'd have thrown myself at him, crushed his neck with my bare hands. But he's talking about my mother, a woman whose only claim to that title is that she pushed me out nineteen years ago. Besides, he's speaking the truth.

'You think you can stop her? Whatever she's planning?' he asks.

I can't look at him. Whenever anybody talks about my mother, I'm filled with shame, as if I'm responsible for all the things she did. Mostly I'm ashamed that we're forever linked. She gave birth to me. I can never escape that.

'She's nothing to me,' I say.

'But if you had to kill her, could you do it?'

I don't answer. Would it change anything? She's been dead to me my whole life.

'Look,' I say. 'You hang around me, you might as well have a bulls-eye tattooed on your forehead.'

'Funny, I was thinking about getting–'

I slam the mug down. 'This isn't a joke. You stick with me, you're dead. Just the way it goes.'

'You can't know–'

'I can.'

He looks confused, touches his scarred cheek. 'Is that what Peng's whole thing was? The *shen* stuff?'

'You survived once,' I say. 'Don't count on getting lucky twice.'

'The garage? You think some kind of bad mojo caused the explosion?'

'That's the way it is with me. Bad things happen. And if you keep giving me the pity look I'm going to break you over this table.'

Bolt shakes his head. 'I don't believe in curses.'

'That's your choice.'

'And it's my choice to stick with you if you insist on going after that psycho.'

'Which psycho?' I ask.

Bolt stares me down. 'Both of them! So what's your plan?'

I've been thinking about this. The next move. We're on a chess-board and we've got to move a piece. Choose the wrong one, you lose. Game over, man. Choose the right one, you can play the other team into a corner. Force them to do something stupid. And the stupider they act, the smarter you become.

Bolt wants to play the game, that's up to him.

'Julian,' I say.

'Your boss?'

'Pretty safe to say ex-boss now. He claimed he didn't know anything, but he's lying. Rose, his assistant, followed me. She was there when I left yours, and she was there again when I checked into the hotel.'

'My place was torched by somebody called Rose. Great.'

'We need to scare him. Julian likes being in control. He was cool as a frickin' cucumber when I saw him yesterday. We need to break him. Make him talk.'

I contemplate the screaming masks on the wall and I know exactly how to get under Julian's skin.

We're back in Bolt's van in less than an hour. He's driving and seems deep in thought. I wonder what he's been doing the past year. Running the shop, most likely. What'll he do now it's gone?

He's an idiot getting involved in this. Without him, though, I'm outnumbered roughly ten to one. Probably more. Ten to two doesn't exactly tip the odds, but it's an improvement. Plus Bolt has the van, and he's bigger than he was a few years ago. The rope-like muscles in his arms stand out even when he's not flexing.

I keep searching him for the telltale signs. Nosebleeds. Headaches. Cramping pain. But there's nothing. Peng's paste is doing the trick. For a moment, I sense what it must be like to be free. To not have to worry about who you're with and for how long. It's bittersweet. It won't last, but I can't help the shiver that travels up my spine.

I shake it off and concentrate on where we're headed. I'm aware I've not showered in days and I'm still caked in the muck of the pit. I must stink, but Bolt doesn't seem to care.

'Julian will be at the office now,' I say, thinking out loud. 'If we get there at 8.30, Rose will be out getting coffee. He'll be alone.'

Bolt grunts a reply.

We travel the rest of the way in silence. When we reach the street where Julian's office is, Bolt pulls the van over a few shops away. My nerves jangle together and I grip the mask in my lap. I took it from Peng's wall.

'You first,' Bolt says.

I scramble over the seat into the back. For a second, I remember the van Nicotine Man bundled me into and irritation plucks my insides. Then I shrug out of my jacket and pull the grey bodysuit on over my torn jeans and bloody T-shirt. The suit reeks of petrol.

I catch Bolt's eyes in the rear-view mirror. Then, without a word, he climbs into the back with me. He hesitates, and it looks like he wants to say something, then he grabs the second bodysuit and puts it on. He slips a mask over his head. A screaming dragon. Then he's back in the driver's seat and I'm beside him, shoving my own mask on. It's identical to his. My hot breath steams up my face and I realise this is it. We're actually doing this.

'Ready,' Bolt says.

I nod.

He eases the van along the kerb, crawling until we're outside Julian's office.

Bolt's dragon mask faces me and his eyes shine. Then he grabs the door and gets out. I jump after him and together we crash into the office.

Julian's exactly where I expect him to be, leaning back in his chair reading. He startles when he sees us, dropping the file.

'What the–' he begins, but Bolt's already on him, shoving him back. Julian crashes to the floor and Bolt flips him, pushing his face into the carpet.

'Quiet.' Bolt's growl is every bit as menacing as I'd hoped it would be.

Julian struggles but I grab his legs and Bolt zip-ties his hands behind his back.

'Whatever you're–' Julian starts.

'QUIET!' Bolt yells. He drags Julian onto his back and I pull the duct tape from my pocket, ripping off a piece and clamping it over Julian's mouth. His eyes are wide with fear.

Good.

Bolt pulls him to his feet and shoves Julian towards the office door.

As I go to open it, Julian makes a muffled sound and turns, charging at Bolt. His shoulder drives into Bolt's stomach and they collapse to the floor. Julian cracks his forehead against Bolt's mask, which splits but holds together.

I hurry over, grab Julian's bound hands and haul him up. He turns on me, forehead shining with sweat, and for a moment, I forget I have the mask and I'm scared he recognises me. Then I snap out of it and punch him. He staggers backwards into Bolt, who's on his feet again.

Bolt deals a blow to the back of Julian's neck and Julian's eyes roll. He sags to the floor.

'The door!' Bolt shouts, hefting Julian's unconscious body up.

I open the office door and dash into the street, yanking the van's side door. Bolt hastens out with my boss slumped over his shoulder and bundles Julian inside. I get into the back with him, slamming the door.

Bolt hops into the driver's seat and we tear off down the street.

CHAPTER TWENTY-ONE

TWO YEARS BEFORE THE HAMMER

A few months after leaving my last foster home, I've forgotten about Frances and George. They've been tucked into the part of my mind that's guarded by the spider. Thinking about them makes me weak. Frances' kind eyes, George's belly-deep laugh. I need to be strong if I'm going to survive. They were temporary. Disposable. The only permanent thing in my life is the curse. I'd better start thinking about what's right for Rumer, and what's right for Rumer is staying the hell away from people.

Sleeping rough isn't fun. I spend a couple of nights a week in the ghost house Frances showed me, but I never sleep for more than a few hours, always waking up with the taste of dirt in my mouth, as if somebody's been shovelling soil on top of me.

One cold evening, I'm on my way to the house when I see a car outside and a woman poking around at the front door. I can't be certain, but I've a feeling she's from social services; she looks the sort. George must've told them I ran off. He wouldn't've had a choice, and they must've read the bit in my file that says I was found here as a kid.

The last thing I want is to get dragged back into the system, shipped off to another home.

Doesn't matter. A month later, I turn eighteen and I'm no longer their problem. I don't go back to the house for a month, though, just in case. I don't know exactly how social services works, but if they've reported me missing, the police might check out the neighbourhood, and if they catch me, I'll be waist deep in shit. Social services is one thing, but the police are another. I'd rather lose a toe than have anything to do with them.

Meanwhile, I'm a lifter, targeting busy stores, taking what I need. People don't pay attention to shadows.

I discover the power in stillness. It's funny what people do when they fail to notice you. I've seen guys selling drugs to kids, old ladies picking their noses at bus stops. One time a guy knocked on a door and an elderly man in suspenders and nipple tassels answered.

Sometimes there are small kindnesses, but I can count those on one hand. Mostly it's a rat race. Elbows and shoving and fighting. Frowns and eyes rolling in sockets and glares that smoulder. Scraps of pavement or squares of Tube space that are yours, but only if you don't surrender them to a smartphone-wielding invader.

One autumn day, I'm picking dried dirt off my jeans in a bus shelter. The leaves are crisping into warm colours and it's so cold I can't remember what it's like to be warm. If I can feel the cold as it needles my bones, though, I must be alive.

I've been watching a guy in a cafe window. He's pretending to read his paper and sipping his coffee. I know he's pretending because he only looks at the paper for a few seconds before staring across the street at a sandwich shop. He looks to be in his thirties, preppy, like he was born with a silver spoon up his arse and nobody ever thought to remove it. The more he fails to read the paper, the more I'm intrigued.

As evening draws in, the light fades and, just as I'm thinking about finding somewhere to sleep for the night, a guy emerges from the sandwich shop, shrugging into a black coat.

I stop chewing my nails as the preppy guy jumps up and leaves, chucking money onto the table as he goes. He pops his umbrella and goes the same way as the sandwich shop man. I should find a place to sleep, but curiosity snicks a fire inside me. Before I know it, I'm following the preppy coffee shop guy down the street, hanging back just far enough that he won't notice me.

The preppy guy looks like he's struggling to keep up. The street's not busy, so I don't have any trouble following him, but when a woman with a buggy emerges from a shop just in front of me, I lose him.

Dodging out of the way, I squint into windows and I'm just about to give up when I notice a side alley. I hear hushed voices and I creep into the alley, which leads into a courtyard I didn't know existed.

Two shapes clash in the dark of the courtyard. One of the men has the other up against the wall and is hissing ugly syllables.

So Preppy Man isn't as good at following people as he'd like to think.

Not my problem.

A flash of silver stops me as I turn back into the alley. Sandwich guy holds a switchblade to the other man's throat.

Still not my problem, but as I think about where I'm going to sleep tonight, I find I've slithered through the courtyard's shadows and kicked the back of sandwich guy's knee.

He goes down and I wrench the hand holding the knife until he's yowling. The switchblade's mine now and it trembles between us, but then sandwich guy's up and turning on me, scowling, eyes bright.

'You want to fuck with me,' I say, 'you'll find out how it feels when an eyeball pops.'

I wave the weapon a little, lick my lips. You go up against somebody like this, the only way out is the crazy road. Pearl and her posse taught me that. People generally leave lunatics alone.

'POP!' I jab the knife at him. 'POP! POP!'

His expression reveals a sliver of fear and I'm enjoying this. That part of me my mother controls, the oozing black sludge of her in my veins. Her hand grips the switchblade, her callous grin contorting my face, and I'm daring him to try me. For a moment I think he'll rush me, but then I see the fight leave his eyes and I know I've won.

'Fucking psycho,' he mutters, backing off down the alley, and my mother's voice spits 'coward', except it's me who speaks.

Preppy Guy stares at me, looking relieved and terrified. I like seeing him squirm, the way his gaze switches between me and the switchblade but, as the fever boils off, a sickness wriggles from my chest into my stomach.

It's not my mother's hand holding the blade, it's mine.

I snap it shut and slide it into my boot.

'Where did you come from?' He sounds as posh as he looks.

I shrug, making for the alley.

'Did you follow me?'

'Wasn't hard.'

'I didn't see you.'

'Nobody does.'

119

He starts fumbling with something but I'm already in the alley. The nearest shelter is a mile away, but the thought of going there turns the meagre contents of my stomach to cement. Their pity looks sting like swarming insects. The too-wide smiles are sinister, inhuman, and the stifling compassion in their eyes betrays their true intentions. Because you're not a person to them; you're their key to back-patting self-congratulation. I go when I'm so hungry I can't think straight, otherwise I avoid it the way I avoid any other human interaction. The handouts can get bent.

'Here,' he says.

I stop and look at his outstretched hand, the crumpled notes. I'm tempted. I saved his life, why shouldn't I get something out of it? The cash feels like an insult, though. This guy's bought his way out of a lot of problems.

Didn't work tonight.

He slowly withdraws the money.

'Are you from around here?'

I'm already regretting not taking the money. I could buy a proper meal. Go into the classiest restaurant I can find and laugh at the way the waiters look at me.

'Are you... do you have anywhere to stay?'

'Eat shit.'

'I didn't mean... Look...' He shoves the money into his wallet and takes something else out. A card. He hands it to me and I swear I'm not going to take it, but there's something weird about all of this and I sort of want to know who the guy is, why he's peering at me like I'm behind glass in a museum, some import from a distant land.

JULIAN HART – HART DETECTIVE AGENCY.

I snort.

'Detective? You?'

That gets him where he lives. He straightens and I can practically see him fluffing his feathers. It's sort of endearing.

To his credit, he doesn't rise to the insult. 'How long were you following me?'

CHAPTER TWENTY-ONE

I shrug again. 'You were in the cafe an hour. Maybe more.'

'And you... watched me?'

'You weren't reading the paper. Wanted to know why.'

His eyes glitter and my insides roll uneasily. It's been so long since somebody looked at me, *really* looked at me, it makes my skin heat up, as if I'm under one of those special lamps. Stay here any longer and I'm going to fry.

'I have a job for you,' he says.

It's the last thing I expect him to say, and just like that, I'm not thinking about finding a place to stay any more. A job. He's offering me a job.

'Talk,' I say.

CHAPTER TWENTY-TWO
THE DAY OF THE HAMMER

The slumped form in the back of the van bounces with every bump in the road. I keep my eyes on him, my breath huffing against the inside of the dragon mask. I hope Julian's out long enough for us to reach the flats. If he wakes up beforehand, I'll have to put him under again and I'd rather not give him brain damage before the interrogation.

I listen to the rain ticking against the roof and finally the van starts to slow. Bolt brings it to a stop. He gets out and opens the side door, wordlessly hauling Julian's unconscious body back over his shoulder. He has his uses.

As I emerge from the van, I scan our surroundings. We're parked in front of a high-rise in North London. It's a solid rectangle against a slate sky. The demolition team is turning up next week and the flats are empty. There's nothing but an abandoned industrial estate down the road. Nobody's going to get in our way.

Grabbing a toolkit from the van, I go after Bolt. He stomps up the high-rise stairs. We climb higher and higher, stopping at the seventh floor. Then Bolt kicks in a door and we're inside a flat.

Whoever used to live here left in a hurry. There's crap everywhere. Newspapers on the floor, toys strewn about the living room, a moth-eaten sofa facing a wall that probably used to hold a TV. There's drug crap everywhere: needles and bits of tin foil.

I check every room but there's nobody else here. In the kitchen, I turn the tap but no water comes out. The pipes rattle like my nerves.

Back in the lounge, I set the toolkit on the table. Bolt's strapped Julian into a dining room chair, fastened his arms and legs with duct tape. Julian's chin rests against his chest. Still out cold.

Funny, not long ago, that was me.

'Think he's faking?' Bolt asks.

I shrug. We agreed Bolt would do the talking. I don't want to risk Julian recognising my voice. Not yet.

Bolt tears the tape from Julian's mouth. 'Hey, buddy. Nap time's over.'

Julian doesn't move. Bolt slaps his cheek and Julian bucks in the chair. He peers blearily around the room, mumbling something. Then he notices us and he grips the chair, struggling against the restraints.

'What's going on?' he demands. 'Where am I?'

'Your new place.' Bolt stands. He's big and broad and I'm glad Julian's looking at him like he's afraid he's going to start pulling teeth. I remain further back, by the sofa, giving Julian less of a chance to look at me – I know I wouldn't look at me if Bolt was hulking over me like that.

'Tell us you like it,' Bolt says.

Julian's pale. I can see his brain working, trying to figure out who we are, what he can offer us, how to get out of here alive.

'If you want money–'

'You think we'd go to all this trouble for money?' Bolt growls.

'Just name your price. Anything.'

Bolt punches him. I hope he won't knock him out again; he'd be useless then. Julian dabs his lip with his tongue. He must have bitten it. Blood dribbles down his chin.

'If it's not money, what the hell do you want?' His eyes become slits. He's probably thinking about how he'll have to explain the cut lip to his clients when he gets free.

'You had a visitor recently,' Bolt says.

I told him to say that. We're assuming Julian knows Reverend Mara, but we have no proof yet. We should be able to bluff our way into him telling us everything.

'You have any idea how many people I meet every day?'

'You know who we're talking about.'

'I'm afraid I don't,' Julian says, and there's something dangerous about his expression, like he thinks he's the one in control, even if he is bound to the chair.

Bolt strides over to the dining room table. He pops open the toolkit and removes a screwdriver. I notice Julian looking at me and I stare back. He won't recognise me like this, I'm sure of it. I can count on one hand the number of times we've met.

Bolt returns with the screwdriver.

'You know how much physical pain a human being can take? You'd be surprised.'

'I don't know anything.' Julian eyes the screwdriver as if it were a scorpion.

'Your visitor. Start talking.'

'I don't know what you're talking about.'

Bolt buries the screwdriver in Julian's thigh. I wince at his scream.

'You're crazy!' Julian thrashes in the chair like it's on fire. 'You're a fu–'

Bolt removes the screwdriver, then taps Julian's kneecap lightly with it.

'I can keep going if you'd like,' he warns.

Julian's trembling, his eyes blazing with anger and pain, but he stops yelling. He's sweating through his shirt. That'll be some dry cleaning bill.

'She'll kill me,' he groans, staring at his skewered thigh.

I frown behind the mask. Who's he talking about? Bolt's shoulders tense under the bodysuit, and I can tell he's surprised, too, but he recovers quickly.

'*I'll* kill you,' he says. 'Tell me what she looked like.'

Julian's eyes are glazed as he stares up at Bolt's mask.

'White hair, like an old woman's, but she's not that old.'

I'm numb. My mother visited Julian? It's the last thing I expected him to say.

'What did she want?' Bolt asks.

Julian looks broken. The man who hired me, the suave detective whose blue eyes seduce every client he meets, has crumbled. In his place is a shuddering wreck.

'What did she want?' Bolt asks again.

'She wanted to know… A girl. There's a girl who works for me. A nobody. She wanted to know where she lives.'

I can't breathe.

'Did you tell her?' Bolt asks.

'I don't know where she lives.' Julian's staring at me again and my stomach turns inside out. Is he playing us? Has he known all along it's me behind the screaming dragon mask?

'Rumer,' he murmurs, and I tense, but then Julian's looking at Bolt again. 'Rumer's in trouble. You have to help her.'

'Rumer's the girl who works for you?' Bolt asks, and I'm impressed he's still able to play the game despite what's coming out of Julian's mouth.

My boss nods. 'They think she has the Crook Spear.'

Am I the only person who hadn't heard of this thing?

'Why? Why do they think that?'

'Because of her mother, Celene.' Julian says her name like it's a bad word. 'She's the one who came to my office. A long time ago, she boasted about possessing the spear, and people think she left it to her daughter.'

'Why would they think that?'

Julian's looking at me again. 'Celene had a daughter who she abandoned. One theory is that when she knew she had to hide the spear, she hid it with the kid.'

'So did she?' Bolt asks, and for a moment I'm not sure if he's asking me or Julian.

'I don't know,' Julian says.

Bolt taps his kneecap lightly again with the screwdriver.

'I DON'T KNOW!' Julian screams and Bolt removes the screwdriver.

My head's spinning. My mother visited Julian, but he didn't give me up, unless he's lying. And he knows she's my mother. How does he know that? He shouldn't know anything about me. Could my mother have really left me the Crook Spear as a baby? I've never seen it and Frances never mentioned it. That's if the spear even exists. I don't know what to believe any more.

'Rumer,' Julian murmurs. 'Whatever you do to me, you have to help Rumer.'

Bolt's trembling as he presses the screwdriver to Julian's shoulder.

'What are you doing?' My boss's voice is shrill, exhausted.

'You're screwing with us,' Bolt growls and I eye the screwdriver, thinking the opposite is true. Bolt's enjoying this too much. I wonder where he'll draw the line. Which body part he'll skewer next. What if he likes hurting Julian too much? And what if Julian really is telling the truth?

I go to Bolt's side, grab his free arm and draw him back to the sofa. He only resists a little, his eyes never leaving the bloodied guy in the chair.

'Cool it,' I hiss, low enough that Julian won't hear.

'He's–'

'Just keep him talking. How does he know all of this? If he's fucking with us, I'll know.'

Bolt stares at me, his green eyes verging on feverish through the dragon mask. If I have to break a chair over his back and knock him out... Well, I could really do without the drama.

Breaking away, Bolt returns to Julian, who shoots him a nervous look.

'How do you know all of this?' Bolt demands.

'I just want to protect Rumer–'

Bolt squeezes the screwdriver.

'Rose recognised her,' Julian adds quickly. 'My assistant. She studied her mother's case at university and when she came to work for me, she saw her mother in her straight away.'

I hate Rose more than ever. I'm nothing like my mother. But I remember her pale face staring at me from the hotel window and squirm. I don't want to admit how similar we look.

'Rumer's weak,' Julian continues. 'She won't be able to stand up to Celene.'

My fingers curl into fists. This isn't getting us anywhere.

'How is she even alive?' I hiss, so low that even I don't recognise my voice. 'Celene Cross is meant to be dead.'

Julian's gaze snaps to me.

'I... I don't know. I suppose too many people had an axe to grind with her. She could have decided to get the law off her back by faking her death.'

That sort of makes sense. By the time she died, Celene had enemies just about everywhere. Starting fresh was pretty much the only option left to her that didn't involve a noose around her neck.

'Look, I'm as surprised as you are that she's still alive and kicking.' The pleading tone to Julian's voice is starting to grate. 'Honestly, I had no–'

'Your assistant Rose,' I whisper. 'She set Mara's men on Rumer. You're working with him.'

'Rubbish!' Julian struggles in his chair. 'For Christ's sake, this is all nonsense. Rose is my assistant. I've known her for years. She's got a fucking PhD. She'd never work for somebody like Mara.'

I can't tell if he's covering for her or if he genuinely believes Rose wouldn't double-cross him. Honestly, I'm sort of beyond caring. If Rose wants to two-time Julian, that's on her. The important stuff is…

'Why does Mara care about Rumer?' I demand. 'What's so special about her?'

'Look, I don't know who you people are–'

Bolt digs the screwdriver into Julian's armpit and my boss shrinks away, making an 'ah, ah, ah' sound that's posh and sort of funny at the same time. Or it would be if my head wasn't pounding with questions.

'The spear. Mara wants the spear.' The desperation in Julian's voice suggests he really doesn't know anything. 'Mara's insane. Thinks he'll rule the criminal underworld if he has it.'

He doesn't know anything.

'Let's go,' I hiss at Bolt, who answers me with a glare. I glare back until he trudges to the toolkit and replaces the screwdriver, snapping the box shut. We both head for the door.

'You're not going to leave me here!'

I look back at Julian, strapped to the chair, dripping blood, dark smudges under his eyes. I don't know if he's been telling the truth, but suddenly I want him to know it's me. I'm not my mother. I'm not weak. I don't need Rose following me around London. And I definitely don't need his pity or help.

I pull the mask off.

At first he looks confused, like his brain got mushed when Bolt hit him. Then his brow darkens and he bares his teeth.

'Rumer... What the hell...'

I step back into the room. 'It's the only way you'd tell the truth.'

'You stupid girl,' he spits.

'Hey,' Bolt barks, raising the toolkit. 'I've still got this.'

'And who's this?' my boss snarls. 'Got yourself a bodyguard? You could have picked somebody a little less unhinged.'

'If you'd been honest with me, I wouldn't have had to–'

'You don't know what you're getting yourself into,' Julian says. 'I wanted to protect you.'

A brittle laugh leaves my throat. 'And how exactly were you going to do that?'

'Rose–'

'Followed me. She set Reverend Mara's men on me.'

'She's been trying to keep them *away* from you.' Julian seems to have forgotten he's strapped to a chair, been used as a pin cushion. He looks annoyed, like I'm a disappointing niece or a pet who's been bad.

'She burnt my friend's place to the ground and she followed me to the hotel, right where Mara's men attacked me,' I say.

'Rose wasn't responsible for any of those things.'

I wonder how much his leg's hurting. How much blood he's lost. He must be in agony.

'Then how did they know where I was?' I demand, thrusting aside any sympathy.

'You're leaving a pretty obvious trail. I told you to lay low and you've done the exact opposite.'

I toss the mask to the floor and scrape a hand through my hair. 'This isn't getting us anywhere.'

'Untie me,' Julian says. 'We need to–'

'Nobody's getting untied,' I say.

'Rumer–'

'No.'

I don't know where to begin. I mull over what Julian said before I took the mask off.

'You aren't your mother,' Julian says, his voice suddenly satin soft. 'Why should I lose a talented shadow because your mother was a psychopath?'

He really wants me to untie him. That won't be happening any time soon and this really isn't getting us anywhere. I can't trust Julian any more than he can trust me. This was a bad idea.

'Come on,' I say to Bolt at the door.

'Hey,' Julian shouts. 'Untie me! I can help you!'

I shoot him a look over my shoulder. 'Help yourself. You're pretty good at that.'

Then I leave the flat and go down to the van and wait for Bolt to catch up.

CHAPTER TWENTY-THREE

'We really going to leave him up there?' Bolt asks, pulling the mask off as he approaches the van.

I'm tempted, really I am. It'd serve Julian right. I don't like being treated like a fool – and I *really* don't like being treated like a damsel. I imagine him chewing at his restraints as the wrecking ball smashes into the flat. He'd probably piss himself before getting pasted. Now who's weak?

'He can sweat it out for a while,' I say. 'Then I'll call the office, tip off Rose. She can come for him, assuming the rats don't beat her to it.'

Bolt grins. 'So who we paying a visit to next?'

'How much of what Julian said do you think is true?'

'That guy? Bullshit artist.'

I nod vaguely. The chat with my boss has only confused things, unsealed a new reservoir of questions. How did my mother know I work for Julian? Is Rose really trying to protect me, or is she playing Julian? And how much of what Julian said was even legit? He's foxy. I can't help wondering if he lied with the truth. If my mother really did leave me the Crook Spear, there'd be some proof of that. A note in my social services file, maybe. Celene could have left the spear to gather dust in a safety deposit. Social services might even have the key. I have no clue what's in my file, and I don't think I have the energy to break into the office.

A new idea thuds in my heart.

Frances had a friend at social services. She might have had a copy of my file. In fact, I'm sure she would. It could still be there, in Frances' house. I baulk at the thought of going back there. She's been dead for over two years, but her husband George could still be living there.

How much intel does my mother have on me? Has she already stopped in to see George? I feel sick.

'You okay?' Bolt asks.

'Yeah, just... I know where we have to go.'

We're back on the road in minutes. It's a risk returning to that house, but I don't care. George is in danger, assuming they haven't already got to him. I try not to think about it. George was always so kind. I stayed away after Frances died and I've not seen him since. I wonder if he'll recognise me, the Rumer I've become.

It takes thirty minutes to drive to High Barnet. It's changed since I was last here. It's still greener than a lot of London but there are new blocks of flats and hipster coffee shops everywhere. My stomach starts rolling when Bolt drives down Abbott Road. I force myself to breathe.

'Want me to tag along?'

Bolt's parked and I'm gazing through the windscreen, bewitched by the sight of Frances' house. The only place that ever felt like home. It's had a fresh smack of paint and the front garden's thriving, but it's the same as ever. My heart skitters over a few beats and I feel a deep ache in my bones.

'Rumer?'

'Come if you want,' I say, getting out of the van. I limp up the steps to the front door and ring the bell. It jingles inside, disturbing a hundred memories.

The door opens and there's George. Softer and more wrinkled than I remember, like an elderly apple, but it's unmistakably George.

'Yes?' he asks. I meet his familiar brown eyes and he stops short. His hand trembles towards me. 'Rumer?'

I can't help it, I take his hand. It's warm and leathery and George has tears in his eyes. I don't know how to feel, but then George has his arms around me and I can smell the house, the scent of old wood and whatever that pink flower is that blooms in the back garden every year, and George feels so frail, but his hug is firm.

'I knew you'd come when you could,' he whispers.

He puts us in the lounge and brings us tea. It's strange having Bolt here. My past and my present butt up against one another, attempting to slot together but not quite managing it. The lounge looks just as I remember it, though there are more framed photos, a couple of Frances. I can't look at them for very long without seeing her laughing in the armchair, then playing the piano, then on the kitchen floor.

'I'm so glad you came,' George says, pouring us tea.

I sit on the sofa. Bolt does his guard dog thing by the front window.

'It's good to see you,' I say.

'You're all grown up.' George hands me a cup. 'And I'm even older than I was when you were younger.'

'You look just the same.'

George laughs. 'Your memory must be suffering, if you think that.'

Something about him softens me. It's as if the past two years never happened and Frances is cooking in the kitchen while George and I play dominoes. I could have been away travelling or at university and I've come home at last.

I feel nineteen and a kid all at once.

'You're still here.'

'No reason to leave, not at my age. I think Frances would like that I'm taking care of the place.'

I nod.

We talk for a while. George tells me about his new passion for painting and asks what I've been up to. I say I've been working for a detective agency and he seems impressed. I leave out pretty much everything else. I want to warn him that some bad people might figure out this is the last place I lived before I dropped off the map, but I don't know how to say it. He wouldn't believe me anyway.

'Can I take a look around? For old time's sake?' I ask.

George nods. 'Please.'

Shooting Bolt a 'play nice' look, I leave the room. I wander upstairs, peering into rooms and the memories slip beneath my invisible armour, no matter how painful they are. I peek into what used to be Frances' bedroom. It's just George's now. The dressing table is where it was before, though. Only the bedsheets and the colour of the walls have changed.

I feel more like myself than I have in years.

Peering up the stairs to the attic, I take a breath and begin to climb. My old bedroom hasn't changed much either. The bed's still under the sloping roof. Stevie Nicks stares out from a wrinkled poster. I'm shaking and I don't know if I want to laugh or cry or run the hell out of here like there are bats in my hair.

I walk into the room. The floorboards creak in the same places they always did.

The sun beams through the coloured window, stamping a pink octagon on the floorboards. I contemplate the shape, then move closer. The floorboard pokes up slightly. I grip it with my nails and pull it up.

In the dark recess rests a shoebox. I take it out. It's covered in dust, which I wipe off as I sit on my old bed, then I lift the lid.

Browning newspaper clippings nestle inside. I pick through them and my mother's face glares up from almost every brittle piece. Frances must have clipped them herself. Maybe she thought I'd want to see them one day. She might have sat me down and gone through this box with me. For a moment, I imagine her beside me, how calm she always was. She'd let me read each article in my own time and she wouldn't say anything, but having her there would be enough.

I keep looking. Some of the articles I've seen before, the ones about Celene going on the run. The missing teenage boys who turned up in pieces. There's one I've not seen before, though. Under the headline – *13 DEAD IN BANK HEIST MASSACRE* – is a blurry CCTV photo of my mother and a man emerging from a building. They carry bags that must be loaded with cash. Her dark hair's blowing in the wind and they're both wearing shades.

I feel suddenly sick. The guy beside her is muscular with a buzz cut and I've seen that face sneering at me. It's Nicotine Man. The article's from the year before I was born and this is Nicotine Man as a young buck. What's he doing with my mother?

I search the text next to the photo. His name's Ellis Jacobs, twenty-five, originally from South London. That'd make him almost fifty now. He has a history of bloody crime and links to local gangsters, including Takehiko Kobayashi, Reverend Mara's father. Ellis' uncle headed up a drug ring and died during a police raid in the mid '80s.

The article says my mother's pretty much the most wanted woman in Europe. Her previous crimes fill an entire paragraph – arson, murder, theft, kidnapping. You name it, she did it. She's linked to Takehiko Kobayashi, too. It seems like she's working for him. Worked for him. And when he died, she went with Reverend Mara instead. Such loyalty.

CHAPTER TWENTY-THREE

A floorboard creaks and I jerk to my feet, paper scattering around me.

'Sorry.' George is in the doorway looking sheepish. 'I didn't mean to scare you.'

I quickly gather the scraps of paper. As I stuff them back inside, George comes into the room.

'She cared about you more than anything in the world.'

I slot the lid onto the shoebox and find George contemplating the porthole with the rose glass.

'I knew her the years before she took you in, and it was like she was hibernating,' he says. 'Then you came along and woke her up.'

There's nothing I can say. I'm not sure I can talk about Frances. The few times I've let myself think about her, I hug the memories to my chest jealously. They're too precious to share. They also come sticky with guilt. Because I killed her. I killed the one person who ever cared about me.

'She'd want only the best for you.' The pink light shades George's cheek as he looks at me. 'She wouldn't want you caught up in this. Whatever it is you're caught up in. This person you're becoming.'

He sinks into the window seat. The space between us seems to have shrunk. I clutch the shoebox.

'Frances knew you were troubled. How could you not be, with a mother like that? But she only saw the best, even if some days it was buried so deeply it was as if it didn't exist at all. She saw it, and I see it now. Do you?'

'I know who I am,' I say. 'And that's fine. I don't need anybody.'

'That young man downstairs seems quite taken with you.'

My head snaps up and George chuckles, though I don't think he's mocking me.

'We must surround ourselves with the people who see the good in us,' he says softly. 'We all have dark thoughts, but they can't control us, not if we have others to help us bleed them of any power.'

Why is he telling me this? I look down at my grubby hands, seeing my equally grubby T-shirt and jeans like it's the first time. Still filthy from the pit. He'd have to be an idiot not to realise I'm in trouble, and he's offering advice, just as Frances would have. He's doing it for her.

He's right, too. Frances saw the good and the bad in me, and she wanted all of it.

'You can stay, if you like,' George says.

There's a loud crash downstairs. In an instant, I'm on my feet, dropping the shoebox and charging for the door.

'Stay here,' I tell George, who's already moving to follow me. 'Please.'

He nods uncertainly and I hurry down the attic stairs, reaching the landing. Shouts and the sound of things smashing come up the stairs and I peer over the banister, attempting to see what's going on, edging down the stairs.

'Rumer! Run!'

Bolt's voice joins the cacophony. It sounds like he's still in the living room. A gunshot cracks and I'm certain it came from there. Pressing my back to the wall, I carry on down the stairs. When I reach the hall, I hurry to the front door and check it's locked. I peer through the glass at the street, but I don't see any of Mara's men. No strange vehicles, either.

A shout comes from the living room and I hurry to it.

Bolt's locked in a fight with another man. The lounge window's shattered – somebody must have smashed their way into the house. Bolt grunts and twists, burying his fist in the guy's ribcage. The guy screams and yanks Bolt's arms, flipping him onto the coffee table. It shatters under his weight.

The other guy turns and I see his face for the first time.

Nicotine Man. Ellis Jacobs. My mother's accomplice.

He's about to say something to me when Bolt pulls his legs out from under him. Ellis hits the floor hard and Bolt scrabbles onto him.

'Rumer, get out of here!' he yells, burying his fists in Ellis' face. I swear I hear his nose break again and Ellis howls.

But I've spotted a gun on the floor. I cross the room and grab it, raising it just as Ellis heaves Bolt off him. Bolt tumbles back and crashes into me. We're both almost impaled on the shards of glass sticking up from the base of the window frame.

I recover first, chasing after Ellis, who's bolted into the hall. I skid to a halt in the doorway.

Ellis is by the stairs and he's got George in front of him, sinewy arm around his neck, using him as a shield. I have the gun pointed at Ellis' head, but I've never held a gun before and I'm scared to risk it. What if I shoot George instead?

'Ladies first,' Ellis says, reaching behind his back. His hand appears, gripping a hunting knife with a serrated edge. He puts it to George's throat.

'Let him go,' I say.

Ellis hacks out a laugh. 'Where's the fun in that?'

'Rumer–' George says. He looks so calm. I want to tell him it'll be okay, but the words won't come out.

'Fine, I'll go first,' Ellis says. He drags the blade across George's throat and all I see is pumping red. Hot, blinding red. And George is collapsing to the floor and I squeeze the trigger.

CHAPTER TWENTY-FOUR

It's dark again. The only light in the basement comes from a bare bulb hanging above Nicotine Man's head. Ellis. I keep forgetting I know his name now. Garden furniture and rickety shelves surround us. Frances liked to keep things neat, even if they were hidden away. It smells like damp and soil and I want to spit.

Ellis is bound to a chair. His nose is definitely broken again. The white bandage has come unstuck and I see ruptured bone. Blood smears his shirt, which was probably white a few decades ago. A gunshot wound puckers his shoulder. I narrowly missed his heart. It'll hurt like hell when he wakes up.

Bolt's by the stairs, listening for Ellis' comrades. I shiver at the knowledge that my mother's on her way, then shove the thought to the blackest corner of my mind.

'We should get out of here,' Bolt says.

'Not yet. Not until he's talked.'

'There'll be others coming.'

'I know.'

It won't take long. I slap Ellis and his head bobs up, his eyelids ratcheting open. He looks confused, just like Julian did, then his lips draw back in a sneer.

'One word,' I say, hefting the hammer in my hand so he can see it. 'And you find out how much this thing weighs.'

He doesn't seem afraid. There's a strange sparkle in the way he looks at me. I don't particularly care what he's thinking until I realise that sparkle is respect. He's impressed I did this. I feel sick. I don't want to impress him. I just want to end this.

'How's the old man?' Ellis asks.

It takes all my effort not to swing the hammer. I clench it until my knuckles hurt and I hate the way Ellis keeps looking at me. Like he knows me. He knows *her*. Are they planning a new job together? Looking to recruit? I wouldn't join them if Stevie Nicks herself enlisted.

'Where is she?' I ask.

'Who?'

'You know who.'

His eyes narrow. 'Hit your head lately?'

I grab the collar of his shirt. 'My mother. Where is she?'

The sparkle dims and is replaced with a tar-stained grin.

'Your mother! Ha! Girl, you're behind the times. She's been dead nearly two decades.'

'That's a lie and you know it.'

His forehead crinkles and the grin shrinks.

'Dead's what she is. Maggot food. Go look at her grave if you don't believe it.'

I don't believe it because I've seen her, but maybe Ellis hasn't. Is it possible he bought into the lie like everybody else?

'It's been so long.' Ellis' sneer is back. 'What was her name again?'

I release his collar and step back.

'You must know it,' he prods. 'Go on. Say it.'

I squeeze the hammer tighter. I hate saying it. The word 'mother' feels alien. Even just by saying it I'm giving her power over me.

'Can't do it, can you? Can't even say your own mother's name.'

'Where is she?' I demand, raising the hammer. 'What does she want?'

Ellis cackles. He's practically daring me to hit him. Would he get some sick pleasure out of it?

'Not seen her for years,' he says eventually. 'Not since they fished her out of the Thames.'

'You're lying.'

He doesn't like that. 'Listen, little girl. You better stop worrying about spooks. You're in deep shit. Could end up like one of mummy's vics. You ever hear about the bank job? Thirteen dead, all done in by her. One of them was a fourteen-year-old girl. Shot her in the eye, I think.'

Ellis starts screaming. I've smashed his kneecap. I've done it before I even realise I've swung the hammer. The popping sound of his kneecap breaking makes me feel euphoric and ill.

'You crazy bitch!' Ellis shrieks, thrashing in the chair. 'You crazy little–'

I rest the hammer on his broken nose. He falls silent, though his chest still heaves, his broken leg trembling.

'Tell me where she is, what she wants.'

'Told you... she's dead. Or pretending. Either way she's gone.'

I start to wonder if he's telling the truth. The sparkle's gone. He's in pain. But he must have seen her. She was there the night he and Reverend Mara's men tracked me down at the hotel. Unless she's working alone now.

'Rumer,' Bolt says. 'We need to move.'

'You better run, girlie,' Ellis says. 'Rev's on his way and he's getting impatient. He likes a chase. Makes the capture all the sweeter. And you're giving him a good chase. But eventually you stop and face the music.'

I punch him. His nose is practically hanging off his face, and Ellis stifles a sob, which makes me hate him more. Pussy.

'He was right about you,' he says, broken-sounding.

'He's talking nonsense, Rumer. Let's go.'

Ellis spits blood to the floor. 'You're savage, like her. Single-minded. She'd be proud.'

I punch him again. I can't help it. His hacking, sobbing laugh says I'm only proving him right, but my fist has a mind of its own now, and I'm punching him again, wanting to beat the laughter out of him. His face is purple and red and puffy and why can't I stop hitting him? I can feel her inside me. My mother's wielding the hammer, rupturing bone and carti-lage.

'Rumer, enough. You don't want him to pass out.'

George's face swims before me. The calm expression when Ellis had him by the throat. The spray of red when the blade bit his flesh.

'Tell me what she wants and I'll stop,' I growl, though I don't know if I can. The hammer throbs in my palm and I want to keep hurting him.

Ellis' non-closed-up eye rolls in its socket and he spits blood to the floor.

We must surround ourselves with people who see the good in us.

There's no good in me, only my mother, all the terrible things she did, and it feels so good to hit and smash and the pain in my knuckles is a comfort. A pain that makes me feel alive and here and *just right here*, nowhere else, not my mother, I'm not her, *I'm not.*

'Rumer.' Bolt's hand closes around my arm and he drags me to him. I hit him, too, and he grabs my fists, knocking the hammer to the floor.

'Rumer. Stop. It's okay.'

I shove him off, panting.

'You'll make a great lapdog for the Rev.'

I turn to Ellis and I see what I've done to him. I'm horrified by the mess of his face. He's barely recognisable.

'Ever since mummy disappeared, he's been looking for a replacement.' His voice rasps between puffy lips. 'You're her daughter alright, and you're passing his tests with flying colours.'

'Tests? What are you talking about?'

Ellis tries to laugh again, but he must be in too much pain because the gurgling stops abruptly. 'You're so close to the truth, and you've been relentless. You've turned on everybody you know, trusted nobody except this meat sack, and you've beaten me, in all senses of the word.'

'Mara wants me dead,' I say.

'How could he recruit you if you're dead?'

Recruit me? That doesn't make any sense. Mara threw me into a pit to die.

I frown.

He threw me into a pit that I escaped from. And then he sent his men to attack me. They shot at me, but they didn't kill me. I got away and then I took a hostage and watched Bolt stab him with a screwdriver. Let him do it. And when Ellis tracked me down, I shot him, bound him to a chair and–

Reverend Mara's testing me?

I don't want to believe it. Besides, I've only evaded him this long because I had help. If Mara's test is proving anything, it's that one person is no match for his army.

I look at Bolt, but I can't tell what he's thinking.

Then I hear the basement door opening and I know we're out of time.

CHAPTER TWENTY-FIVE

Bolt charges up the stairs. I seize the hammer from the basement floor and dash after him. Better to fight them at the door than get trapped down here. Bolt trades blows with a figure all in black. One of Mara's ninjas. They're wily, but Bolt's like a solid wall. He slams the ninja into the brickwork and the black-clad figure tumbles down the stairs. I get out of the way just in time.

'Here! Down here!'

Ellis is yelling. I forget about him. He's tied up. The ninjas aren't. One of them slips by Bolt and flips towards me. I manage to duck and the figure swings from the banister rail, doubling back to kick my legs from under me.

I hit the stairs and manage to roll onto my back just in time to heft the hammer as the ninja pounces. I hear a crunch, though I don't know what I've hit. Whatever it was, the ninja crashes down the stairs.

'Rumer,' Bolt shouts from the door. I scramble up.

'Run, little girl! Run run run! Ha!'

Ellis' shrieks fade as we bowl into the hall. I try not to look at George, who's still slumped against the wall. The floor's wet with his blood, but I won't succumb to the sucking grief. Not when Mara's men are swarming over Frances' house. My house.

The anger's a shard in my ribs. How dare they? This place is sacred and they're shitting all over it.

More figures spill into the house and the next few moments are a blur of thrashing limbs and shouts. I wield the hammer and duck and try to make sense of all the figures trapping us in the hallway. Try to imagine a way that this could end with us still alive.

Something whistles past my ear.

They have guns.

'Down!' Bolt's holding most of Mara's men at bay and I know I'd be long dead if it wasn't for him. Except Ellis said Mara doesn't want me dead. He wants to recruit me. Was he just having fun scrambling my brains?

Bolt yells as two ninjas grab his arms and force him back against the wall. I rush forward, but Bolt throws them off. A third figure loops a chain around Bolt's neck and jerks him sideways. Bolt gags, hands clutching at the air.

Another figure lunges for me and I bury the hammer in his head. He drops to the floor.

'Enough!'

My gaze wheels to the front door.

Reverend Mara stands observing the scene. His hands are clasped together and he's wearing an intricate kimono, his hair cut in blades to skim his cheekbones. He stares at me with the eye that isn't smoky.

'You've been busy, Ms Cross.'

I don't say anything. Bolt's still struggling with the chain around his neck.

'Tell your guard dog to cease his struggles, or I'll be forced to put him down.' That soft accent, implacable but strangely soothing.

I look at Bolt, who relents.

Behind Reverend Mara, a figure shuts the front door and goes to his side.

'Rose,' I utter, and I shouldn't be surprised, but after interrogating Julian, I'd discounted him and his assistant as players. But now Rose is standing by Mara, her dark hair tied back so her bony face is fixed in an even more unforgiving expression than usual. Her eyes glitter at me and she's smarter than I've ever seen her in a dark green suit.

'You're already acquainted,' Mara purrs.

'She'll be acquainted with my fist soon.'

Mara laughs. His men line the hall and he strolls towards me, half smiling as he fixes his shirt cuffs.

'You didn't like my pit.'

'It was draughty.'

He laughs again. He knows he's in control.

'And you have Ellis,' he says.

'What's left of him.'

Mara's face changes ever so slightly. The skin tightens around his eyes. I imagine Ellis has served him well over the years. Is Mara afraid of losing him?

'He's alive,' I add. 'Mostly.'

'And you, Ms Cross? Do you value your life? The fight in you says one thing, but your eyes tell a different story.'

I don't answer.

'Let us talk.'

'There's nothing to talk about.'

Reverend Mara strolls into the lounge, Rose gliding after him, her lips twisting at the corners, mocking me, enjoying this. I glance at Bolt, who nods, signalling he'll fight if I want us to, but he looks exhausted. We could try to fight our way out of here, but we'd die in the process. I don't have a choice. I follow Mara into the living room.

He's standing with a photo frame in his hands. A picture of Frances. My stomach churns but I resist the urge to smash it in his face.

'Frances Ahearn,' Mara says. 'I had wondered who took you in after your mother abandoned you.'

I stand by the sofa. Evening's drawing in and the room's blushing autumn orange. Rose stands by the window and I want to scream at her to get out of Frances' house, but I chew the inside of my cheek and force myself not to look at her. I wonder if Julian's nearby. If he's working for Mara, too, or if Rose has played him.

'Tell me about yourself.' Mara sets the frame down. 'Anything.'

'I'm a Sagittarius and I think chickens are weird.'

'Smart mouth. You remind me of your mother more and more.'

I bite my tongue. The last thing I want to talk about is her. Though if Mara's working with her, knows why she's after me…

'You're curious about her,' Mara says. 'It's only natural. She birthed you. We all need to know where we came from.'

'I don't.'

Mara sits in the armchair and contemplates me. I don't like him looking at me. It's the same way Ellis did, as if he knows me just because he knows my mother. Or knew her. I honestly can't keep up.

'What is it you want most in the world, Ms Cross?'

To punch that smug look off your face and get the hell out of here. Forget I met any of you.

'It's not a trick question,' he says. 'Please.'

'Freedom,' I say, and I mean it.

'Ah.' Mara sighs, tipping his head back. 'Freedom. Something only the wise know to wish for. The wise and the doomed.'

Doomed. Like everybody I ever met.

'I don't have the Crook Spear,' I say. He has to believe me. If he doesn't, I don't know what'll happen next. Bolt's still with the ninjas. Mara won't kill him, though. If he kills Bolt, he'll never get me to work for him.

'We'll get to that. First, I want to tell you a story.' He gestures at the sofa – Frances' sofa – inviting me to sit and listen. Clenching my fists, I perch rigidly.

'My mother used to tell me about the Greek goddess Eris, who oversaw the domains of chaos and discord,' he says softly. 'Such was the size and scope of her domain that she was split in two. The first Eris was nicknamed Strife. She was a heartless warmonger whose cruel acts resulted in bloodshed and death. The second, though, was named Nyx. She understood the toils of men and, though she wrought hardship wherever she stepped, her nature was more benevolent.'

'They sound delightful. Can I go now?'

Mara's expression tightens. 'It's a clever man who plays the fool.'

I press my lips together.

'Family,' Mara continues. 'It's more than the people around us, the bodies birthed out of our heritage. It's the basics of our genetic makeup. The unique qualities passed down from mother to child. You've never met your mother, so you wouldn't know, but you're the image of her.'

'I'm nothing like her.'

Mara laughs. 'Every word you speak reveals your likeness even more. Have you ever heard of parthenogenesis?' He eyes me, knowing I'm too stupid to have ever heard of anything like that. 'It's the term, for lack of a better phrase, for immaculate conception. Certain insects and reptiles are able to give birth without the process of fertilisation. The mother is quite literally the sole parent, passing all of her genes on to her offspring. Fascinating, don't you think?'

At first I don't understand why he's telling me this, but then his words start to sink in. I have no idea who my father is. I'm not sure anybody does, except my mother, and I've never really thought about him. Only her. Mara's suggesting I don't actually *have* a father. I'm entirely hers.

It sounds like madness, but I find I've caught my breath at the thought.

Mara sighs. 'You're young. You don't know what's good for you, but I do. You will come with me and you'll never want for anything.'

'Other than freedom.'

'You will earn your freedom,' he says. 'You've proven yourself resilient, shrewd, wilful. Just the qualities I require.'

I stand. 'I'd rather die.'

'Perhaps.' Mara waves a hand at one of his guards. 'You will come with me and I will spare your friend.'

On cue, Bolt is hustled into the living room. One of the ninjas kicks the backs of his knees and he collapses to the floor. The ninja holds a gun to his temple.

'Leave him out of this.' I turn angrily on Mara, avoiding Rose's probing gaze behind him.

'You brought him into it.' The Reverend's teeth snap around his words. 'Every choice has a consequence, Ms Cross. You brought him into this, and it's you who must get him out of it. What do you say?'

I lock eyes with Bolt. Mara's right. It's my fault Bolt's here, and now he's being used as a pawn in whatever game Mara's really playing. As a shadow, I've learnt to pick my moments. This isn't one of them, but one will come. I just have to watch for it.

'Fine. Let him go and I'll come with you.'

'Rumer, no–' Bolt begins.

'Don't.' I cut him off.

'I'll find you,' Bolt says.

'Find her?' Mara sneers. 'You won't have to look very hard.'

Before I can stop them, Mara's men haul Bolt from the room. I hear the front door opening and I round on Mara.

'You said you'd let him go.'

'I said no such thing. Come, we haven't a moment to spare.'

Something inside me snaps and I go to throw myself at the Reverend, but somebody seizes my arms before I get anywhere near.

'Let's try to keep it civilised, shall we, Ms Cross?' Mara says softly, leaving the lounge, Rose sailing after him as if she's attached to his wrist like a balloon. I'm hauled after them.

'I can walk,' I grunt, attempting to pry myself out of the guard's hands.

'You heard her,' Mara says.

As I'm released, I spot George's slumped form. His blood has soaked into the rug and his skin's a horrible chalky white.

'What about George? We can't just leave him here.'

'Somebody will be along to clean him up.' Mara says it like he's talking about dog shit. 'Come, Ms Cross.'

I hate how he says my last name. The name I share with her. It sounds like he's used it for years. Which he has, I guess.

A guard shoves me away from George, through the front door.

Four black SUVs hum at the kerb. Darkness has fallen and their red tail lights cast Reverend Mara in a devilish glow as one of his guards opens a door and he slides in.

Bolt's wrestled into one of the other SUVs and Rose gets in beside him. My blood boils at the thought of her with him, what she'll fill his head with.

I'm directed to Mara's car. Clenching my fists, I get into the back and one of the guards slips in beside me. The door slams, then the car's engine roars and we're on the road again.

CHAPTER TWENTY-SIX

It's raining. Two guys ride up front and they're talking in a language I don't recognise. Hungarian, maybe. The masked guard beside me hasn't said a word. I eye the guns strapped to his belt and wonder how fast I can move. The thought of him moving faster and popping a cap in my leg – or worse – stops me from finding out.

Mara peers out the window, watching the neighbourhoods rise and fall around us.

'You may ask me anything you wish about your mother.'

I don't think so.

I press my lips together. I'm done talking. My head's full of George. His body in the hall. Those kind eyes telling me everything was going to be okay, and Ellis proving him wrong.

The best man I've ever met, gone.

My temples throb with anger and guilt and hatred. Hatred for this thing I am. Ellis might have wielded the knife, but I'm the one who killed George, just like I've killed everybody who ever got too close to me. I'm so angry I want to scream, but what good would that do?

Mara. I can be angry at him.

Even as I resolve to keep my trap shut, I feel the questions coursing into my mouth and I hear myself speak.

'Tell me about the spear.'

Stupid mouth.

His long hair swishes and a smile tweaks the corners of his lips.

'The spear. Yes, of course. They're linked, your mother and the spear, but you already know that.'

If he's trying to irritate me, it's working. I clasp my hands together, squeezing my knuckles.

'We talked of family before; perhaps I should tell you about mine. My father was a great man. Cruel, but it is a cruel world.' Mara briefly caresses his cheek beneath the smoky eye. 'He was the head of a powerful corporation, The Silver Tower. Perhaps you've heard of it. No? I suppose the world of business is of little interest to you.'

He's got that right. I keep my expression neutral. I realise I actually want to hear whatever he has to say. His voice is like the rain. Cold but comforting. A soft patter. We're on the motorway now and the humming of the SUV is oddly soothing.

'Like all powerful men, my father had enemies,' Mara says. 'He did things others disagreed with and many sought to dethrone him. They say the bounty was close to a billion pounds. My father was never concerned, though. His advisers were all trusted friends. He had a fleet of bodyguards working around the clock. The closest anybody ever came to putting him in the ground was when an asp was delivered to his office. The post boy was too stupid to check the contents of the box before it landed on my father's desk. My father was bitten twice but he sucked the venom from his arm himself.'

Mara tells the story like it's a fairytale passed down through the generations. I wonder how much of it is true.

'He was a romantic, though, and a collector,' Mara continues. 'A lover of stories and ancient artefacts. When he was travelling in Morocco, he came across a shop run by an old man. My father asked to see the shop's most interesting piece, and the old man showed him an intricate gun. Its chamber held four bullets, pure silver. It had only been fired once, to kill a much-loved Moroccan prince. It was forged by one of the prince's enemies, a sorceress. She was hanged, but by then her allies had smuggled the gun out of the city. Nobody wanted to keep it. They feared the sorceress had cursed it and it was sold to the first street merchant they encountered.'

I roll my eyes. 'Henchmen are always wusses.'

Mara doesn't seem to hear me. 'My father bought the gun. He did not believe in curses, but he liked the story. A conversation piece for his parties. He hung the gun on the wall in his living room, and there it stayed, until a young woman took it down and shot him with it. Can you guess who that woman was?'

I'm squeezing my hands so tightly my knuckles hurt. There's a glint in Mara's eye but I don't know what it means.

'Your mother disappeared with the gun, and neither has been seen since.' Mara traces a ring on his finger. 'Curses are tricky things, Ms Cross. My father should have paid attention to the Moroccan man's story; he might have lived. If he'd been clever, he could have used the gun to cement his power forever. You see, according to the Moroccan man, every bullet the gun held was forged to destroy. Every bullet save the last.'

'All bullets destroy,' I say.

'Yes, all *normal* bullets, but these were different. The last grants the victim immortality. That was the sorceress's plan. Kill her three enemies, then use the final bullet on herself and rule Morocco for eternity.'

I stare at him blankly. He's deadly serious and I daren't laugh. It's obvious that even though Mara's father didn't believe the story, Mara does, fiercely. He's even crazier than I gave him credit for.

'What's this got to do with the Crook Spear?' I ask.

Mara smiles and he's beautiful.

'A spoon is not always a spoon,' he says. 'The Crook Spear *is* the gun. Perhaps it was an actual spear once. The metal could easily have been fashioned anew. It has always been referred to as a spear, though. Perhaps to protect it from those who would seek it out. A cloak of protection. But I know what it is and I must have it.'

I'm speechless. The spear's a gun? A mystical weapon that has the power to turn a man into an immortal. Anger prickles through me. Everything that's happened over the past few days has happened because some power-hungry maniac wants to get his hands on a fucking voodoo gun. The pit. Bolt. George. The killer assassins firing at my head.

'You're insane.'

I shouldn't have said it. Mara's expression darkens and he bares his teeth.

'At last count, there were only two bullets left, which means I have one to spare,' he growls. 'Would you prefer I use it on you or your mother?'

Stupid question.

I need to change the subject. There's only so much crazy I can take. Better to deal with the here and now. I'm nervous, though. If there's anything I understand better than anybody else, it's curses. I've been one for the past nineteen years. What if there's some truth to Mara's story? What if the gun really does make you immortal?

It's not something I can think about. My head hurts and I still have to figure out how to get out of this mess without me or Bolt being killed. The chances of that happening are getting slimmer by the minute.

'Where are we going?' I ask.

Mara retracts his claws. He looks out the window again, watches the rain as it pebbles the motorway.

'Somewhere safe. Somewhere you can think about what you really want to do with your life, such as it is.'

Nice and vague. I'm still trying to understand how this all fits together. According to Nicotine Man, Ellis, my mother's been AWOL for the past two decades. Mara says she betrayed his father, shot him dead. Is it possible she isn't working for him any more? And if she's not working for him, who is she working for?

The SUV swerves suddenly and I'm thrown against the guard.

'What the hell–'

The shriek of tyres cuts me off and something slams into the side of the car. Somebody's ramming us. Another car is hurtling along beside us. A grey jeep with tinted windows. It crushes us into the barriers at the side of the motorway and sparks fly as metal grinds metal.

Up front, the driver jerks the wheel, yelling in Hungarian or whatever. Mara's guard yells back. Mara's quiet, though he grips the door handle tightly.

We're rammed again and the driver throws on the brakes.

The seatbelt slices into my chest as we screech to a halt. I rock back in the seat.

Wailing car horns become distorted as other vehicles shoot by. They weave around another car that's stopped just ahead of us. The jeep sits there. Nobody gets out. What are they waiting for?

A prick of hope disturbs my belly. Has somebody come to rescue us from Mara? One of his enemies perhaps? Julian?

No. There's nobody who'd rescue me. I grit my teeth. This may be my moment. If I get caught in a fight between Mara and whoever's driving the jeep, I may be able to escape. Grab Bolt and run.

'Get us out of here,' the guard beside me shouts.

The driver revs the engine, then slams his foot on the accelerator.

We tear down the motorway, whisking past the jeep. We shoot past it and out onto the open motorway.

I whip round to stare out the back. The jeep's speeding up.

It's coming after us.

'Who is that?' I ask. I realise I've lost sight of the other SUVs. Bolt's gone.

The car bucks again. The jeep's ramming us from behind.

I turn to look out the back again and I stare right into the jeep.

My blood freezes.

A white-haired woman is in the driver's seat.

It's her.

CHAPTER TWENTY-SEVEN

This is it. There's no escaping. If Mara doesn't kill me, my mother will. I can't bear to look at her. I swing back round in my seat, but her face is seared into my mind. So full of rage. A screaming phantom swooping down the motorway. There's nothing she won't do. If I've learnt anything from what I've read, it's that she'll stop at nothing until the job's done.

So I'm her latest job. Suppose I should feel honoured.

'You aren't pleased to see her,' Mara says. Though he's mocking me, he's pale, his expression drawn. Like me, he's afraid of her, but there's admiration, too. A desperate kind of respect.

The guard beside me lowers his window and leans out, gun aimed at the jeep. Shots ring out and I hear the jeep swerve, tyres catching on the tarmac. We're rammed again and the guard nearly topples out onto the road.

I eye the other gun holstered at the guard's hip. He's distracted. I could grab it, take him out, turn it on Mara.

'Off the motorway,' Mara orders the driver. 'Lose her. Now.'

I glance from the gun to the motorway and the breath catches in my throat.

'Look out!'

The driver's been so busy watching his rear-view mirror he doesn't notice the truck in front of us. He spins the wheel and the SUV careens to one side. For a moment I think we'll make it, but then there's a crunch as we clip the back of the truck and the world explodes in a spinning, crunching nightmare of roaring metal and ringing glass.

The seatbelt threatens to slice me in half and my ears ring as the motorway somersaults. It seems like we'll tumble forever, but finally we rock to a standstill.

I cough.

My chest is killing me and my head feels weird. Pumping with blood. My arms hang upward, scraping the ceiling, and I realise the SUV's upside down. The seatbelt's pinned me in place.

The vehicle creaks and I feel like I'm dreaming, only I can't be because dreams never hurt this much.

The guard lies half out the window. There's blood everywhere and I know he's dead. Another one bites the dust. When your time's up, it's up, right?

Gradually my ears stop ringing. I hear the whoosh of cars on the other side of the motorway. And something else. A door opening somewhere and footsteps crunching calmly on the tarmac.

The jeep.

My mother.

I fumble for the seatbelt. Panic threatens to bubble up, flood my mouth with frantic mumbling, but I can't let it. This is my moment. If I can get out of the car and run, I'll be free. It's my only option. Run like fucking crazy.

Click.

The seatbelt comes undone and I slump to the car ceiling. I'm all tangled limbs, flailing like a newborn lamb, and it's gone eerily quiet. I manage to untangle myself and flip over onto my hands and knees, wincing as shards of glass slice into my palms.

Mara's unconscious. He's suspended the way I was, slumped against his seatbelt, long hair covering his face. I'm trembling and my hand hurts and I realise I'm clutching a shard of glass, blood thumping between my fingers.

All thoughts of running vanish.

George. The pit, all those dead bodies. Bolt.

I inch closer to Mara's slumped form, forgetting everything else. Killing him is all I want now. I can end it right here. He's going to die anyway. Everybody who gets close to me ends up dead, but it could be months, years. Mara doesn't deserve that long.

I've been a killer my whole life. Why not become a murderer?

Before I get any nearer, boots appear at the side of the car and I freeze. Whoever it is – my mother? somebody working for her? – drags at the car door, inching it open.

Fast. I have to move fast. I thrash towards Mara and grab him, shoving his hair aside to expose his throat.

I raise the glass shard.

'Rumer!'

I've never heard my mother speak before. Her voice is sing-song sharp, cotton wool coiled in barbed wire. It cements my joints and I can't move. The shard shakes in my grasp and my gaze flickers to the face that's appeared through the open door.

She looks at me.

There's electricity in the air. A storm in the crumpled car. I can't breathe.

'Rumer–'

No. I have to do this before she kills me. I raise the shard and now my mother's scrambling inside, a wild animal, her teeth exposed, hands scrabbling. She grabs my wrist and the shock of her touch makes me gasp. I try to wrestle free but she's too strong. I drop the shard and my mother drags me out onto the tarmac. I could never imagine she'd be so strong.

I lash out, try to shake her off me, but she hoists me to my feet.

'You're injured.'

Again that voice. Glass sprinkled over ice cream.

I'm caught in her gaze.

A popping sound breaks the spell. The other SUVs in Mara's fleet have returned and his men are leaning out with their guns aimed at us.

As I turn to duck away, my mother seizes my wrist and yanks me towards the grey jeep.

'Get off me!'

Her expression is deadly and I can't shake her grip. She opens the back door and bundles me inside, slamming the door. I move to open it but there's no handle on the inside. I raise a boot and pound it against the window but it must be some kind of reinforced glass.

My mother jumps into the driving seat and then we're tearing down the motorway.

Article from *The Sun*

'Razor' Stanley makes dog's dinner of mob links

By JIM GREEN
Reporter

A London tycoon eaten alive by his own guard dog was killed by a rival gangster, his ex-wife claims.

Vile criminal Bob 'The Razor' Stanley, 45, died after he was torn limb from limb by Daisy, a Rottweiler he'd purchased a week earlier to protect his new £3 million penthouse in Canary Wharf.

The CEO of Bright Tech was in the middle of a £35 million divorce from his ex-wife, glamour model Suzy Price, 32, and had fielded numerous accusations that he was in league with local mobster Gino 'Smiffy' Smith.

Price, whose tell-all book *I Married A Mobster* is being published next month, said: 'Bob pissed off too many people and they finally got him. That dog was always going to kill somebody – she hadn't been trained properly yet. Somebody let her out and she went straight for Bob.'

Cops are trawling CCTV footage for evidence of a break-in at Stanley's home amid claims a hit squad van was spotted in the area the same night the mobster died.

Part Four
THE CAMP

CHAPTER TWENTY-EIGHT

I'm being driven to my death by a ghost. It sounds nuts, but it's no more nuts than anything else that's happened over the past few days. The chill of certainty floods my veins and all I can do is stare at my mother's reflection in the rear-view mirror.

Not my mother. The Red Widow. Celene. When has she ever done anything remotely motherly?

Celene doesn't acknowledge me. Her misty grey eyes are trained on the road. Her hair's ash white and her bony hands throttle the steering wheel.

A thousand questions cram into my mouth and I can't chew them into any order. I'm light headed and my vision swims. Must've hit my head when the SUV rolled. I stare at the car ceiling, marvelling at the flickering stars, then not marvelling, because I remember I'm screwed.

My mouth fills with saliva and I vomit all over the backseat.

'Try to relax, Rumer.'

If she means to be comforting, she's failing spectacularly.

'Sure, why not?' I slur. My tongue's too big and my throat's on fire. 'Never heard of an unrelaxed murder victim.'

Her eyes flicker at me in the mirror, eyebrows pinching together. Is that surprise? Confusion? Her expressions are alien to me.

'What you going to use? A knife? A gun? Bit of rope?'

'Quiet,' she says. 'Save your strength.'

'Yeah, gotta struggle when you kill me or it's no fun, right?'

'Nobody's going to kill you.'

I hurl a laugh at her. Then my mouth floods with saliva again and I swallow hard, crushing the seat in my grip, desperate not to throw up again. I come close. I feel like a kid in one of those stupid TV shows. A sixteen-year-old who's drunk too much cider in the park and now Mum's driving me home, so cross that she can't speak. I should feel something more than this maddening sense of unreality, but I'm trapped in the bad dream.

A thrumming ache ticks in the back of my skull, like somebody's tapping against it.

Rap, rap, rap.

I try to focus on the road, counting the white strips as they disappear beneath us. It helps. I get to fifty before I realise we're not on the motorway any more. At some point, we slipped off onto a side road and we're the only car around. It's so dark all I can see in the window is my reflection.

I'm not going to lie, I've looked better.

'You're dead,' I murmur. 'Why are you here?'

My thoughts tumble the way the SUV did. Is Mara still alive? He was unconscious in the SUV, or I assumed he was. The crash could have broken his neck. The others came back to get him, and Bolt must've been with them. He was in the first SUV. Have they taken him somewhere? The pit? Or is he strapped to a chair like Ellis was? Something tells me Mara's dogs will make me look restrained when it comes to interrogation.

And I'm in the car with my mother.

I'm with her.

In her car.

Hysteria buzzes, static in my brain, and I try to shake it off, but it gets louder with every second. If I give in to it, I'll start thinking about how I'm trapped in here, and how the most dangerous woman who ever lived is taking me somewhere remote so she can pop a cap in my head. Or maybe she'll do it slowly. Tease out every strip of pain. Savour the sight of the life trickling out of me.

And there's part of me that always knew it would end like this.

I had it coming.

It feels right that it's Celene who's going to end me.

She's the one who started me.

The hysteria latches on with steel claws.

'Why aren't you dead?' I slur. My voice sounds wrong. Un-me.

Maybe I can take her down with me. Make my death count for something. She could be the first person I kill on purpose, and it'd mean something. It'd mean nobody else ends up a victim.

Now. I need to do it now, while she's distracted by the road.

I brace myself, deepen my breathing.

As I prepare to lunge forward, she catches me in the rear-view mirror.

'Don't do anything stupid, Rumer. I know you don't believe me, but you're safe.'

For the first time, she sounds convincing, even if what she's saying is ridiculous. Safe with her? Was I born yesterday?

Weariness sucks the strength from my limbs. Weighs them down. The buzzing in my skull has spread, cramping my neck and shoulders so that I hunch in a ball on the back seat. Is this what concussion feels like? I curl up like a woodlouse and listen to the rain.

What feels like moments later, the jeep turns and the road feels different. Stones tic against the chassis and we're on a dirt track. Trees muscle in around the car and the darkness is complete.

Then, ahead, glimmers of light appear. Orange flames.

We creak to a standstill. A chain-link gate rests in front of us and Celene opens her window as a stony-faced woman approaches. They exchange a few words I can't hear, then the woman heaves the gate open and we drive into some kind of compound.

Wooden huts stand on stilts. Gas lamps flicker on porch steps raised off the ground. We drive by a guy who's clutching a shovel, which isn't creepy at all. He's dressed like a janitor in a pressed white shirt. He blinks and raises a hand as he's caught in the SUV's headlights, and I catch a strange look between him and Celene.

Then we're past him and I'm not comforted by the fact that there's nobody else around. The place almost looks cosy, until I realise what it is. This is why my mother hasn't been seen for over twenty years. Her cult upped sticks, relocated here.

I'm in the middle of nowhere with a load of devil worshippers, and that's why Celene didn't kill me on the spot, because what's the one thing devil worshippers do?

They offer up human sacrifices.

Celene parks by two other grey jeeps and gets out. She pops my door and insects churn in my belly. I try to resist her, but she snaps at me and something about her tone turns me to jelly.

She drags me out of the car and I lean against her. I can't help it. The ground's spinning and I smell the rain in her hair.

'Just do it,' I murmur. 'Just do it already. I don't care any more.'

I'm not even sure what I mean.

CHAPTER TWENTY-NINE

I must have passed out. I don't remember closing my eyes. When I open them, it's dark and I'm lying down. Wood beams criss-cross the ceiling and my stomach turns at the smell of coffee coming in under the door.

I sit up with a start and regret it. My head feels like it's split open and I'm so sore it's like somebody's been playing piñata with my unconscious body. Which isn't too far from the truth, considering the car crash.

The room's small. Just a bed, a sink and a cracked mirror. There are orange flickers outside the window. A fire spits in my belly. The window. I'm alone and there's a window. I need to get out of here. Now.

I have no idea what sort of life Celene's been living in this place, but I don't want to find out. She's trying to trick me. She's been tracking me for God knows how long and now she has me.

I don't particularly want to be a human sacrifice – tonight or any other night.

Screwing up my face, I ease myself off the bed. My muscles are solid rock and I'm sweating, but I can't let that stop me. I count.

One. Two. Three.

And I'm up. Steadying myself against the bed, I shamble over to the window. I'm just about to push it open when the door clicks behind me.

'You're awake.'

I spin around, almost toppling over. The room splits into four, then two. Finally I'm able to refocus.

'What did you do to me?' I demand, clutching the windowsill.

Celene's face is expressionless but I know she's drugged me. Why else would I feel this groggy?

'You were in pain.'

We stare at each other and I can't tell what she's thinking. She looks so different in the flesh. Not the phantom I feared and not the skull-faced assassin from the newspapers. Something else. Harder and softer. Older.

'Where are we?' I ask.

'My home. Come, I made you supper. You'll feel better.'

'I'm not eating anything.'

'You want to starve?'

'Better than being poisoned.'

'Nobody's going to poison you.'

'Says the mass murderer.'

Nothing. No reaction. She's like a robot and her laser eyes burn into me.

'You're dead,' I say.

'We'll talk about that when you've rested.'

'There's a grave. They found your body.'

Her gaze flickers. Is that anger or am I making her uncomfortable? 'I'll be outside. Let me know when you change your mind.'

'So I'm your prisoner now?'

She starts to leave. Casually, she says, 'There's no lock on the door. Oh, and the window's a thirty-foot drop to the ground.' The door shuts behind her and I want to scream at it, blast it into splinters, but I don't have the energy. I turn and throw the window open, freezing air snarling in my hair, shocking me awake.

Celene wasn't lying.

The ground looks impossibly far away. Compacted dirt. If I jump, I'll break both legs and a hundred other bones besides. This isn't the way out. I dig my nails into the windowsill, wanting to tear strips out of it. I'll have to wait for my moment again. Play along until I spot my chance, then grab it with both hands.

For now, I need to rest. To get strong. Find out where Bolt was taken and make Mara pay for all the shit he's brought into my life. I won't be able to rest until I've avenged George. Except... is that what George would want? Me going up against a dangerous criminal, which'll either end with my death or somebody else's?

My bones weigh me down and I don't know what the right thing to do is. There *is* no right thing.

I glance at the bed, but it seems almost as far away as the ground. I slide to the floor, resting my back against the wall.

It's still dark when I wake up and a shadow's watching me.

For a second I imagine it's Mara but, as my sight adjusts to the dark, I see it's a grey-haired man. The click of the door closing woke me up and his eyes glint like ten pence pieces. He looks about sixty. There's barely any flesh on his bones.

I push my hands under me, but they barely move. Whatever Celene gave me worked. I'm as useless as a person can be, and knowing that makes me afraid. Whoever the old man is, he can do whatever he wants.

'Rumer? Is that you?'

His voice is a whisper like dead leaves and he's hunched by the door. He can't possibly be afraid of me. That doesn't make any sense. I'm paralysed on the floor, my back against the wall.

'Rumer?'

I don't answer. We stare at each other.

'It's you, isn't it? She finally found you.'

'Who are you?' My voice is a croak.

'I can't believe you're really here. After all this time.'

I'm starting to think this guy isn't playing with a full deck and that thought only increases my anxiety. What if he has a knife on him? Or some kind of sacrificial doohickey? What if he's come to carve out the first bit of flesh?

'Get out.' I try to sound stronger than I feel.

He doesn't move, which gives me the impression of a coiled snake. He's stick-thin but that doesn't mean he's not strong. The state I'm in, he could probably overpower me easily.

'How do you like Camp Virtus?' he asks.

I hesitate before answering. Talking to him won't make him leave any quicker. Unless it will. Eventually I push my chin out and stare into his face, swallowing the anxiety like a stone.

'It's heaven,' I say.

'And your mother? She's what you expected?'

'How do you know–'

'You're the image of her.'

My patience is wearing thin. 'Who are you?'

'A friend of Celene's.' He shakes with sudden laughter. 'Friend! Never imagined I'd call her that. If you'd told me thirty years ago that's something I'd say, I'd call you a liar.'

'You've known her that long?' The uneasiness floods back. Is this one of Celene's old mob buddies? He looks so frail I can't imagine him ever wielding that sort of power, but he was young once. Maybe life as a mobster took its toll.

He ponders me and the curiosity in his face makes me want to shrivel into a husk.

'Been around her, yes,' he says. '*Known* her? As well as anybody could know a shadow.'

Shadow. Paranoia bristles through me, but he can't possibly know what I do for a living. *Did* for a living. No way Julian's keeping me on the payroll after I got Bolt to use him as a crash dummy.

'Just get out of here,' I say, but I sound less determined than before. He's got me curious and I need answers about this place. He might just be crackers enough to give them up.

He must notice my curiosity because he chuckles softly, then grows serious. His eyebrows are bushy, deep lines carved into his leathery skin. I'm reminded of George and my chest aches.

'She's made a good life for herself here. We both have. She's private, keeps to herself. Sometimes she goes off for days. Weeks, even. When she gets back, she's always exhausted. I worried what she was doing, but now I know. She was looking for you.'

I hold his gaze and wonder what he's trying to tell me. I feel like he's leading up to something. Does he know what Celene's really up to? Or is he just a sweet old man who wants to see a mother have her happily-ever-after with her daughter?

I remind myself I'm in a camp of devil worshippers.

He stares over my head, out the window. 'Everybody here knows about her past. Perhaps not the dirtiest details, but enough. They were shocked at first, but shock has a habit of dulling and being forgotten.' His brow darkens. 'I remember.'

'What do you remember?' My heart's jack-rabbiting and I stiffen against the floorboards, trying to wake up my body. Queasily, I manage to push myself up off the floor and lean against the window ledge.

'Did you ever wonder who named you?'

'What?'

That twinkly half smile's back and I swear if I wasn't using all my energy on just standing, I'd help him remove it.

'Rumer... it's an odd name.' His knowing look infuriates me. 'I think I chose well.'

I want to throw him out face first. Slam the door on his rambling. There's nothing I can do, though. I'm stuck to the spot, waiting for him to speak.

Questions smash at the inside of my skull. He named me? I've never seen this guy before, but if he gave me my name, does that make him my–

'I saw her do things I'll never forget,' the man says. He swings an arm and I notice he's clutching a bottle. Caramel-coloured liquid sloshes around inside and I eye him with sudden scepticism. He already sounded like a loon before I noticed the bottle.

'Terrible, terrible...' the guy goes on. 'She claims she's changed, but I see it sometimes. In a look or the way her shoulders creep up. She's keeping it in check, but sometimes I wonder...'

'You were in the cult with her.'

It's obvious. No other way he'd have known her this long.

He massages his hip absent-mindedly. 'When she fell pregnant, she tried to get rid of you. When she couldn't, she sank into despair.'

This all sounds weirdly familiar but I can't think why. Whatever Celene gave me, it's making me slower. My thoughts bleed together.

'Despair,' I say. 'Because she couldn't get rid of me.'

'She said she wanted to change.' The guy takes a swig from the bottle and wipes his lips on his arm. 'I gave her a fresh start. Found a way. Wiped it clean.'

I'm hugging myself so hard I think I'll crack a rib.

'Fresh start?'

He turns to me and his eyes are bloodshot and glistening, his lips still wet.

'I was different then, too. I didn't think... But then you were born, and she ran, and I didn't know what to do with you. I should have ended it there, but you didn't look like a monster. So I gave you a gift – a name – and I left you with a friend... and then I ran, too.'

I'm shaking. Every bit of me is trembling, as if the temperature's plummeted, but I can't feel the cold. I try to make sense of what the stranger's telling me. That he was the one responsible for the curse. It all goes back to him.

'How do you know all this? Who are you?'

'They call me Domhnall here. Before that, I was Kieran. And at one point I went under Dominic Waters, but that was years ago.'

Dominic Waters.

THE CURSE OF CELENE CROSS.

The wind's knocked out of me. There's roaring in my ears. Dominic's the one who sold his story to *Crystal Visions*, the spiritual magazine. The one about how Celene fell pregnant, and they cursed her newborn so that it would bear the weight of all Celene's crimes. That's why it sounds so familiar. I'm face to face with my maker.

My ears are ringing and my head's heavy with confusion. And somewhere in there is grim relief, because somebody's finally confirmed what I've always feared.

My voice is a rasp. 'You did this to me?'

He nods and then his eyes are bulging out of their sockets because I've clamped a hand around his throat. I've thrown myself at him without realising it, without even knowing I had the strength, and I spin him around, forcing him back into the windowsill.

The bottle smashes on the floor, but even the sweet scent of liquor can't mask the reek of alcohol ingrained in his skin and clothes.

'You did this!' The growl vibrates up from my gut and I don't care if Celene hears. Let her see what she created. Just because I don't look like a monster doesn't mean I'm not one.

'Please, it was so long ago.' He gulps for air, his breath foul with booze. 'I didn't...'

His eyes are practically on stalks and the fear shining there is intoxicating. I wonder if he looked at my mother this way when she was pregnant and threatened to kill him if he told anybody. He's staring at me like I'm mad, and he's terrified because, even through his drunkenness, he knows mad people are impossible to predict.

I see George and Frances and Troll and I want to tip this sack of bones over the edge of the windowsill. Watch his body fall and hit the hard ground. He's so frail he'll smash into a hundred pieces.

'Rumer.' His hands flail for the windowsill, but he can't break free.

I imagine what it would be like to watch him die. There'd be some poetry in it. He cursed me so that everybody who gets near me ends up dead. Maybe he can be one of them.

'There's a way out.'

He chokes on the words and I clench tighter.

'What do you mean?'

His Adam's apple twists in my grip.

'If... you kill her... it goes away...'

My grip slackens and I let him push my hand away. He coughs and backs off a few paces, clutching his throat. Finally, he meets my gaze.

'It's true,' he wheezes, almost doubled over as he cradles his throat. 'You can fix what we did. All you have to do is take her life. Take hers to reclaim yours.'

I sag against the windowsill feeling like I've finally lost my mind.

'You're nuts,' I say, because even though he's confirmed everything I've ever feared, this is one step too far into Crazy Town. All my life I've known I'm cursed, that somebody did this to me and there's no way to undo it, but now this guy, this *boozer*, is telling me something even more terrible. It can't be true.

There's a noise.

The door opens and Celene casts a look around the room, seeing me clutching the windowsill and Dominic cowering by the door.

'What's going on?' she asks. 'Domhnall, what–'

Dominic, or Domhnall, whatever his name is, shoots her a look of terror and then darts out onto the landing. Celene doesn't try to stop him. I hear his footsteps clomping down the stairs and then a door slamming.

Celene's gaze flicks at me. 'Are you okay?'

I grip the sill, drained, my head spinning. My legs give and I slump to the floor.

Is it true? Can I fix what they did to me? Is it as easy as that?

Easy as killing my mother?

She hurries to me and I flinch. She must notice because she stops a foot away.

'Are you okay?' she asks again and she's so good at sounding concerned I almost admire her.

'Just leave me alone.'

'Did he hurt you?' she asks.

Apart from confirming my worst fears?

'Rumer, did he hurt you?'

'No. He couldn't hurt a barfly. Too drunk and old and–'

'Crazy.' Celene considers a wooden chair in the corner but doesn't sit down. 'He's troubled, Domhnall. I'm sorry he... I don't know how he got past me. Maybe when I was in the bathroom. What must you think?'

She paces from one side of the room to the other.

'Worried what we talked about?' I ask, because I have to know. I'll be able to tell from her reaction if what Dominic, Domhnall, said was true. That the curse is real and I can break it by taking her life.

'He's a pathological liar,' says Celene, and of course she'd say that. In four words she can make me doubt anything he might have said. But I've seen liars, shadowed enough of them, and she doesn't look afraid or angry or suspicious. She looks sad. Tired.

'I do my best for him,' she says, 'but there's only so much you can do for an alcoholic. Ever since he lost that job at the paper. They raked him over the coals. He told too many lies. Domhnall has... Well... He lives in his own world. I've never understood him.'

So there it is. She denied it without denying it. I'm staring at her as if trying to read her mind. See past the white hair and the ageing rock-chick look she's going for. I want to find the woman who did all those things in the nineties. Find out the truth.

The fight with Dominic has eaten up the last of my energy, though and, as much as I fight to stay conscious, it's a battle I quickly lose. The last thing I see is Celene looking at me and I could swear she's close to tears.

CHAPTER THIRTY

TWO YEARS BEFORE THE HAMMER

The last person I killed didn't die. I've been shadowing for a year and I've turned into something new. I'm not Schoolgirl Rumer, raw and miserable, and I'm not Soft Rumer, the one who lived under Frances and George's roof. I'm different. Quieter. More focused. Living for the packet of money Julian leaves under the floor in the old phone box.

He didn't mean to take me on full time, I'm pretty sure of it. The first job he sent me on was following a man suspected of cheating with his wife's cousin. All I had to do was catch them in the act and take photos with the phone Julian left in the envelope. I had the photos in two days. They didn't suspect a thing and I got a £100 bonus, which may as well have been a million. I stuffed my belly so full that night I almost vomited the crisps and fizzy drinks back up.

Julian must've been impressed because he kept giving me work, and who was I to refuse? Life's all about standing on other people's shoulders, shouting the loudest, finding a way to survive despite the odds, and here was my ticket to a roof, a meal and something resembling a life.

It's hard to keep track of time, but I notice the front page of a paper a week after my eighteenth birthday. By now I have my own flat, a damp den above a newsagent. It has bare bulbs, something masquerading as carpet, rags for curtains. But it's mine. Comics and movies are my friends. I watch DVDs on a cruddy old TV my landlord sold me at a steal, mostly because it flickers between colour and black-and-white every five minutes. But I don't care. I have my own frickin' TV.

I've lived here almost a year when things get weird again.

The sun is scorching the day I'm shadowing a guy who's supposedly ripping off his boss.

Jimmy Long is forty, overweight, crammed into a suit, sort of like a hippo with a degree. A long-serving London chancer who's got by as a salesman for a car parts company. At least, that's his story.

I've been assigned to catch him selling drugs to a mechanic, whose business is a cover for some kind of pharmaceutical empire, but so far all the guy's done is take me on a merry dance across London. He has meetings in greasy cafes even I have trouble stomaching.

Eventually, he travels the entire length of the Central Line, gets out at a stop I've never heard of, and leads me to Mick's Motors, a garage that resembles a cavernous corrugated shack.

Sweating into my jacket, I peer into the dark of the garage. My hair sticks to my face and my throat's scratchy and dry because I guzzled an entire bottle of water half an hour ago and didn't think to save the rest for later.

Jimmy's having a heated conversation with a guy in a dirty blue boiler suit. The guy turns and the name stitched on his chest is BARRY, because of course it is.

Jimmy says something like 'your boss ordered the product, I'm delivering it', but Barry says he doesn't 'want that filth here, what'd he bring it here for?'.

I notice Jimmy's knuckles are bone white around the case he's carried all the way to the garage, and his throat is reddening like somebody's strung string around it.

Slipping my phone out, I snap some pictures of them, but it's too dark. Julian needs shots that leave no room for doubt. Cursing, I slide into the garage, melting into the shadows. Crouching low, I move between cars with missing bonnets and wheels.

'You wanted the stuff, now it's here. Where's the dough?' Jimmy's cherry cheeked. I watch them through the windows of a scrapheap car.

'Come back when Mick's here.'

'Mick said you'd finish the deal. I'm not going—'

Jimmy stops mid-sentence because Barry's grabbed his arm and growled something under his breath.

Bad move, Barry.

In a flash, Jimmy's slipped a hand into his jacket and then Barry steps back, arms above his head, going 'woah, woah woah'. Jimmy's clutching a gun. Good for him, didn't think he had the balls.

Raising the phone, I snap a few pictures. They're clearer. Not amazing, but they'll do, and it all looks very dramatic now the gun's made an appearance. Maybe I'll get another bonus.

I'm not supposed to interfere with the people I follow, and I could really do without the hassle of stopping Jimmy doing something mur-der-y, but before I can slink away from whatever mess he's about to create, a car screeches to a stop in the garage door, blocking it.

Red and blue lights dart inside and I spit another curse under my breath. What the hell are the cops doing here?

An officer hops out of the car and assesses the situation with bright eyes.

'Jimmy.' His voice echoes through the garage. 'You really want to put holes in this guy with the law watching?'

'Stay back,' Jimmy says, his complexion now fish-belly white, his collar damp with sweat.

I've been following Jimmy all day and I didn't notice the police hanging around. Have they followed us both here? No, I'd have spotted somebody tailing us. Somebody must've tipped them off that Jimmy was closing a deal at Mick's. Now I'm trapped in here with them.

All I can do is crouch where I am and hope they don't see me.

Already, the clock's ticking in my head. My gaze sweeps the garage, from the oily floor to the cans of petrol and the cars; rusty, decrepit death traps all by themselves.

I've gone over a year without anybody dying and it felt good. I could almost forget about the curse. But it's always been there, hiding just out of sight, like the spider in my mind, and I can feel it in the garage with me, breathing down my neck, deciding who it'll take this time.

'Jimmy—' the officer says.

'Quiet! I need to think!'

'Jimmy, you're not this guy. You've not done anything yet. Just put the gun away and—'

My leg's gone dead from crouching and I shift my weight. My boot scuffs the cement loudly and every muscle in my body tenses.

'Who's there?' Jimmy yells. I see he's squinting across the garage at me.

Shit.

The officer turns to peer in my direction, and then Jimmy grunts, because Barry's gone for him. They struggle and the officer draws his baton, then a shot rings out, but it's come from the mass of limbs that's Jimmy and Barry. They're fighting for the gun, and another shot pops loudly, hitting something, and then suddenly there's fire.

Flames erupt from a petrol can, spewing into the air. The blaze spreads swiftly. Mick's Motors has sponged up decades of flammables and the place goes up like a haystack.

The jig's up. I can't hide any more. I hurtle from my hiding place, running for the exit as a wall of heat presses in around me. As I skirt around the police car, a horrible groan rumbles through the garage, and I turn just in time to see the ceiling collapse.

Jimmy and Barry and the officer are in there somewhere.

I hesitate. My boots cement to the floor and I know this is my fault, but what can I do? There's nothing to stop the fire with – nothing I can see, anyway – and I've never been able to save anybody before. Why break the habit of a lifetime?

Something shifts in me, though, something I've never felt before, like meat straining away from bone, and for the first time I decide to try. My eyes water as I peer into the black smoke, then I edge into the flaming garage, my arm over my mouth. The voice in my head screams at me to run, to save myself, but it sounds too much like what I imagine my mother sounds like, and the thought of somebody else dying because of me – because of her – is too much to bear.

The air's thick with smoke and fire and I'm light headed because of what I'm breathing in. I keep searching, and the more I search, the more I realise this is a suicide mission. Maybe I'll finally kill Rumer.

Then, out of the smoke, a flaming figure thrashes, coming right at me. For what feels like an eternity, I don't move, mesmerised by the column of fire, but then my instincts kick in.

Not even feeling the flames, I grab the figure, throw it to the ground and roll it until there aren't any more flames, just a charred person who lies motionless.

I grab his shoulders and drag him across the floor. He's so badly burnt I can't bring myself to look properly, focusing on each agonising inch of cement. I have no idea if I'm going in the right direction, but I've committed to it now. If we burn, we burn.

I spot the police car in the garage entrance and I heave the unconscious figure out into the open air. When we're clear, I retch and cough until I'm sure I'm going to choke a lung onto the pavement.

Exhausted, I crouch by the figure. His clothes are burnt to a crisp. The police officer. In the smudged black mess of his face, a shockingly green eye rolls, then blearily trains on me.

'I'm sorry,' I murmur.

Sirens are wailing so I know he'll be found. I begin to get up, but the officer grabs my wrist.

'Th–th–'

I shake him free and run.

In the days after the fire, I keep thinking about the cop. I saved him, but I don't know what that means. Has the curse worn off? Was I just lucky? Or was the cop somehow different? Immune?

I think myself in circles for a few days, obsessively checking the news to see if the officer died in hospital.

Curiosity overpowers me and, even though I shouldn't, I go to the hospital where he's being treated. He's asleep when I get there, half his face bandaged up, and a nurse scares me off when she asks if I'm a relative.

But then I go back a second time.

The fourth time, he's awake and asking questions before I can bolt out the door. I talk. Small stuff. If he asks the wrong questions my mouth clamps shut and he changes the subject.

Maybe he can see the guilt on my face.

The board over his bed says his name's WINSTON, which is so ridiculous I decide to call him Bolt, because that's what I want to do every time he looks at me too closely, like a strange bug he's spotted crawling up the wall.

The next time I visit, he's not there. The nurse says he was let out, and because I'm an idiot, I find out where he lives. I watch his flat a bit. I have to know what was different, why he lived.

One day, I'm at the bus stop just down his street when somebody sits next to me.

'Going somewhere fun?'

I look over and it's him. His eye's bandaged. I glimpse the scarring at the edges and feel guilty looking. His one brilliant green eye gleams like a lighthouse beam. He's studying me and I pick at the sleeve of my hoodie. He seems to be the only person in London who can see me, which both revolts and excites me. I've not had a friend since Troll.

'It was raining,' I say, which is true, but the rain never bothered me. It's obvious he knows why I'm here, ten doors from his place, but he doesn't get me to spell it out.

'Don't know about you but I'm parched,' he says. 'Want a tea or something?'

I'd be an idiot to accept – apart from anything, it's a twentysomething guy asking a teenage girl into his flat. I've stared at enough newspaper headlines to be able to come up with one automatically.

COP BUTCHERS GIRL WHO SCARRED HIM FOR LIFE.

But my curiosity gets the better of me and I relent, following his broad back up the street, all the way in to the flat above his dad's old shop.

'Needs a woman's touch,' I tell him.

'I'm conducting an experiment,' he says. 'Seeing how filthy I can make the place before the furniture starts talking.'

It's been so long since I've talked to anybody, I've forgotten how to have a conversation. You ask questions, right? That's polite and shows you're engaged. I try to think of something to fill the silence. Anything that isn't an apology.

'When you going back to work?' I ask.

'I quit.'

'Why?'

He points to his bandaged eye. 'Don't fancy desk work for the rest of my life.'

The guilt quadruples, hardening like an ugly hunk of metal in my chest.

Bolt goes into the kitchen and comes back with a tray that holds a teapot and mismatching mugs. As he crosses the lounge, his foot catches a floorboard and he crashes to the floor. The teapot smashes, hot tea covering the floorboards, and I react too slowly. Bolt grabs a mug and smashes it against the wall.

So this is my fault, too. He's so angry, I get out of the flat quickly, leaving him in the lounge.

The next time I visit Bolt, he's drunk. His tongue rolls around his mouth lazily and the conversation's weird. We sit in the dingy lounge playing poker but he can't sit still for long. I only stay an hour.

The time after that, he's sober – or seems it – and we drive out to the coast. It's bitterly cold but bright. We draw in the sand.

After a few weeks I realise I've seen him more and more and the hunk of metal in my chest has grown so heavy I'm surprised I can still move. Troll's face keeps surfacing in my mind. The sight of him broken in the junkyard. I find I can't look Bolt in the eye.

One day we're driving and I feel a warm weight on my knee. Bolt's hand.

He must feel me tense because he removes it again almost immediately.

'You okay?'

'Yeah.'

We drive a lot. Aimlessly. There's something comforting about it.

And when did I start saying 'we'?

The van suddenly feels tiny and I swear the metal chassis is creaking inward, trying to crush me, but slowly. So slowly it's torture. I resist the urge to hurl myself out of the moving vehicle and manage to breathe until we're back outside Bolt's.

'Tea?'

I'm not going in, I'm not going in.

'Rumer–'

'I'm not going to be your girlfriend.'

He opens his mouth then shuts it.

'This isn't right.' I stare at the street through the windscreen. It's drizzling rain and there's no colour in the world. 'Sorry.'

I get out and hear him do the same.

'You think you're the only one with problems?'

I shouldn't take the bait but still I turn to face him, blinking through the rain.

'I've never said that.'

Bolt shakes his head. 'Rumer, this doesn't have to be complicated.'

'You're complicating it.'

'I like you.'

'You don't know me.'

He steps towards me. 'I know enough.'

It seems like he wants to put his arms around me. Kiss me. Tell me everything's going to be okay, but he can't know that. They'd be empty words. Words that can only ever be disproved.

There's a churning in my chest and I don't know what it means. It feels like we're not really here. I'm going to wake up in a second or he is.

'See you around,' I say and I can't bear the expression on his face so I turn into the rain and walk away.

He doesn't try to stop me.

I don't see him again until the day I go back and ask him about Mara and the Crook Spear. I don't know why he survived the garage but, if I'm around, that will change.

It's better if I'm alone.

CHAPTER THIRTY-ONE

I passed out again.

When I peel my eyes open, grey light's filtering in through the window. A blanket's been draped over me. I throw it off, my skin crawling at the thought of Celene coming in and watching me sleep. Why the hell did she put a blanket over me? Did she sit on the bed and contemplate my sleepy face? Did she think about finishing the job quickly while I couldn't defend myself?

My hands go to my throat, but it's not been sliced open, even if that's the sort of thing Celene loves doing.

I don't know why I'm alive. What's she waiting for? A waxing moon, maybe, whatever that is. Or perhaps some kind of mystical alignment of the planets like in *The Dark Crystal* or the weird comics Troll gave me. Then they'll strap me to a tree or something and carve out my heart.

The Celene of the nineties would have already chopped me up, tossed my pieces into the Thames and fried herself a full English. What's stopped her?

My neck creaks and I hoist myself up from the floor. The room doesn't spin and my skull doesn't feel like it's going to crack open, so I know the drugs have worn off. I press my ear to the door. Nothing.

Holding my breath, I ease onto a narrow landing. There's no sign of Celene, so I go downstairs, my boots thumping loudly no matter how hard I try to be quiet, and I find myself in a cluttered living room. Dark curtains let in gauzy light and plants sprout in little pots on a bookcase. The books aren't what I expect. *The Art of War*. And *On Guerilla Warfare*. And a load of spiritual crap I'd laugh at if I still had a sense of humour.

I never imagined her as a reader. She's a killer. Pure and evil. But now here she is reading up on battle strategies. Because she's planning something? I don't want to think what and the unease that's settled in my abdomen doesn't let up, only becoming more leaden by the minute.

I go to a window and peer out at the cabins nestled among the trees. I have no memory of coming through here last night. Did she carry me up the stairs? Exactly how strong *is* she?

We arrived in the dark and I can see the camp for the first time. It's a bizarre compound of buildings. A handful of cabins at ground level are rotting and deserted. A dozen more cabins are on stilts between the trees and look like they're inhabited, well kept even. I can't see the gates from here, but to the far right nestles a decrepit portacabin, and beside that is a building made out of breeze blocks that looks like it could contain toilets.

It's a bizarre, half-dead place that might once have been a holiday camp. Except I can't imagine anybody ever having fun here.

I notice a crowd has gathered at the steps leading up to one of the cabins. They're all murmuring and crossing their arms and touching their foreheads, ignoring the mizzling rain. I can tell from the light it's early.

The crowd makes me nervous. It's happening already. I've been at the camp for one night and somebody's died. I know I'm right. Unless… Unless this is normal. God knows what kind of people live here. If they're anything like my mother, they'll be hardened criminals, egos the size of jumbo jets. Fighting's probably an everyday occurrence, and people like these fight to the bitter, bloody end.

Before I know what I'm doing, I'm out the front door and hurtling down the wooden steps to the ground. I'm drawn to the commotion the way people are drawn to car crashes and burning buildings. I know I should stay away, but my feet won't listen.

About fifteen people elbow in around the stairs leading up to another cabin. The knot in my chest tightens. Nobody stands about in the rain unless it's something big.

Slipping through the crowd, I reach the steps but my way's barred by a stony-faced woman. My heart's in my throat and a familiar nag huddles like a spider in a corner of my mind.

This always happens.

'Nobody's allowed up there,' the stony-faced woman says. She's the one from the gates last night.

'What happened?'

'You're Celene's girl.'

I don't know what to say so I try to push past her, but she slams a hand on the wooden railing.

'Nobody's allowed up there.'

A man joins me at the stairs. He's in his forties and has an impressive beard.

'May, why don't you tell us what's going on?'

'Dr Scott's up there, she'll be down when she's finished,' May says.

'Finished what?'

'Yeah, what's Dr Scott doing up there?' a woman asks.

'If Domhnall needs help—' The man tries to push through and May grabs him by the collar, dragging him away from the stairs. Seizing my moment, I lunge past her and hurtle up the steps.

Domhnall. That's the name Dominic used.

The front door's already open and I'm heading inside when I see him.

He's hanging from a beam in the living room.

His face is grey and swollen. His eyes milky and bloodshot.

The rope creaks.

'Shit.'

A woman wearing latex gloves turns from the body. 'What are you doing up here?'

'Rumer.'

Another woman stands on the other side of the body. Celene. Beside her is a man, the one I saw holding the shovel when we arrived last night. First Celene looks angry, then her forehead smoothes out and her gaze softens. She hurries towards me but I'm already stumbling backwards, feeling top heavy, like my skull's turned to stone.

'I have to get out of here,' I murmur.

An overturned chair rests under Dominic's dangling feet. It looks like he killed himself, but I know better. He spent ten minutes in a room with me and I was so angry, I almost strangled him. I could feel the pulse ticking in his throat, counting one, two, three, and I wanted to squeeze it until it stopped.

Now he's swinging from a beam.

I almost fall down the steps to the ground, tearing my nails on the rail.

Being here has made it worse. Nobody's ever died this quickly. I can't breathe. Can't think. My thoughts are snarled and thrashing tentacles, searching for something safe to cling to, but finding nothing. I shove through the crowd at the foot of the steps.

'Did you see Domhnall?'

'Is he okay?'

I ignore the devil worshippers. The rain gets in my eyes, but I charge on, thinking of Dominic's bloated face, his bloodshot eyes, and then I reach the camp gates.

As I throw myself at them, I'm only vaguely aware of a voice.

'Rumer, please.'

Hands pry me away from the gates and I whirl to face her, shoving her off me. Celene steps back, raising her hands.

'Okay, okay. Just please take a moment and breathe.'

I want to hurt her so badly. Everything's her fault. My jaw aches, I'm clenching my teeth so hard, and I wish I could get rid of her the way I get rid of everybody else. With a look or a touch or a thought. And why is she alive? All these years I thought she was dead. Everybody did. She shouldn't be here.

Celene's big-eyed and panting. The look she's giving me could mean anything. Pity. Shame. Fear.

'So that woman they pulled out of the Thames wasn't you,' I say. The grave I've been to just once in nineteen years wasn't even my mother's.

'I wish you hadn't seen that,' she says. 'Domhnall.'

'Don't change the subject! You say he lies... *lied*, but you... You're meant to be dead!'

'I don't expect you to understand.' There's no emotion in her voice. If anything she sounds tired, like this is a conversation we've had a hundred times before and she's bored of it.

'Who was she?' I demand, because whoever the woman in Celene's grave is, she could've once been a sister or a friend or a mother to somebody. And she got caught up in Celene's games, all so Celene could disappear.

'That doesn't matter now. It's raining. Let's go inside.'

The more I stare at her, the more that robotic expression seems to suggest fear. Why would she be afraid of me? She's not afraid of anybody, any*thing*. I attempt to slip through the tentacles in my head, stop them thrashing, and the breath catches in my throat, as if an answer has lodged there.

I saw Dominic. He told me what they did to me, and then he turned up dead.

'You killed him,' I say.

Maybe it wasn't me, the curse. Maybe it was her.

Her expression hardens and blood thunders in my ears. She's angry that I know. She's going to finish it now. Screw whatever ceremony she had planned. I'm too much of a liability. She wasn't able to stop Dominic confirming my biggest fears, but she stopped him from revealing them to anybody else. And she can stop me, too.

But what comes out of her mouth next isn't a confession.

'I had no idea you'd be so cold.'

Her white hair is slicked into grey string by the rain.

'What the hell's that supposed to mean?' There's so little space between us I could reach out and slap her.

'You've had it tough. I wish you hadn't. I wish…'

'That you hadn't killed the woman in your grave? Or Dominic?'

'How do you know that name?'

'Just admit it. You didn't like that he knew all your secrets, so you found a way to make sure he kept them.'

'Domhnall… Dominic… I told you. He was troubled, always has been.' Rain spits between us but I barely feel it. 'He's tried to kill himself before. This time he actually managed it. Look, if you want to know more about him, I'll tell you. Just come inside.'

'Tell me now.'

'Inside.'

I give her a look that tells her I'm not kidding and her jaw sets hard.

'He was a journalist once,' she says. 'Worked for one of the broadsheets. *The Times* maybe. It's been a while. He was ruthless, successful… but he had problems. He was addicted to just about every drug going, and then he wrote something that wasn't just untrue but completely fabricated. Probably while high. He lost everything. He couldn't sell a story because nobody believed a word he said. Then he came here and he's better… Was better. He could curb the mania, but when he drank…'

I think of the liquor bottle smashing at my feet and Celene's so convincing. My head's spinning again, all tangled tentacles and fear like stones, and I don't know what's real. Of all the things I thought when I saw her in the hotel window, I didn't think she'd be like this. Sad and brittle. Desperate.

Maybe she didn't kill Dominic. Maybe she got somebody to do it for her.

Or maybe he really did hang himself.

Maybe maybe maybe.

'What do you *want*?' I demand. 'What am I doing here?'

'I want to…' She lowers her gaze. 'I never wanted you to be part of that world. Mara's world. I've been searching for you for twenty years and then I discovered you were caught up in his games. I realised the worst had happened.'

Worse than being abandoned as a kid? Worse than sleeping rough on the streets?

Worse than killing children and never being punished for it?

Cursing your own daughter?

'I want to help you,' she says.

'You're crazy.'

'Maybe. But I'm trying to be the good kind of crazy. I'll tell you about it if you just come inside.'

It's a trick. As soon as she gets me into the cabin, she'll shackle me to a pipe or the bed and then she'll have won.

'You should eat,' she continues. 'You'll feel better.'

'I'll feel better when you let me go.'

'You can leave whenever you want.'

The gates cut into my back and I consider digging my boots into them, hauling myself over the top and escaping into the forest, but I don't feel well. My body's heavy and my head's pounding. All I want is to lie down and think. Straighten out the confusion knotting things together in my brain.

'You'll tell me everything,' I say.

She nods.

'And answer anything I ask.'

She pauses, then nods again.

'And I'm not eating anything,' I say, because I still can't trust that she won't drug me or poison me or serve me the flesh of one of her enemies.

Without a word, she turns and strolls back into the camp. She only looks over her shoulder once to check I'm following, but she needn't have bothered.

CHAPTER THIRTY-TWO

It takes me a moment to realise she's not leading me back to her cabin. She must be taking the 'no eating' thing seriously. The huts on stilts all look so alike, the rotting cabins at their feet even more so, I'd feel disoriented even if I wasn't attempting to think through a crashing headache. It's only the crowd dispersing from Dominic's place that helps me get my bearings. They hunch into the rain, some in pairs, some alone. A solemn mood has settled where anxious curiosity had buzzed before, though a few of them flash looks at me, that same curiosity burning through the misty air.

I peer back. They look normal; nothing like devil worshippers. Not that I have any idea what devil worshippers are supposed to look like. The girls at school thought I was one with my dark hair and black nails.

The guy who had the shovel flashes a hooded look back at me and then crosses the centre of the camp. He strides like he owns the place, his black boots buffed to a high gleam, and then he disappears inside the portacabin. I wet my lips. Something about the portacabin makes me nervous. Its windows are blacked out and it crouches under the canopy of trees like a toad. Maybe that's where they torture people. Or cut up the bodies.

As we pass the other cabins, I crane to look up at them, wondering why they're on stilts.

'Flooding,' says Celene. She must have noticed me sizing up the camp. Her ability to guess what I'm thinking makes my gut spasm. 'Place was condemned, but only after they'd blown a load of cash on the stilt experiment. It worked out for us, at least.'

I trail after her even though I shouldn't. My insides strain in the opposite direction, attempting to pull me back to the gates, but something else overrides them. As wary as I am of Celene, there's a part of me that wants to see her. I can't explain it and I don't understand it. I don't believe in a static crackle of magic that binds members of a family.

Maybe it's because I've started seeing what everybody else has said

191

my whole life. That I'm her mirror image. We're on opposite sides of a pane of glass, except if I reached out, I'd touch flesh and skin. A real person. My mother's replaced the yellow photographs of the Dead Room.

My boots sink into the mud and it takes a huge effort to wade on, but I keep up with her, scanning the cabins as we pass them, looking for anything out of the ordinary. Satanic symbols carved into wood or heads on pikes, but there's nothing. It could be a frickin' holiday camp, except there are no kids. I spot a guy who looks to be in his fifties, but he's too busy tipping rainwater out of plant pots to pay me any attention. There's a surreal quality to the whole place. This could be where serial killers come to retire. It's a great advert for serial killers. Except everybody seems so normal.

'What is this place?' I ask.

'Home,' Celene says. 'Has been for almost a decade.'

'I love what you've done to it.' She ignores my brittle tone. Perhaps she can't believe what a bitch her daughter is, but I can't help it. The world's been turned upside down and I'm supposed to just accept it?

'All these people... They're–' The word 'cultist' won't come out of my mouth. It sounds too ridiculous.

'Everybody here has been wronged in some way,' says Celene. 'They've either suffered at the hands of some nutcase, or they've been roped into doing things they regret.'

Boo-frickin'-hoo. 'So it's a retirement village.'

'Village, yes. Retirement, no. Everybody here works in their own way, contributing to the community.'

'Yeah, they're all saving the world, I'm sure.'

She gives me one of her looks. I've touched a nerve. What did I say? *Saving the world.* Why would that upset her? I scan the camp to avoid her eyes. The run-down cabins. The strange portacabin standing separate from the others, its windows blacked out, antennas forking from the roof.

I try to puzzle it out but all I see is a commune for murderers and rapists. I think about the books on Celene's shelves. *The Art of War* and the one about guerilla warfare. There was something about the security woman, May, and the guy with the shovel. The way they walked. The polished boots and the ramrod postures. They looked like they'd either served time or been in the military.

I stop and stare at Celene's back.

'You're training them,' I say, and I almost laugh at the way it sounds.

When she doesn't say anything, it's like a cold hand has slipped under my collar.

'You're *shitting* me,' I say, my voice tight with hysteria. 'You can't actually be training people, killers and Christ knows what else. What are they? Wannabe soldiers or bounty hunters? What the hell does that get you? What, you're planning a coup or a heist or a—'

She turns to face me. Her granite expression could mean anything and I'm struck again by how much older she looks. I've spent years staring at photos of a young woman. Someone in her prime. There are cracks in her skin now and her eyes are different.

'They're not soldiers,' she says eventually. 'But they have been trained. It's a dangerous world out there and nobody's doing anything about it.'

My ears are playing tricks on me. It sounds like she thinks she's running some sort of military operation. One served by murderous headcases. What exactly is going on around here?

'So you've trained them to kill,' I spit.

Was that a flinch? Or just a shiver because of the wind shushing through the trees? She stares at me for a long moment, and it seems like she's ready to spit some words back at me, but then she traipses towards the woods and it's only my curiosity that makes me go after her. The air smells of fresh rain and wet soil and the world keeps somersaulting so that I'm having trouble distinguishing between fact and fucked-up.

Celene stops and sits on a log. I stand a few feet away, not sure what to do with myself.

'I wasn't prepared for the way you'd look at me.'

Her voice verges on a whisper and an icy shock travels through me. How do I look at her? Like she's the worst person I ever met? Like it's painful to stare into her face and imagine what it was like for her victims. Hers was the last face they ever saw.

Get used to it.

'I'm guessing you know all about me,' she continues, snapping leaves off a nearby plant and raising them to her nose. 'What I did when I was younger.'

'It was good bedtime reading.'

'I'm sure you think I'm a monster.'

She talks so matter-of-factly it throws me off.

'You care what I think?' I ask.

'You're the only person I ever cared about. When you were born, I thought you were dead. I ran. I wasn't exactly in my right mind back then. When I found out you'd survived, I tried to find you, but you were gone. I thought maybe it was for the best. Who needs a mother like me?' She meets my gaze. 'Now I can't help wondering if I was wrong.'

I'm dumbstruck. Did she really search for me? She can't have looked hard; I never left London. With all her contacts and skills as a killer it should've been easy for her to track me down.

No. Celene Cross lies. Just like her daughter. Just like everybody who ever had anything to hide.

'Tell me about yourself,' she says.

'Like you give a shit.' She doesn't care. She just wants more intel. More things to use against me for when she finally strikes. If I tell her anything, it'll come back to get me in ways I can't even imagine.

'I know I haven't been around,' she says.

'No kidding.'

'But that doesn't mean I don't care. I want to know you. Everything.'

I want to yell at her, but then for some reason I'm talking. I don't know why. Am I flattered that she wants to hear about my life? Is it nice that somebody cares?

No. I want her to know what it's been like. What she did when she abandoned me. What she turned me into. I tell her about the foster homes and the idiots pretending to be my parents. I miss out Frances and George because just thinking about them makes my throat close up. I tell her about shadowing for Julian and how I spend most of the money I earn on rent and food and comic books.

'But you already know that; you went to see Julian. You scared the crap out of him.'

'I don't like him.'

I'm not sure, but I think the corner of her lip has curled up a little.

'You were looking for me again,' I say. 'Why?'

She crumples the leaves and lifts them again, closing her eyes. I can't tell if she's toying with me. I'm not buying this Mother Earth crap for a second.

'Our last target was a man named Cyril Berry,' she says. 'This was about a month ago. He was a small-time crook using immigrants as slaves. He had ambition, though, which we discovered when we interrogated him. He was romancing a new power in London, trying to climb the ladder. He gave up Reverend Mara within minutes and blabbed about his obsession with finding the Crook Spear in another few. He was pathetic.'

Her eyes flash and I see disgust, maybe even hatred. It stuns me how quickly those emotions flicker across her face and then vanish, replaced with ghostly indifference.

In the swimming soup of my mind, a stray thought bobs to the surface. A few weeks ago, I read an article in the paper about a London mobster, Bob 'The Razor' Stanley, who was eaten by his dog. There were reports of a hit squad van being seen around that time.

'You've been taking out gangsters,' I say. 'Bob Stanley. Is that what you've got going on here? You're getting revenge on all the guys who crossed you in the past.'

'Revenge? No.' Celene merely stares back at me, her face as grey as her hair.

'What, then?'

Saving the world. When I said that, everything about her had changed.

'You can't seriously be trying to save the world,' I probe. It doesn't make any sense. It goes against everything I know. Why would a self-confessed killer suddenly decide she's a superhero?

'I did a lot of things I regret,' murmurs Celene. 'A lot I wish I could change, but I can't. This… it helps. In some small way, it helps.'

She's messing with me. Maybe it's the drugs she gave me last night, or the concussion from Mara's car flipping, but she's so convincing I almost find myself believing it. I *want* to believe it. Because if she's no longer a monster, maybe I'm not either.

But she's lying. I think of the Dead Room and all the articles about the havoc she wreaked in the nineties. The blood. The way everybody who's ever got near me has died. And the fact that she and Mara are two sides of the same coin. Vicious. Manipulative. Crazy.

'You worked for Mara,' I say.

Celene nods, her hair getting in her eyes. 'He was small fry in the nineties, but he's grown.'

'You killed his dad and you took the Crook Spear.'

'You missed your call from the FBI,' Celene says. Is that pride in there? It turns my stomach.

'Why'd you kill him?' I demand.

'I had my reasons.'

Hello vague. 'And where's the Crook Spear?'

'I hid it where nobody would find it. Tell me about growing up. Where did you live?'

Nice try. 'Wherever I was sent. The spear–'

'You didn't have it easy.'

'Who does? Look, Mara thinks I have the spear, and he wants to recruit me or something, he has some crazy idea that killing runs in the family. And he has Bolt.'

'Bolt?'

'My friend. Sort of.' She doesn't need to know he used to be a cop. I've got a feeling that would only push him to the bottom of her list of priorities. 'I need to help him – and stop Mara.'

'You can't stop him. Leave it to us. He's next on our list. Last, actually.'

'What are you planning on doing? What did you do with Cyril Berry?'

'He's in jail.'

'You mean you didn't–' I put a finger to my temple.

Celene looks at the ground. 'I don't do that any more.'

I think about being in the upturned car with Mara and holding the shard to his throat. My chest starts to burn. George would be alive if it wasn't for Mara, and Mara would be dead if it wasn't for Celene.

'You should've let me kill Mara when I had the chance,' I growl.

She peers at her hands. 'I couldn't let you do that.'

'I have just as much right to want him dead as you do. More, actually. His lackey killed George and he's taken Bolt and he locked me up–'

'You're no killer, Rumer.'

Except I am. I've been killing ever since I was a little kid, thanks to her.

'You made me one.' I'm trembling.

'I don't understand.'

'You want to know what it was like for me growing up? Imagine everybody you ever got close to dying.'

Her expression is blank.

'You did something to me. I read about it. Dominic Waters or whatever his name is, he sold his story to some magazine.'

Celene doesn't say anything. She seems confused. 'Dominic?'

'I know all about the curse. What you did when I was born.'

'Did? Rumer, I don't know what you're talking about.'

I want to scream or hit her. *Something* to get her to stop lying. 'You did this to me. You made it so everybody dies.'

She's on her feet, taking a step towards me, but I step back and hug my ribs, hating that I'm trembling but I can't make it stop.

Celene's gaze is heavy on me and her mouth droops at the corners, like she's only just realising how much she fucked everything up.

'I told you about Dominic,' she says. 'Christ, I wish he hadn't snuck into the house. Whatever he said to you, you can't believe any of it. It was the rambling of a maniac. You saw him. He was drunk and he knows... *knew*... he wasn't supposed to drink on his medication.'

'The story in the magazine,' I say, and my voice is trembling now, too. 'The Divine Order and all that bullshit. You belonged to a fucking cult and you did this to me.'

Celene shakes her head slowly and I can't escape her eyes. I've stared into them for so long, the ones stuck to the Dead Room wall, but now they are staring back and seeing me, and the pity in them makes me want to tear out my hair.

'I was naive back then,' she says softly. 'I joined the Order and they had strange customs. It's true, I wanted to escape that life, and Dominic... Well, he had his ways. He helped me give birth and his methods were unconventional, but there's no such thing as a curse, not a real one.'

She's still lying. Saving her own skin because, for some reason, she wants a relationship with me now. She knows that wouldn't be possible if she admitted what she did. Does she know what Dominic told me? That if I kill her the curse goes away?

I'm sick of lies. It's getting harder to distinguish them from the truth. And what is 'truth' anyway? Something printed in a newspaper? Or on a website? Or is it looking into somebody's eyes and seeing their pain and not turning away from it?

Celene reaches a hand towards me.

'You're not cursed, Rumer.'

She makes it sound like I'm being ridiculous. A melodramatic teenager. Everything in the Dead Room tells me otherwise. She's the one who belonged to a devil-worshipping cult.

'Come on,' she says, 'let's get back inside.'

CHAPTER THIRTY-THREE

I shower and I can't believe how good it feels. My clothes had practically grown into my skin and I had to pick them off like a scab. I've not washed since the pit and the water massages my skin the way a lover might, soothing the tender knots in my shoulders, not that I know much about lovers beyond what's in the movies.

The broken tooth's still throbbing, though. Every once in a while it stabs at my gum, the pain sharp as a scorpion's stinger, and I'm sick of it. Sick of being a broken thing trapped in a broken world.

Pushing my face into the water, I dig my fingers into my mouth, feel out the cracked tooth. Just touching it makes it angry, like I've disturbed a rattlesnake, but I ignore the shooting pain and twist, attempting to unscrew it from my gum.

A coppery tang floods my mouth and the pain multiplies like a virus, firing through my jaw and into my throat. I wrench harder, not making a sound, feeling the water on my face, imagining it dissolving the pain and, just when I start seeing black spots, something crunches, clicks and the needling shard is out.

Choking blood, I spit, inspecting the near-black thing in my fingers, and sigh with relief.

It's been rotting in my head for days. I turn the tooth before me, washing it clean. A piece of me that's not a piece of me any more. If only it was as easy to dig out everything else rotting inside me.

'So long, sucker.'

I drop it and it rattles down the drain.

When I look in the mirror, I look more like my old self. The one who quietly works shadowing people and doesn't know anything about Crook Spears or mobsters. I'm even paler than usual, though, and I know Celene's right. I need to eat. My hands quiver as I attempt to claw stubborn knots out of my hair.

For the first time I let myself really think about where I am.

With her.

In detective novels, this is what they call a 'golden opportunity'. A chance to see for myself what she's really like. I've only ever read about Celene. Had her described to me by newspapers that weren't exactly tripping over themselves to write flattering things. Not that her life lends itself to flattery.

Will I see the killer in her? Or is it buried under years of denial and indifference?

Celene's left fresh clothes on a bench. A purple T-shirt with the emblem of some ancient rock band. Black jeans. Scuffed boots somebody would pay a fortune for in a retro sweat shop. I eye my discarded clothes and, though I'd rather die than wear anything of Celene's, the thought of struggling back into that crusty scab makes me itch all over.

Fine. Let's do this.

Celene's standing in the hall when I emerge from the bathroom. I can't help jumping. She really is like a ghost. Both here and not here, silent and unknowable. If she notices my reaction, she doesn't say anything.

'Come here,' she says, walking down the landing and stopping at a door at the end. Clutching my old clothes to my belly, I join her. She pushes the door open and doesn't move. Warily, I peek around the frame, expecting to find a cell with chains or something worse that my mind can't think of quickly enough before I see it's a bedroom.

Nothing fancy. White walls stencilled with purple patterns. A paper night light rests in one corner, turning shadows over and over so that the room seems to breathe. Pillows are piled up on the bed and the rug looks like it was stitched together with bits of old fabric.

'I always thought you'd like purple,' Celene says, and I realise what I'm looking at. What she's made.

My own room.

My heart pulses a beat I don't recognise and my palms grow clammy.

'You can go in. If you want.'

The spider in my mind whispers it might be a trap, but for once I don't care. I'm walking on cotton wool as I go and stand in the centre of the room – *my* room – letting the night light's shadows wash over me. I can't feel the floor, only a strange sensation of falling and being lifted up, like I'm being gently stretched.

The only room I've ever had, one that really felt like mine, is nothing like this. How did she know? If she'd crawled into my head she couldn't have known that this is perfect, because I don't know what perfect is either. Definitely not my grotty flat above the newsagents. Not the bars and seedy hotels I've shadowed people in. Not the Dead Room. Not even Frances' house, which was only mine for a while and then suddenly wasn't.

'I wanted you to have somewhere.' Celene's still at the door.

My cheeks are burning and I think she sees something in my expression because hers changes.

'I'll be downstairs,' she says, and then she's gone.

How can something feel right and wrong at the same time? This isn't home. It's the house of a maniac playing mother. This is why Celene's dangerous. It must be how she earned her reputation as a ghost. She charmed her way into the homes of her victims, then snapped her jaws. She did it in the nineties and she's doing it now.

Except her expression is imprinted on my eyelids. The same tangle of emotions tentacling through my skull. When I think about the way she looked at me just now as I stood in the room she's made for me, all I see is hope.

What does she hope for?

Carefully, I place the bundle of my clothes at the foot of the bed, peering around again, knowing the room means something to her.

I hate myself for knowing it means something to me, too.

A sizzle of cooking food comes up the stairs and, begrudgingly, I leave the room.

'I'm glad the clothes fit,' Celene says as I enter the kitchen. She hands me a plate of scrambled eggs, bacon and toast. I'm no idiot. I know it could be laced with something, but I can't remember the last time I ate and my stomach seizes control of my hand. I manage to resist for about five seconds, then I'm at the table, ravenously shovelling forkfuls into my mouth, not caring. At least I'll die with a full belly.

I don't even notice Celene watching me until I've swallowed the last mouthful. She stands to the side of the kitchen, her arms crossed.

'When's the last time you ate?'

'No idea,' I say.

'That's not good.'

'When can we get out of here?' I ask. 'Bolt's still–'

'Bolt's dead.'

She doesn't sugar-coat it. I admire and hate her for it.

'You don't know that.'

'If Mara has him, he's dead.'

'He won't kill him. He knows how much–'

I stop. *How much he means to me.* I hadn't realised that until I almost said it. Bolt's the closest thing I've had to a friend since Troll. When I went to him for help, he didn't hesitate, telling me everything he knew about Reverend Mara and rescuing me when his hounds pelted me with bullets.

And when Mara torched his place, he didn't yell at me, which he had every right to. There was no simmering resentment. He was there for me, fighting off assassins and stopping me from demolishing Ellis' skull, and all I cared about was saving my own skin.

Not any more.

'I have to try.'

'You'll die in the process.'

'Sounds like a fair trade,' I say.

'It's not. You're safe here–'

'According to you.'

Her jaw hardens into a line. I wonder what she's like angry. *Really* angry; when her blood boils and her vision swims. Does she get violent? Would she hit me? Or worse? Her nails are digging into her arms and I imagine the whistling kettle in Peng's kitchen, wondering if she's ready to erupt.

'We're infiltrating Mara's regime the day after tomorrow,' she says evenly. 'I can't promise anything, but I'll try to look for your friend.'

'Try. Great.' I stand. 'If you're going up against Mara, I'm coming with you.'

'No, you're not.'

'You said I could leave whenever I wanted.'

'Not if you're going to run off and get killed.'

'So I'm your prisoner after all.'

CHAPTER THIRTY-THREE

'I'm trying to do the right thing–'

I cut her off with a laugh. Annoyance crosses her face and my pulse quickens. If I keep lobbing flaming grenades her way, she's going to have to either take the explosions or hurl them back.

Was there a lock on the bedroom door? I can't remember.

'We can discuss this later,' Celene says, grabbing a khaki jacket from the back of a chair. 'Let me show you the rest of the camp. You'll see for yourself we're more than capable of taking on Mara.'

She's at the door before I can protest and then I'm going after her again like some irritating little yappy dog that doesn't know what's best for it. I can't shake the feeling she's got me on a leash.

Outside, the rain has stopped, but fog creeps between the cabins. They look so strange on their stilts and I wonder if there are wild animals out here. Maybe the fences are for keeping more than just Mara at bay.

Curiosity keeps threatening to make me ask questions. I have so many of them multiplying inside me I'm practically vibrating. I clench my fists. I don't want to make this easy for her. The more we talk, the less I'm able to see the monster.

Celene leads me towards the portacabin resting at the back of the encampment, away from the other cabins, and suddenly I'm on high alert again. This is the place that looks like a torture chamber. Or somewhere dead bodies are hacked apart to be used in satanic rituals.

I consider slipping away. Celene has her back to me and I could probably make it all of twenty feet before she notices I'm not behind her. What the hell's in the portacabin? I wish I had the knife in my boot, the one I always have for emergencies, but it's long gone and I feel more vulnerable than ever.

We reach the portcabin and now all I want to know is what's inside.

If Celene really does want me to believe she's changed, here's her chance to prove it.

First chain dripping blood I see, though, I'm out of here.

An armed guard stands at the door. More guards stroll around the perimeter.

'What was this place? I mean, before you moved in.'

That one slipped out before I could stop it.

'It was a holiday camp. Something bad happened, a fire, and there was flooding every winter. They tried to get around that by building cabins on stilts but by then the place wasn't earning a penny. It lay unused for a decade. I bought it at a steal almost ten years ago.'

She goes up the steps to the portacabin. The guard tips his hat at her, then blinks at me.

'She's with me,' Celene says and my insides flutter strangely.

The guard stares at me a moment longer, then nods. We go inside.

What light there is comes from little lamps swinging from the ceiling. There are a few desks. Somebody sits wearing headphones, scribbling notes. Another hunches over a laptop. They're monitoring news feeds. Some are staring at CCTV footage, others seem to be listening in to police radios.

'This is operations,' Celene says as we move between the desks, and I almost smile. They're shadowing people.

No, these aren't shadows. They're hunters. Killers. Like me but not.

'The camp population is thirty-five.' Celene leads me between the desks. 'We have ten monitors in operations, two trained infiltration units, ten fighters apiece, and then there are the heads of operations. There are two of us.'

'You're a head of operations.'

Celene nods.

Mama's earning the big bucks.

We've reached the back of the room. Turning a corner into a side room, I stop short. For a moment I thought I was back in the Dead Room. The wall contains an elaborate montage of headshots and maps. The headshots are arranged in a triangle. Mara's at the top and a number of smaller shots spread out below him.

'The Wall,' Celene says, joining me as I stare up at it.

A lot of the smaller shots have red crosses struck through them.

'Mara's dangerous because he's different from past power players,' Celene says. 'Usually, reaching the top of the pyramid means killing the competition. Mara's plans are more insidious. He wants to unite the factions under his rule, create an empire.'

She points at four pictures directly under Mara. Two women and two men.

'These are the four heads of the main factions. Mara wants them working together with him.'

A smaller photograph snags my interest and I lean in closer to it, squinting at the image of a young man with sandy hair. He's directly under the picture of one of the crime bosses, and I recognise him immediately. It's Skinny, the boy from the pit in Mara's warehouse, except under his picture reads: Viktor Kumiega.

'Rumer?'

Celene's voice is an echo.

The last time I saw this face, I was reaching across the front seat of the van, attempting to drag him inside. Then the bullet hit, making a sound like a stone hitting a watermelon, and there was red everywhere.

'He's dead,' I murmur.

'This one?'

Celene touches the photo of Skinny and I nod.

'You know him?'

'He was in the pit with me,' I say.

'Pit?'

'In Mara's warehouse. He has a pit full of dead bodies. Viktor was in there. He helped me escape. They killed him.'

'His mother is Agnes Kumiega, a powerful player. It sounds like Mara was using her son as collateral. If Mara killed him, I can't imagine it will have helped his cause.'

I don't care about that. All I can think about is Bolt. I remember reaching for Skinny when the bullet hit and, in my mind, it's Bolt I'm reaching for. Bolt whose brains get splattered against the window. Bolt I leave for dead in the road.

I've already decided I'm not staying here. Celene can argue all she likes. Even if I don't leave with her tomorrow when her team go to confront Mara, I'll slip out when there's nobody here to stop me.

Celene doesn't have to know that, though. For now, I have to play along. Let her think I'm interested in how she's going to take down Mara. Let her think she's convinced me it's best she deals with him.

And I am interested, but not because I need convincing. I need to know everything she does if I'm going to kill Mara and save Bolt.

That means I'd better start asking questions.

'How are you going to stop him? Mara?'

'The Crook Spear. After I took it from Mara, I sold it to a collector, a Swedish investor called Magnus Vinter. He promised to keep it under wraps, and he paid a decent amount for it. Security at his mansion is airtight. Cameras, electric fences, armed guards. I knew it would be safe with him. Mara can't be the only lunatic who believes it has supernatural properties. Even without them, it's still a weapon. Better not to tempt anybody to do something stupid with it.'

'So he's the one who has it now?'

Celene nods, her gaze drifting up to another picture tacked to the The Wall. It's an illustration of an exotic woman standing against a rising sun, her arm outstretched, a gun pointed at something or someone off-page.

The gun looks completely unremarkable. Not what I expected.

'Magnus is hosting a party tomorrow evening in London. That's where we'll get Mara.'

'He'll be there?'

'We leaked intel on the whereabouts of the gun to Mara this morning. He's not stupid enough to try to crack Magnus' security, so he's going to use the party to infiltrate Magnus' home and steal back the spear.'

'Where you'll stop him.'

'I have my own invite to the party. I'll walk right in the front door.'

'What about the gun?'

'It can stay where it is.'

'But the legend. Mara thinks–'

'Mara can think all he wants. If he gets the gun, I'll have no choice but to shoot him with it.'

Just like his father.

'Why did you steal the gun in the first place?'

Celene casts an eye over the cabin. 'To buy this place. I knew I had to get out. This was my best bet. A chance at freedom.'

A shaft of light cuts through the gloom of the cabin as somebody comes in. He's square shouldered and tall, striding towards us. As he passes under the lamps, his face is illuminated. Lined. Tired looking.

It's the guy I keep seeing around the camp. The one who was clutching the spade the night Celene brought me here.

'Celene,' he says when he reaches us.

'Rumer, this is Frank,' Celene says. 'The second head operative.'

Frank seems distracted as he nods at me, barely making eye contact before he returns to Celene.

'Figures have been sighted in the woods,' he says. 'May has headed out to patrol the area.'

'How many?'

'May reported two, but she couldn't confirm.'

'Mara's?'

'For our sake, I hope not.'

Celene's demeanour changes. It's like she's grabbed an exposed wire and the electricity has jolted to life every nerve in her body. She grabs my arm and ushers us back through the cabin.

Outside, it's just as gloomy. Fog hangs in ghostly wreaths and the air's wet. We hurry through the camp. Celene's hand is clamped around my arm and the contact unnerves me.

'I want guards at all access points,' she tells Frank. 'Anybody with a gun.'

We reach Celene's cabin.

'Rumer, go up and lock yourself in,' she says.

I want to protest, but her no-nonsense look says I'd be stupid to. I wouldn't want to help protect a camp full of serial killers anyway but, if Mara's turned up, I'd rather do anything than lock myself in Celene's cabin. She's playing the protection card, though. Maybe she's worried I'll die before she can use me in whatever she's got planned. It's easier to let her think I'm going along with her. Easier for *her*, anyway.

'I won't be long.' She stares at me until I turn and hurry up the steps. She watches until I'm inside, maybe listening for the sound of the key clicking in the door. Her expression's strained and I find myself wondering if she's having as much trouble trusting me as I am her. Does she think I'll try to escape if she's not got an eye on me? I have to admit, it's the first thought that enters my head.

I watch through the window as, wearing that same conflicted expression, she finally takes off through the camp, Frank at her side.

If Mara's here, that changes everything. Does he have Bolt with him? And if Mara knows where the Crook Spear is, what use does he have for me now anyway?

Celene betrayed Mara and killed his father. This is revenge. Mara won't stop until he's taken Celene out, and I can't help thinking he'll do the same to me. I've made it pretty clear I'll never work for him.

Below, campers and the guards race around clutching guns. I don't see any of Mara's men, though. What if they break in? That'll give Celene a chance to prove once and for all whose bite is worse than their bark.

If they get past her, they'll sweep every cabin until they're sure they've destroyed the whole nest.

And if they find me here, I'll have nothing to defend myself with.

I spin about and hurry into the kitchen, zeroing in on a knife block. I grab the biggest knife and squeeze the cold steel into my palm, feeling better already. But there's no gunfire outside. No shouting. Was Frank wrong? The figures in the woods were just poachers or dog walkers? If it *was* Mara's men, did May manage to head them off?

Minutes tick by and my focus trembles on the front door, waiting for somebody to crash through, imagining what I'll do then.

Nobody appears. It's unnaturally quiet out here in the middle of nowhere. It's never quiet in London. There's a constant drone. Buses and kids in parks, the Tube rattling under your feet.

Silence means death.

My focus blurs, the quiet like a shroud, and I'm suddenly aware I'm alone in Celene's home. I could kick myself for wasting so many minutes. This place has me on edge and my natural instincts are smothered under a blanket of static. I shouldn't be guarding the front door, I should be doing what I always do.

I cast a look around the cabin. Now is the perfect time to find out what secrets Celene's hiding.

CHAPTER THIRTY-FOUR

By the mid-afternoon light, I pick over the living room. Self-help books with stupid titles. A few trinkets on the table by the sofa. Shells. A carved cat. A pair of slippers by the stairs. Where are the weapons? The relics of her crimes? The cupboard under the stairs is stacked with tins and jars, a couple of backpacks. The most incriminating object is a small axe resting against the wall, but it's not stained with old blood. If anything, it looks brand new. She might actually chop wood with it.

The kitchen's like any other. Cleaner, maybe, but then Celene was always good at cleaning up after herself.

It can't be that easy. Celene... what? Finds Gaia and becomes a whole new person? If shadowing taught me anything, it's that people aren't like that. They don't change, they just become more extreme versions of who they always were. Thieves become criminal masterminds, worriers end up never leaving the house, daytime drinkers become booze-a-holics. The thought of a more extreme version of Celene makes the hairs on my arms stand up and I throw a look at the door to make sure she's not back yet.

One woman I followed was a shoplifter. She was crafty, though. She'd shoplift expensive clothes, get dolled up, then target the shops in New Bond Street, playing on the shopkeepers' prejudices. I sort of respected her. She'd found a way to survive, just like everybody else.

Looks like Celene found a way, too.

At best, her crimes could have landed her behind bars for life. At worst, she'd have been tortured by her enemies. Perhaps turned up at a police station in boxes. Or even washed up on the Thames, like the woman everybody assumed was her back in the nineties. Divine justice.

Seems Celene's as clever as she sounded in the reports I hoard in the Dead Room. She tricked these gullibles, played on their sympathies, perhaps even constructed a story of domestic abuse (so tragic) and they'd be cold hearted to turn her down now, wouldn't they?

Celene said everybody else in the camp has a history as messed up as hers. Are they all killers? Or were some of them victims? Dominic didn't seem the killing type, but then he killed himself. Possibly.

My gaze drifts to the stairs.

Her bedroom.

If the cabin contains any incriminating evidence, it'll be in there.

Still clutching the knife, I go upstairs. Four doors line the landing. The bathroom. The spare room I slept in last night. The room she made for me. That just leaves–

I open the final door.

I don't know what to expect. After discovering Celene was alive, I've pretty much learnt not to have expectations. I stare blankly at the neat room with its single bed and bookcase. It could be a prison cell.

Going inside would be an intrusion, but that didn't stop Celene kidnapping me. If it wasn't for her, I'd still be with Mara, potentially even rescuing Bolt by now. Instead, I'm here, looking at the place where my murderous mother sleeps.

'Rumer?'

My shoulders tense, but Celene's not caught me in the act. Her voice comes up the stairs. I shut her bedroom door and slide the kitchen knife into the chest of drawers in the other room – my room. It might come in handy.

'False alarm,' Celene says as I come down the stairs.

'Poachers,' Frank adds. He's in the kitchen, filling the kettle, then setting out three mugs, taking a spoon from a drawer. He seems awfully at home in Celene's house.

'You look tired,' Celene says.

'I'll live.'

My mind's still in her bedroom. The secrets she's hiding in there. I want her gone so I can keep snooping. What if I don't get another chance? Celene didn't leave me in the house alone for more than ten minutes. She must be afraid I'll find whatever it is she's hoarding.

'Tea?' Frank's already stirring the contents of the mugs. I'd prefer coffee, but for once I need to play nice. Be a good girl. Ask the right questions. Throw spaghetti at the wall and see what sticks. It's about time the shadow started speaking.

'You get a lot of false alarms like that?' I ask.

'The guards are jittery,' Celene says. 'We're closer than ever to stopping Mara and that means we're even more of a target.'

'So far, we've gone undetected, though.' Frank hands me a mug. 'Quite an accomplishment, given the world we're dealing with.'

Celene cradles her mug by the window, leaning against a wooden beam. She doesn't seem to like to sit, as if relaxing for a moment will put her at a disadvantage. Frank sits on the sofa, presumably so he can watch the door. Old tricks. I can't shake the feeling I'm among people who share my haunted mentality.

'What's happened to Dominic?' I ask, perching on the arm of the sofa.

'Dominic?' Frank's brow creases.

'Domhnall,' Celene murmurs. 'He'll be laid to rest later this week, when everything's settled down.'

Frank winces as he sips his tea. 'A shame. Some of us fight our demons, but some of us tire of fighting.'

So Frank doesn't suspect foul play. My mother's face is blank as a whitewashed sky, but her eyes are dark and stormy.

'Look at us.' Frank tuts. 'Rumer, tell me about yourself.'

I give him a few breadcrumbs. Stale scraps of my life to satisfy his curiosity. In return, he talks about his time in the military, how he fought in some war somewhere, how Celene befriended him when he was at a low ebb, brought him here, what a wonderful woman she is.

So Celene's into recruitment. And, going by the way she and Frank are staying on opposite sides of the room, carefully avoiding eye contact, there's more than business between them.

'Did you recruit everybody who lives here?' I ask her.

'Some of them. Most people just need a hand, a nudge in the right direction. Lots of them were homeless, or addicts, or both.'

'And they repay you for giving them a roof over their heads by fighting the scourge of London.'

'Basically.'

The idea of Celene as some kind of Christ figure would make me cackle if it wasn't so sinister. Everybody here is in her debt. I wonder if she'd kick them out if they refused to fight.

'They want to fight.' Celene's looking right at me, as if she's read my mind. How does she do that? 'The thing you have to understand is that nobody wants to be a victim. Not if they've been through the worst kind of degradation imaginable. People want to feel empowered, and that's what they get here. They can stop others from suffering the way they did.'

'And Mara's the Golden Goose,' I say.

'He's a ruthless, conniving egomaniac and he must be stopped,' Frank says.

Because he's on a mission to kill your girlfriend.

It's almost sweet.

'But killing him won't wipe the criminal underworld clean,' I say.

'It'll knock it back a few steps,' Celene says.

'Meanwhile, you get your revenge.'

'I'm not doing this for revenge.' She sounds like she means it but I smell bullshit.

'Mara made you public enemy number one and you don't have a problem with that?'

Celene doesn't blink. 'How I feel doesn't matter. Mara's dangerous and the police are under his thumb. It's up to us to stop him.'

'Because he believes a gun can make him immortal.'

'Because he holds no regard for human life.' She meets my gaze. 'I know I'm the last person you'd expect to say that.'

You said it, sister.

'I did terrible things and I live with that every day. Believe me, I do, but Mara's a sociopath. He's tried everything. The black market, drugs, importing weapons. At one point he traded in slaves, shipping girls over from China. Now he thinks he can harness some kind of feminine power, this transvestite act, the thing with the Crook Spear, but he's a fraud. Nothing he does comes from a place of honesty.'

'Do you think the Crook Spear has some kind of power?'

Her gaze is steady. 'Rumer, none of that matters. It's smoke and mirrors. It's a distraction from what does matter, which is life. Freedom from fear and persecution.'

And suddenly I realise Celene knew all along that Dominic visited me last night. She knows what Dominic told me. That I could break the curse by killing her. She's been playing me ever since she brought me here. It's the only reason she'd start spouting all this stuff about valuing human life – because she wants me to value hers.

'I guess so,' I say, because what else can I say? *You're a liar. You're only out for yourself. You're scared I'll take you down.*

Does she think I'll succeed? Or is she scared she'll have to put me down, the way she thought she'd put me down all those years ago when I came out of her looking dead and purple?

Frank gets up from the sofa and goes into the kitchen. 'I should get back to cabin one.' He washes up his mug and leaves it on the drier. So domesticated. Does he bring order to Celene's life? Is that why they're together?

I try to focus on what's important. Cabin one, that's the base of operations around here.

'Can I come?' I ask.

Frank shoots Celene a look.

'I need to go over the directives for the Mara hit,' he says uncertainly. 'I'm not sure–'

'I won't get in the way. I want to see how this place works. It's... interesting.' A little ego-stroking never hurt anybody. 'Besides, I've been around Mara, there may be some way I can help. Not that I really know anything...'

'Let's all go.' Celene sets her mug on the coffee table next to mine and goes to the door. I'd been hoping for a little alone time with Frank, a chance to pick his brains about my mother, see how much she's brainwashed the campers, but that can wait.

On the way to cabin one, I catch Frank looking at me strangely, but I ignore it. Inside, he goes ahead of us to the operations room and unrolls a sheet of paper, laying it out on a workstation.

'Vinter's mansion,' Celene says as we gather around it, a spotlight illuminating the blueprint.

I try not to look too interested, but Celene must sense I want to know how they're going to execute the job. I've already shown some interest. Perhaps she thinks we'll work through our issues and she'll train me up next. Train me to be a killer.

'This is the entrance hall, and this is the ballroom,' she traces a finger over the plan. 'Most of the guests will be in there, going by my expe-rience of Vinter's parties. But Mara will probably head for the collec-tion, where Vinter keeps the Crook Spear. That's on the first floor, here.'

My gaze runs over the whole plan. Vinter's place is big. Like Buck-ingham Palace big. The kitchens are at the back, and the front of the house contains the ballroom and a couple of living rooms. The first floor has a number of smaller rooms, including a library, and one of those rooms contains the gun.

The spider in my mind cranes forward, attempting to memorise the plan.

'How do you know the Crook Spear's in one of those rooms?' I ask.

'Vinter told me about it the last time I saw him,' Celene says.

'Which was?'

'A month ago, when he assured me I'd have an invitation.' She taps the workstation. 'The gun's the bait. Mara will want to get up there as quickly as possible.'

'Vinter knows you're planning on taking Mara out at his party?'

Celene doesn't blink. 'As far as he's aware, I'm coming for the kicks.'

Vinter's in for a treat.

'And then what? You grab Mara, cuff him and haul him out of there?'

'I'll be the first from camp to arrive because I have an invite,' Celene explains. 'Once I'm sure Mara is at the party, I'll open the gates using the control panel in the entrance hall, letting Frank and the others in. We'll subdue Mara and take him out through the back.' She points to an atrium at the rear of the house that leads into the gardens.

'What about Mara's guards?' They'd be pretty conspicuous at Vin-ter's party in their black masks.

'Vinter won't allow them in. He'll be alone.'

'And if they force their way in?'

'We'll be armed,' Frank says.

'Okay,' I say, filing the information away. I've asked too many questions already, but I'm hoping they think I'm interested in their plan, rather than forming a plan of my own. I wander to the wall with the photos and clippings. My eye's drawn to a photo labelled *Magnus Vinter*. He's undeniably Scandinavian, striking sea-green eyes set into a chiselled face, his blond hair slicked back.

Celene and Frank talk over the floorplan and the room's starting to feel crowded, mostly with my thoughts.

'I'm going for a walk,' I say.

Celene looks up from the blueprint, the spotlight bright on her face. For a moment I think she looks suspicious, but then her gaze softens.

'Be back for dinner.'

I nod and make my way through cabin one, emerging into a drizzly afternoon. I consider going back to Celene's cabin, rooting through her bedroom, but I have no idea when she'll be back and it's too risky. Besides, I really do need to clear my head, so I avoid the camp, slipping into the woods. I walk for a while, my mind crowded with Mara and Bolt and my mother.

I have two nights before Vinter's party. Plenty of time to figure out an attack plan.

CHAPTER THIRTY-FIVE

Celene makes us dinner, but I don't have an appetite. My stomach's sick with thoughts of Mara, what he's doing to Bolt, and I can't go more than a few minutes without Dominic's bloated face bobbing into my mind. His body dangling by the neck like a duck in a Chinatown window.

If my mother's offended I don't eat the vegetable stew, she doesn't show it. She doesn't give much away, which I suppose is what Frances used to say about me. I hate that even though Celene didn't raise me, not even close, there's a shard inside me that's all her. A needle-like sliver of ice embedded deep down and, even if I tore at my flesh, there's nothing I could do to prise it out.

Frances knew how to help me forget about it. Frances got it.

I clench my jaw. Missing Frances isn't going to help.

'I'm going to bed,' I say, leaving the table.

'Sleep well.'

I wish she'd give up the concerned mother act. Balling my hands into fists, I go upstairs and into my room. The room she made for me, with the purple cushions and the wheeling night light. Shutting the door, I check the knife's still in the top drawer, then slip it under my pillow. I doubt I'll have another midnight visit from one of Camp Virtus' unstable residents, but it can't hurt to take precautions.

Just in case, I get into bed fully dressed, hugging my knees to me as I watch the door. There's no lock and the thought of Celene checking in on me while I'm asleep makes my skin itch.

I barely sleep all night. At one point I hear Celene's bedroom door clicking shut, and then it's just me and the shadows in my perfect room. If it really was perfect, I'd be able to sleep, but there's something off about it. It's on the wrong side of Stepford. A dream room, intangible, unreal. A room that imagines me and my mother could have some kind of life together. That we can be happy. That I'll settle here. Bygones and all that.

I must fall asleep at some point, because there's a moment where I'm not in my room any more. I'm soaked to the bone, clawing my

217

way out of a grave, grabbing my swollen belly with filthy hands, dirt prising my fingernails away from the soft flesh underneath. Pain tearing through my abdomen, I scream, and then a second scream joins it. Something slithers wetly from between my legs and, when I grab the shrieking baby, it has my mother's face.

When dreary morning light nudges into the room, I get up and go downstairs. Celene isn't up yet, so I go out and sit on the porch, trying to get my thoughts into some sort of order as morning steals through the camp.

'You're up.'

Celene's coming up the steps to the porch. I'd assumed she wasn't in because her door was closed, but she looks like she's been up for hours. Maybe she's been checking the camp perimeters after yesterday's alarm. I didn't hear her leave. Did I sleep longer than I realised? The thought sends spiders skittering down my spine.

'Hey.'

'Sleep well?'

I nod, though the bags under my eyes probably tell her otherwise.

'I'll get some breakfast on.'

I watch her through the window as she sweeps about the kitchen. I can't help it. Whenever I thought of my mother before, how she'd been in the nineties, I imagined her scratching a living in a filthy squat, maybe eating rats or boiling pigs' heads. I never imagined she'd be almost normal. Like everybody else. Killing aside.

She's a decent cook, too, serving eggs on toast with a sprig of something green. I watch her over the table as we eat, waiting for her to reveal her true face, the one I see in my nightmares, but she's unreadable. She might even look content, in her own quiet way. Does she like having me here? Do I complete the picture of domestic perfection in her head?

We walk in the woods after breakfast, barely talking, just existing together. It feels weirdly easy, being with her. Almost natural. I fight that feeling, knowing it's wrong. Knowing I can't even think about relaxing here.

After lunch, Celene lays things out on the coffee table for the Mara hit. A hunting knife. A mobile phone. A pair of handcuffs.

Watching her, I replay my plan in my head. Or the parts I know already. The catering van. The layout of Vinter's house. The only thing I'm stuck on is how I'm going to get out of the camp without anybody noticing. I'll need wheels. A map of the area.

'Want some fresh air?'

Celene's by the front door. I go after her and we sit on the porch, looking over the camp. A faint mist hangs in the air but it's stopped raining.

'I never thought it was possible to miss somebody you've never known.'

She's staring into the trees lined up behind the cabin opposite, Domhnall's cabin, and I realise she's talking about me.

'You've been my phantom limb for almost twenty years.'

I don't know what to say. I'm trying so hard not to buy into her bullshit, but she's so good at it.

A horn resounds through the camp and Celene shoots to her feet.

The horn sounds again and I jump up.

'Inside,' Celene says, already heading for the steps.

'Another false alarm?'

'Get inside and don't come out until I'm back.'

I'd argue, but she's halfway down the steps, and as I close the front door behind me, I realise I'm alone again. Alone in Celene's home. Before I know it, I'm hurrying up to the landing and then I'm back outside her bedroom door again.

This time I don't hesitate.

CHAPTER THIRTY-SIX

I've stepped inside and it's done.

I've crossed that line.

The smell of something like cedar and fabric softener meets my nostrils and I don't hang back to think about what I'm doing. If it's another false alarm, I probably don't have much time. And if it's Mara, well, that would present a whole other set of problems.

The wardrobe contains a lot of black clothes and scuffed boots. The mirror on the back of the door has a faded sticker of a rock band.

Where are the pagan stick figures and sacrificial knives? I thump the wall at the back of the wardrobe, but there's no hidden alcove. I tug the carpet up in the corner, but the floorboards are firm, revealing no cubbyhole.

This isn't right. I don't have much time; she could come back any moment and I've still not found anything. Sweat breaks out over my top lip and I frantically cross the room again and again, crouching to peer under the bed, then peering behind the bookcase.

Nothing. Not a thing.

I scan the books and they don't help. Some detective novels, more self-help trash, a copy of Winnie-the-Pooh.

One stands out from the rest, though. There's no title on the spine and I realise it's a photo album. I slide it free and flip the cover.

I stare at a miniature version of me. I'm maybe seven years old, scowling at a boy on a swing. We're in a park and I'm unaware there's a camera on me.

'What the–'

Did Celene take this?

I flip the pages and they're all the same. Me outside school aged fourteen. Me walking somewhere, Troll hopping along next to me. Me in a car. Me and Frances at the supermarket.

Me me me.

How did she get these? How the hell did she get them?

I can't believe what I'm looking at. It's a portal into my past, but through somebody else's eyes. Celene said she searched for me after she abandoned me in Enfield, but according to these photos, she found me a long time ago. Has she followed me all this time? Has she been shadowing me my whole life?

The irony of that isn't lost on me.

At the back of the album, there are newspaper clippings.

MAN DIES IN FREAK ACCIDENT.

It's the story about Mr Carmichael, who sliced open his own throat with a malfunctioning power tool.

TEEN DIES IN FREAK SCRAP YARD ACCIDENT.

Troll.

CHARITY WORKER DEATH ROCKS COMMUNITY.

Frances.

They're all here. Everybody I've killed. Collated and preserved.

Did she want me to find this?

She sent me back to the cabin alone. She knew I could do anything I wanted without her supervising. Did she expect me to snoop around and find her little book of the dead?

I want to tear my hair out. The constant doubt is splitting me right down the middle, cracking open my ribcage and dragging my guts across the floor. Any more of this and I'll lose my mind.

Gunfire rattles outside the window and I snap the album shut. I edge over to the window and peer out into the woods at the back of the camp. Dark shapes dart between the trees. I can't tell if they're Celene's fighters or Mara's. I don't know which is worse.

Whiteness flares and the window smashes into lethal shards.

I drop to the floor, pressing myself flat.

Across the room, the closet doors are shredded by gunfire.

A low *whooshing* sound is accompanied by orange light and a flaming object sails through the window. Even as I look up, the wardrobe catches fire.

Gripping hold of the album, I worm across the floor, straining with the effort. The closet's ablaze and choking black smoke ripples over the ceiling. Wood spits and pops.

At the door, I heave myself onto the landing. I reach into the room, grabbing the door and swinging it shut.

That should buy me some time.

A terrible thought hits me.

What if Celene's the one who tried to shoot me through the window?

I know it doesn't make any sense, not after the way she's been. And the album. Why does she have the album?

Racing down the landing, I take the stairs two at a time. At the bottom, I crouch low. The windows don't exactly offer much protection. If somebody's in the cabin opposite, they'll be able to see right inside. I'm a sitting duck.

WHUMP.

Another flaming object ricochets into the cabin on the other side of the encampment and it goes up in flames. Within a few seconds, the front door flies open and a burning figure thrashes out, toppling over the railing and flailing out of sight.

I force myself to take slow breaths. Mara's men have found the camp. Or one of the other factions has. It doesn't matter who's attacking, we're under attack. At least two cabins are ablaze – including this one – and that means soon the entire camp will go up. I need to get out, escape into the woods, hole up somewhere and wait for the siege to pass.

Where's Celene? And Frank? They could be dead. I'm not sure how that makes me feel, so I don't think about it. All I know is that if I stay here, I'm dead, too.

Smoke pours down the stairs and I watch as the kitchen ceiling blackens, begins to buckle.

White lights flash outside. There's the crackle of gunfire. Whoever it is, they've made it into the camp.

I can't go out the front door. They'll shoot me on sight. Same applies to the windows. Is there a back door? I peer round the banister rail into the kitchen, but there's no way out.

My mind works quickly the way a trapped animal's must. It's growing unbearably hot and the thought of burning alive spurs me on.

Crouching low, I shove the photo album across the floor, into the kitchen. On all fours, I crawl after it and duck into the cupboard under the stairs. Not wasting a moment, I seize one of the backpacks and scan the shelves. Tucked into the back is Celene's axe. I grab it and peek out into the cabin just in time to see a burning projectile smash through the front door and land on the sofa. It bursts into flames.

'Great. That's just great.'

I have even less time than I thought.

Squeezing the bag to my chest, I inch into the kitchen and fumble for the album, shoving it inside and zipping the bag up. Above me, the ceiling sags and crackles as the inferno in Celene's bedroom spreads like some furious plague.

Hopping onto the sideboard, I throw open the kitchen window and immediately shrink back behind the wall, waiting for the frame to splinter and shudder under an onslaught of bullets. But there's no gunfire. Whoever was in the woods earlier must have moved on. I peek around the frame.

Still nothing.

Are the odds finally turning?

You're trapped in a burning building. I'd say the odds are as bad as ever.

It's now or never.

I edge onto the windowsill, squatting low, digging my nails into the wood – which is made difficult by the fact that I'm still clutching the axe – and not daring to look down. If I look down, I won't do this, not even with a wall of fire behind me.

The cabin's on stilts. All I have to do is get my feet on them and I'll be able to shimmy my way to the ground.

Positioning myself on the outside of the window, I find myself staring back into the cabin. It's a vision of flames and smoke like velvet. There's no going back now.

For an insane moment, I think of my bedroom – the one Celene made for me – and it's like somebody's skewered my gut with a hook and is tugging it to one side. Come sunrise, my room – the whole camp – will be gone.

The kitchen ceiling collapses.

I cry out as I slip. My heart stops as I'm momentarily airborne, but then I catch hold of the windowsill and my heart's jerking around in my chest like it's trying to escape a leash. I dangle there, my legs kicking thin air, my shoulders screaming.

'Stop being a baby,' I grunt, and heave my legs up, steadying myself against the side of the cabin with my feet.

I look down.

'Shit.'

It seems more than thirty feet now I'm dangling from a windowsill but I don't stop looking down because I've spotted the stilts. They criss-cross under the cabin, like the inside of a jack-in-the-box. If I can inch down just a few metres, I'll be able to slide onto one of the beams and clamber to freedom.

Gritting my teeth, I take the pick axe and slam it into the wood below the kitchen window. Testing it to make sure it's not going to wobble free, I suck in a few short breaths and then let go of the windowsill.

The axe creaks in the wood as I cling to it with both hands, but it stays firm.

My feet fumble for one of the props supporting the cabin, and for a moment I think I'm still too high up, I'll never reach it and I'm going to fall and break my neck and that'll be the end.

Then my feet make contact with something solid.

'Come on, come on, come on,' I whisper, easing myself down, splinters needling my palms. Then I'm on the beam and sliding down it, tumbling onto the earthy ground beneath Celene's home.

I lie on my back for a moment, panting, staring up at the darkness of the cabin's belly, knowing that at any moment the whole thing will collapse. But not yet.

Finally, I pry myself up.

For somebody who's spent her whole life counting the ways the universe has screwed her over, I've been unbelievably lucky these past few days. Alright, I might have ended up in a pit and hunted by a ruthless mobster, but I'm still going. I'm still alive. That has to count for something, right?

The gunfire has been going on for so long now I've grown used to it, but then it abruptly stops, and only the snap of burning wood fills the silence.

I have to move. Getting out of the cabin was one thing. Now I have to get out of the camp. I can only hope that the fighters have all killed each other. At least that way I can just stroll out of this place.

Hands outstretched, I go from beam to beam, heading for the front of the cabin. Then, huddling low to the ground, I scan the area. Not a person in sight. Not a sound other than burning. Plates cracking in the heat. Things falling over as the fire eats away at everything it can fit its teeth around.

Is everybody dead?

This place has been Celene's home for a decade. I turned up and twenty-four hours later it's a pile of ash. Celene can deny the curse all she likes, but I know this place is burning because I'm here. For once, I'm glad. The camp's an abomination. A hiding place for serial killers. They don't deserve it.

I'm going to have to run for the gates.

If I head into the woods, I'll get lost. Woods all look the same. At least the gates lead somewhere. The road will take me back to the motorway and then I'll hitch a ride back to the city.

I count to ten. When there's still no movement, I crawl out from my hiding place and skirt around the building. Then I hop to the next cabin. Still no sign of life. There are only three cabins between me and the gates. My muscles yell at me to run, but that's the stupidest thing I could do. I have to move slowly around the camp until I'm at the gates.

I'm about to move to the next cabin when I hear something. Rustling leaves or a breath. My shoulders tense and I strain to hear so hard I'm sure my ears are bleeding.

Somebody grabs my arm and spins me round.

I stare into Celene's face.

'You got out,' she pants, relief in her voice.

I nod. 'We have to get out of here.'

'The cars.' I remember the jeeps parked outside headquarters and kick myself for not thinking of them earlier. Stealing a car is a much better plan than heading out onto the road unarmed.

She pushes me to one side and surveys the camp.

'We should–' she begins, but I see movement before she does.

CHAPTER THIRTY-SIX

There's the angry clap of a bullet firing, and then we're both on the ground.

Dazed, my ears ringing, I try to figure out what just happened.

Celene's back up in an instant, aiming her gun at a figure on the other side of the camp. She fires and the man goes down in a burst of red. Then she's looking back at me and she's wearing an expression I've not seen before. Her mouth pushes up on one side and I remember what I did.

I saw the man rise from behind the steps, his gun trained on Celene.

I grabbed her and pulled her out of the line of fire.

I saved her.

CHAPTER THIRTY-SEVEN

I'm shaking as we make our way through the camp. My teeth rattle and my head's full of raging fire. Celene's a few feet ahead of me, sweeping forward with the gun clasped in both hands, keeping it high so she can take out anybody who pops up to say hello.

I'm a bundle of raw nerves, my body following her, but my mind's half here and half somewhere else.

The question keeps tearing chunks off me, exposing my bones to the freezing air.

Why did I do it?

Why did I drag her out of the bullet's path?

Why did I save her?

I don't have an answer, and the questions clang through me, like I'm a pinball machine and it can't find the right slot to win the grand prize. All I know is that when I saw the man with the gun, my instinct was to stop him hitting his target.

Because I care about her?

That doesn't feel right.

If you kill her, it goes away.

Dominic's words surface in my mind. He told me I could break the curse by killing Celene. If the shooter had killed her, I'd have been robbed of that chance. I saved her so I could save myself.

'Rumer.'

Celene hisses my name and I snap to attention. She uses two fingers to point at her eyes, and then she gestures to the right. A jeep sits outside headquarters a hundred yards away. The two jeeps behind it are already ablaze, their windows shattered, the metal warping into wretched shapes.

'Quickly,' she says.

I run for the vehicle, tearing the door open.

A crack like thunder echoes across the camp and the window shatters. I throw myself into the jeep, hearing Celene returning fire, and then she appears. I crawl over into the driver's seat and Celene jumps in, slamming the door, slivers of glass shaking loose.

'Here.' She hands me the key and I gulp down the surprise, quickly shoving it into the ignition.

'Rumer,' Celene says, an edge to her voice. I catch movement in the rear-view mirror. Five masked gunmen fan out behind the jeep. Mara's men. They fire at the exact moment I hit the accelerator. The back window explodes, but I don't pay it any attention, revving through the camp. The jeep groans as it's pelted with bullets; kernels of popcorn bursting all around us. I swerve a corner, the gates appearing ahead, and I speed up, preparing to bomb through them.

'Seat belt,' I say, hurriedly clipping mine in. Grimacing, Celene does the same.

I press my boot to the accelerator, the gate drawing closer and closer. We're going so fast I have to clench the wheel to stop the jeep careening out of control, and then the vehicle shrieks and bucks, smashing through the gates, tearing them apart like pages in a book. I pump the accelerator and we shoot through, swerving out onto a dirt track.

'Stay off the motorway.' Celene's voice sounds strange. I notice she's pressing a hand to her shoulder, red oozing between her fingers.

'You're hit.'

'Just keep driving.'

I don't have any problem with that. As we zip down the road, I keep an eye on the woods either side of us, but there are no shapes racing between the trees. No gunmen. Perhaps they're all in the camp. I wonder how many there are and if Mara's with them. I doubt it. He'll be relaxing in his penthouse while the others get their hands dirty.

There are no other vehicles on the road. Nobody chasing us. The track behind us is deserted, bathed in the jeep's tail lights. Red like Celene's hand. I try to concentrate on the road, but as I think of the red oozing between Celene's fingers, I become aware of the blood hammering in my temples and have to remind myself to breathe.

What if it's her turn to die?

Is the invisible clock counting down Celene's life about to go bust? Spit springs and cuckoo feathers over the inside of the car?

It looks like she was hit in the shoulder. Probably just a flesh wound. If it gets infected, though, any number of things could happen. If the bullet's still buried in there...

'What happened to the others?' I ask.

'Frank escaped into the woods with some of the others.' Her voice is fainter than I'm used to. 'Others were shot or burnt.'

'How many?'

'I don't know.'

'Do you think there's anybody left in the camp? Alive, I mean.'

Her voice is smaller still. 'I don't know.'

'How did they find the camp?'

'They must have followed us...'

My shoulders ache and I realise I'm still wearing the backpack. The photo album digs into my back. I want to ask her about it, demand to know what the hell she's been doing all these years, following me without ever showing herself. There'll be time for that later, though. First we need to get to safety.

'The woods,' Celene says. 'There's camping stuff in the boot. We can pitch a tent. They won't find us.'

'No way. We'd freeze to death.'

'Rumer–'

'Just trust me on this.'

I already know where we're going and she won't change my mind. I just have to figure out where we are. When Celene took me to the camp, I was concussed, strung out with exhaustion. I have no idea what route she took away from the wreckage on the motorway. There's a small screen on the dashboard that's probably a GPS but when I dab it, nothing happens. Technology never liked me.

We've got a full tank, so I turn right at a junction and follow a country road through quiet fields, not worrying about where we're headed, trusting that a road sign will turn up eventually. I resist looking in the rear-view mirror, not wanting to see the smoke rising from the camp.

Considering Camp Virtus was meant to be home to the kinds of people who can take down mob bosses, the place collapsed pretty quickly. They didn't seem prepared for the attack.

Had they grown complacent? Celene said she'd been there for over a decade. If nobody had ever attacked before then, it stood to reason they would feel safe, tucked away in the countryside.

Mara proved them wrong.

Celene's gone quiet and when I check her out of the corner of my eye, I see she's barely conscious, staring intensely at the road, not blinking. She's deathly pale and her breathing's shallow.

Finally, road signs start appearing and I recognise the names on them. I steer clear of the motorway, weaving through the B roads. There are hardly any cars out here and, as the gloomy evening turns into night, I start to relax.

When we reach the outskirts of London, I take a breath. This is what I know. Not creaky camps and weird cults. The city is my home, corrupt as it may be. It's good to be back.

I drive through the suburbs, not needing the road signs any more.

Forty minutes later, Celene's eyelids are drooping as I pull up outside the house. The neighbourhood's dark. Most of the street lamps don't work and a shroud-like darkness has settled over the run-down houses.

I pop my door and go round to Celene's.

'We're here,' I say, tentatively touching her shoulder. She peers up at me, her eyes dull slits.

'I didn't mean it,' she mumbles. 'I didn't– I–'

'Come on.' I cut off her rambling, helping her out of the jeep. Getting her into the derelict house is a struggle. I don't have a key for the front door and I have to lead her around the back to the hatch I always use to get into the basement. After a lot of huffing, she's in, clutching her shoulder protectively.

'Just a little further,' I tell her, shouldering her weight, taking her upstairs and leading her down the landing to the room with the black door. I settle her in the Dead Room, then go back to the jeep. The boot contains camping gear, a night light, some sleeping bags and weird foam pillows. I root around a little more and find a first-aid kit.

I grab what I can and lock the jeep.

When I go back into the Dead Room, Celene's slumped against a wall, but she's not unconscious. She's staring at the wall opposite, which is plastered with newspaper reports and pictures of her. Her expression is torn between wonder and horror, like she's not sure if she's asleep or awake, alive or dead. The wall might as well be talking to her. *'Celene Cross, this is your life.'* I doubt she likes what she sees.

'Here,' I say, crouching down and attempting to pry her hand from her shoulder.

'No, no.' She fights me but she's too weak and I firmly remove her hand. It flops into her lap, slick with blood. I pull down the shoulder of her jacket, revealing a war zone of smeared, gloopy red, and snap open the first-aid kit. As I clean the wound, I reveal the ragged circle of flesh where the bullet entered. There's no exit wound.

'I'm going to have to leave the bullet in there,' I say, more to myself than her. 'Safer that way.'

I bandage her up and then rock back on my heels. She looks up at me, raises her bloody hand and touches my face. Her fingers slide down my cheek.

'My girl. What did I do to you?'

Then she's unconscious.

I ease her onto her side, place one of the foam pillows under her head and cover her in a sleeping bag. Then I sit and look at her. She's lost a lot of blood. If she manages to sleep, she'll feel better in the morning. I'm sure it's not the first time she's been shot.

My gaze roams the wall opposite.

This is the only place I know is safe. Was I wrong to bring her here?

Maybe some unconscious part of me wanted her to see. Wanted to see how she'd react to the wall; her life pieced together from snippets and monochrome snaps. My unsettled history referenced in newspaper articles. It paints a pretty bleak picture of us both.

Grabbing the other sleeping bag, I wrap it around me and then sit flipping through the photo album again. Slower this time. Scrutinising every picture, seeing that some seem to have been taken through gaps in fences or from a high window. Across a street. If Celene took them, she was close when she did.

The thought of her following me around for years is darkly funny.

I've always felt like my mother's ghost was breathing down my neck. Now I find out she sort of was.

A strange sensation inflates my chest, pushes my ribs apart from the inside. An odd sort of yearning. I look from the album to the sleeping shape on the floor, then to the wall. I need to remind myself of all the awful things my mother did. Immerse myself in the reports of slaughter and destruction. Remind myself what she did to me. The people who died because of my curse.

And still I saved her. I dragged her down when the bullet snapped at her, and I drove us to freedom, patched her up, cleaned her wound, wrapped her up to sleep, like she was a harmless old lady.

Horror movie shadows twitch across the ceiling. I watch them for a while, imagining they're creating a network of secrets, each connected to the next, like the photos and articles pasted on the wall.

There's no way I can sleep. Somebody's jammed chopsticks into my skull and given its contents a whisk. My eyelids itch like they're plastered with sand, but I can't relax.

The house creaks and I think I hear something. Maybe just the wind. Quietly, I go through the house with the camp light, checking each room, making sure it's as secure as a derelict house can be. I close all the doors, then I return to the Dead Room. Cocooning myself in the sleeping bag, I rest my back to the wall and wait for morning.

CHAPTER THIRTY-EIGHT

My eyes snap open. I feel like I only closed them for a second, but now daylight's struggling through the gaps in the boarded-up window and I can't remember where the night went. I'm still propped up against the wall, wrapped in the sleeping bag. I wince as I stretch my legs out, then notice a thin figure standing across the room.

Celene looks as beaten and bruised as I feel, though she's the one who was shot, so she wins. She has a hand to her shoulder and she's peering at the clippings on the wall. I can't see her face. Is she wearing the same inscrutable expression she always does? Or has the wall undone it somehow?

Her head turns slightly as my movements rustle the sleeping bag, but she doesn't face me.

'This all seems so long ago.' Her voice is husky with pain and exhaustion. 'You really must think I'm a monster.'

I can't deny that; I did, for the longest time, and I'm still not sure I think otherwise. Just because she seems different doesn't mean she is. She's still the person who committed all those atrocities in the nineties. Death followed her, just like it follows me. The only way I can stop it is by killing Mara and – if Dominic was right – my mother. A chill prickles through me.

'What's it like? Killing somebody?' I ask.

Celene contemplates the wall. 'I'm not comfortable talking about that.'

'Because you feel guilty.'

'Because I don't consider myself to be the same person who did those things.'

'But you are.'

'It's not as easy as that.'

Not for the first time, I wonder what it would take to push her over the edge. Make her lose her temper.

'Don't you ever think about the things you did? How many people died?'

Celene doesn't reply and I think maybe we're done talking about

235

that, but then she murmurs something so quietly I lean forward to hear.

'I was an angry person then. I hated everybody. The people I killed, I didn't see them as people. They were a job and hurting them felt good. I suppose I wanted them to suffer the way I had.'

She doesn't explain what she means by that. How she suffered, if she really did, and I'm not sure I want to hear about it. It'll sound like lies anyway. Like her trying to explain away the terrible things she did. How she's the real victim. Yeah right.

The articles on the wall stare at me. Stories of wanton slaughter. On one occasion, she killed teenagers, but most of her victims were criminals, people who knew exactly what they were getting into by allying themselves with mobsters.

'Seems to me a lot of them deserved it,' I say.

'No. They didn't.'

I remember what Frances said to me when she first showed me the derelict house I spent the first four years of my life in.

It's important for a person to know where they come from.

Even if they come from the worst place possible.

Especially then.

My past is standing in the room with me.

Has Celene accepted hers? Or is it a tug of war inside her? Does the guilt hit her in waves, late at night, ice water rushing into her mouth so she chokes? Can't breathe? Begs for mercy?

'You knew where I was,' I murmur.

Celene turns and looks at me. Ashen and slightly bent over, like somebody's hollowed her out. Her hand absent-mindedly goes to her wounded shoulder. At her questioning look, I drag the photo album across the floor.

'I should've guessed you'd find it,' she murmurs.

'You took all these. Some are from when I was a kid.' I try to keep my voice level but the stew of confused emotions keeps threatening to bubble over. 'You've known where I was my whole life.'

'There's a–'

'It looks like stalking. And fear. And not wanting to accept responsibility for anything.'

I can't tell if I'm just imagining Celene swaying slightly, as if my accusation has rushed at her in a gust that her weakened state can't withstand.

'Imagine if I had approached you,' she says wearily. 'Just imagine if I had done that when you had this... view of me.'

My gaze switches to the wall behind her and I hate myself for understanding where she's coming from, at least a little bit. If she'd approached me out of the blue when I was younger, I don't know how I'd have reacted. Probably with my fists. Somebody would've called the police. Troll would've attempted to tackle her to the ground and then he'd have ended up even worse off than he did anyway.

'It would've been suicide,' I say.

Celene doesn't say anything, though she could gloat over the fact that she's right. It sort of annoys me that she doesn't.

'By the time I found you, you were already with a foster family. I hoped you'd be happy, have a good life, be raised by decent people.'

'Ha.'

'I couldn't interfere. I lost any right to you the moment I left you. You stopped being mine.'

Would she be proud of the shard of ice in me that she created, despite her absence? The spider in my mind whispering and watching and constantly looking out for danger?

Celene trails over to her sleeping bag and slides to the ground, still clutching her shoulder. She grimaces, going even greyer than before, but she doesn't say anything about the pain. She nudges the album with her boot, then grabs it and picks it up, turning to the first page.

'Your past is a part of you. Always and forever.'

I want to ask if she regrets leaving me, missing out on knowing me, always keeping her distance, but the words get trapped in my throat and I can't find a way to release them.

'I tried outrunning mine,' Celene continues, staring down at the album. 'I tried hiding. Now I have to tackle it head on.' She pauses. 'It won't be enough. I'll never escape my past, not until it chases me down and buries me in the dirt.'

Does she have the same nightmare as me? Soil cramming into her mouth?

There are no comforting words and I'm not sure she deserves any.

Celene reaches into her pocket and pulls out a phone.

'What are you doing?' I ask.

'If Frank's alive, he'll have tried to contact me.' She slips the phone back into her pocket. No Frank.

'So it's just us,' I say, getting to my feet. 'What time does the party kick off at Vinter's?'

'Seven.'

'Which gives us a couple of hours to get ready. Come up with a plan. Make ourselves pretty.'

'You're not coming, Rumer.'

I don't say anything. Instead, I sidle up to her and squeeze her injured shoulder. She flinches.

'Oh yeah, taking down Mara and his men is easy when you're in such good shape.'

Her gaze burns into me but she knows I'm right.

'You won't get past the front door without an invite,' she says.

'I'm not going as a guest.' I've been thinking about this ever since she told me about the party. I've never been to anything like it, but I've seen enough movies to know how these things work. Big parties like Vinter's require a lot of people. Decorators, chefs, waiters. Luckily, I'm pretty good at being invisible.'Vinter's place is airtight. You won't make it over the garden wall.'

'Trust me.'

'And even if you get in, somebody will notice. Mara definitely will.'

'Which is why I'm not going anywhere near Mara. I'll be in the back, watching, ready to help you.'

'And just how *are* you planning on getting inside?'

'Leave that to me.'

Celene's gaze doesn't break from mine. I'm not asking her permission. I'm offering her a plan she hasn't considered. And she can't stop me going. If she says no, I'll go anyway, and then she'll have no control over me whatsoever.

She probably already suspects that.

And she's right. I'm going to that party but I won't be hiding out back.

I'll be searching Vinter's for the Crook Spear.

CHAPTER THIRTY-EIGHT

Then I'll use it to get Bolt back.

Part Five
THE CROOK SPEAR

CHAPTER THIRTY-NINE

Wind howls across the open road, whipping my hair into my face so I have to keep raking it back behind my ears. I lean against the car bonnet and drag on a cigarette. All part of the show. It's freezing, but that's okay. I'm not against playing on somebody's sympathies, especially when that somebody can get me into Vinter's mansion.

The car bonnet's cracked open so it seems to be mid-gasp, steam puffing out. I've fried the motor out here in the middle of nowhere. Vinter lives north of the city, on the way to Colchester, and there's only one road that leads to his place. Across the field I see the motorway full of weekend traffic and wonder if I've made a mistake.

My watch says it's gone midday but the light's so grey it could be early evening. I tug at the collar of the shirt. It itches like it's got built-in barbs and I feel like an idiot standing out here. I'm all in black. All the better to shadow in. Black shirt. Black skirt. Black tights.

I can wear this to Mara's funeral. Hey, I feel better already.

My mind drifts back to Celene. I used the last of Julian's money to go clothes shopping and I picked up a cheap suit for her, too. Dark, to hide the shoulder wound if it bleeds. The state she was in, though – ash grey, eyes barely open – makes me doubt she'll make it to Vinter's. She has to, though. The plan doesn't work without her. She has a bullet in her shoulder but she's been planning this for months, and I'm pretty sure she won't pass up her chance to confront Mara, send him the way she sent his father, even if it means getting herself killed in the process.

Does she really believe killing Mara will change anything? Cutting off the snake's head usually just creates more. I think of her expression when she said they won't stop coming after her until she's dead. So certain. Her eyes stark smudges.

A vehicle appears on the horizon and I watch as it races closer, anticipation fraying into annoyance when it turns out to be an old van that can't possibly be heading for Vinter's. I've been here for three hours and I'm starting to worry nobody useful is going to come along. I need a rich idiot to take pity on me and get me into the party.

When the driver of the approaching van spots me, he begins to slow down but I wave him on, growing bored, a headache splitting my nerves one at a time. He's the fifth person to think about helping me – being a lone girl in this wasteland has its benefits – but I've moved them all on, frustration causing the spider in my mind to thrash.

Each hour that crawls by is a special kind of torture. It gives me time to get nervous. My plan doesn't kick in until I'm inside Vinter's. And even then, any part of it could fail at any moment. If nobody picks me up I won't even get past the front gates.

Even if I manage to trick somebody into giving me a lift there, who's to say they'll let me in? I wish I'd had more time in the portacabin to study the operation. I could have forged an invitation by copying Celene's or at least got enough intel to blab my way past security.

A pair of headlights appears on the horizon. I toss the cigarette to the tarmac, stub it out with my boot. The headlights draw nearer and my heart raps against my ribcage. Another van.

As it approaches I see what looks like a chef's hat painted on the bonnet.

It's a catering van.

This road goes right past Vinter's, so there's a tiny chance this is the company he's hired to cater the party. This could be my ticket. I step away from the car and throw my arm out.

The van doesn't slow down.

I wave my arm, then put both arms above my head, striding out into the road, the van's engine growing louder and louder until it's a roar fighting the howl of the wind, and then the van shoots by.

'HEY!'

I whirl around, ready to spit. My only way into Vinter's gone in a blast of exhaust smoke.

Then the van's tail lights flash red and it eases over to the side of the road. My hair flapping in my face, I give myself a silent high five and hurry over to the passenger window as it winds down.

A twentysomething girl leans across from the driver's seat. There's a spray of freckles across her nose and her strawberry blonde hair's pulled back into a ponytail. For a second, I think it's my foster sister Pearl. She looks just like those girls who tried to destroy me as a teenager. Joke's on them – now I know exactly how they think.

'Didn't see you there. You got car trouble?' she asks, and she even sounds like Pearl.

'Piece of shit's been threatening to die for weeks. Typical it does it just when I need to get to a job. My boyfriend will kill me if I have to call him out here.'

'Job? Where you headed?'

'The Vinter place. I'd walk it but–'

'Are you with Sophie?'

Thanks for the intel, I think, registering the way her nose crinkles at the name, the way it might when you're talking about somebody you hate.

'She's only my favourite person in the world,' I say in a tone that could either be interpreted as super friendly or unbelievably sarcastic.

'Any enemy of Sophie's is a friend of mine. I'm heading to the Vinter place. Hop in.'

I could kiss her.

'You're fucking kidding. That's insane. Thanks.'

I'm already opening the door, not giving her a second to change her mind, and then I'm inside the van that's going to get me into Vinter's, but I don't feel triumphant, because suddenly I realise this might actually work.

My crazy plan is actually going to work.

And when I come out, I'll have killed somebody for real.

My chauffeur flicks the radio, filling the cab with shrieky pop shit. 'You need to make a call?'

'What?' I can barely hear her over the music.

She turns it down a little. 'About the car. Do you need to call AA or something?'

'Already did, thanks. They should be coming to tow it away this afternoon.'

'Cool. What's your name? You're new, right?'

'Jaime,' I say. 'Yeah, new. I get the feeling Sophie's staff don't stick around long.'

'You're telling me. I'm only sticking it out until college. I'm Lily, by the way.'

Of course you fucking are.

Memories nettle through me. Pearl yelling. Her coven giving me a shared, stinging stare across the school courtyard. Lola calling me 'Oddzilla' and 'Tumour' and a hundred other things so horrible they left lifelong scars.

I push the memories away and force a smile.

'What's the deal with this Vinter guy? He rich?'

Lily's eyes saucer. 'Oh God, don't go there. He's not one of those James Bond billionaires. He's super paranoid about anybody who shows him any interest. I mean, not that you're not pretty–' Her eyes flick over me briefly and it's obvious she's lying.

'Rich guys are boring,' I say, rescuing her from the hole she's digging. 'I've always been more into the hot jocks. Give me a man with biceps the size of my thighs and I'm happy.'

I count the lies as they come out, building a picture of Jaime in my head. She's an art school dropout who thought about studying at law school but then she remembered lawyers are all assholes. She actually quite likes waitressing but only because it funds her art.

Lives alone, but her sister's on the same street.

She's a cat person.

Loves TV shows about rich teenagers.

Lily's saying something about how much she loves jocks, but not the meatheaded ones who go out on a Friday night and drink so much they end up fighting in the street. She likes the sensitive meatheads. You know, the ones who read poetry and can do electrical stuff around the house.

I fight the impulse to throw myself out of the moving van.

Keep it together. Having to share a ride with Lily is nothing compared to what I'm going to have to do this evening. I should be embracing the distraction but all I want is to sit quietly and go over the plan again and again until I know it by heart.

Vinter's profile was pretty straightforward. Inherited his fortune from his mother, a Swedish sculptor whose creations sold for millions all over the world. He collects art and seems to spend most of his time investing in theatre projects. Which, let's face it, means he's probably not interested in female attention. Works for me.

Lily's stopped talking and I notice she's looking at me.

'Sorry?' I say.

'I asked if you've been doing this for long?'

Infiltrating a rich guy's home to steal a cursed artefact I intend to kill with?

'No. A few months. I'm bricking it to be honest.'

Lily waves a hand. 'Just stay out of Sophie's way and you'll be fine. Oh and there'll be so much champagne, they won't even notice we've hidden a few bottles out back for after. Perk of the job, right?'

'Oh yeah.'

'There aren't many– Oh! This is it.'

My grip on my knees tightens as we approach a turning in the road. Lily eases down a tree-lined driveway and my heart feels like it's pulsing in my throat. We roll towards a set of sturdy gates. Beyond them, I glimpse turrets and chimneys high up against the stormy sky.

The van crawls to a standstill at the gates. Lily reaches through her window for an intercom, pressing a button.

I try to relax. I'm Jaime. Nothing suspicious about me. I feel stiff, though, my shoulders ratcheting up around my ears. I unclench my fists and thrust away the doubts. Nobody's interested in me. I'm the help. A bottom feeder funded by the rich socialites on the other side of the gate.

So much is riding on this, though.

And you'd be nervous, too, if you were able to pull a trigger on somebody. Become more than a killer; a murderer.

'Yes?' A voice crackles through the intercom.

'Catering,' Lily sings, grinning into the round bubble that must be a camera.

The gates shudder and then glide open. Lily drives us through and I can't help craning forward in my seat, peering through the windscreen at the Vinter mansion. It's bigger than I'd imagined, with pillars either side of the front doors and statues posing in little alcoves.

'Guy's loaded,' I murmur.

'Shame he's a psycho.'

I sit back. 'What?'

Lily shrugs. 'He pretty much never leaves, and people who've worked for him have these insane stories about what he gets up to in there.'

I didn't read anything about that in the operations room. Either Lily's making it up or somebody's been telling her tales. But then, Vinter knows my mother, so it stands to reason he's unhinged.

We circle an ornate fountain with a marble mermaid, passing into the shadow of the house as we skirt round to the back. This must be the maids' entrance. It's not like we were going to traipse through the front door.

Lily parks up and flashes me a dazzling smile.

'This is it.'

'Thanks. I owe you.'

'You can make it up to me by making Sophie's life miserable tonight.'

'You're on.'

Dammit, Lily. You're actually okay when you're not blathering on about something idiotic.

For a brief moment, I wonder what it would be like if we were friends. I could forget the Crook Spear. Hide out back for the duration of the party, or feign sickness, let Celene and Mara scrap it out. Then I could leave with Lily, say I forgot my keys and crash on her sofa. She'd wake me up with a coffee and we'd talk for a few hours–

'Better get to it, I guess.' Lily opens her door and gets out. My hand twitches for a moment as I reach for the handle.

'Get a fucking grip,' I tell myself.

'Give me a hand with these?'

Lily's at the back of the van taking out trays of food. I go round and she hands me one.

'The kitchen's through there, I think.' She gestures at a small door.

Clutching the tray, I head over, push the door open with my elbow, and just like that I'm inside Vinter's home.

CHAPTER FORTY

The kitchen's enormous. I could fit my whole flat in the sink. It's all silver and white surfaces and the ovens must be on because it's so warm my body's already thawing. I hadn't realised how cold I was until I came inside.

At the workstations, a couple of chefs chop vegetables and throw them into tubs, chatting and laughing. Steam hangs in the air and the smell of cooking meat makes my stomach twist irritably. I've never smelt anything like it.

Countless sharp objects lie around. The ovens are gas, open flames spitting on the hob, chefs getting dangerously close in their uniforms, which could be flammable for all I know.

So many hazards my head spins. If I spend too long in here, god knows what would happen.

'Just put that over here,' Lily says, appearing by my side and loading her trays onto a counter.

'I'm guessing Sophie's not here yet,' I say, doing the same.

'Let me ask Harry. Hey, Harry!'

A tall guy in a chef's uniform looks up from stirring a cauldron of soup. He breaks into a lopsided grin and sets the ladle down, ambling over.

'You're early.' His voice is deep and he has an accent. I can sort of understand why Lily blushes.

'Nina wanted the trays earlier than usual,' Lily says.

'Nina's a pilled-up control freak.'

Nina sounds like a hoot.

Harry's eyes swivel in my direction. 'Who's your friend?'

Something about the way he looks at me is unnerving. His eyes are chocolatey and soft and for a moment I think of Bolt. Why is he looking at me like that?

I put my hand out. 'Jaime.'

He shakes it firmly. 'Harry. You're with Sophie?'

'Unfortunately.'

'You planning on drowning yourself now or after the champagne?'

I'm smiling before I know it. The first time I've smiled for real in a long time. It sends a warm ripple through my abdomen.

'Oh, I want my share of the champagne,' I say.

His laugh is booming, as warm as the steamy air.

I find Lily looking at me strangely, then she shoves Harry. 'Nobody's drowning. Where's Sophie?'

'I banned her from the kitchen until the guests show up.'

'Bet she liked that.'

'Not even a little.'

His lopsided grin returns. Why am I noticing his grin? I feel hot colour flooding my cheeks.

'I'll look for her,' I say. 'It can't be that hard–'

Lily pushes Harry out of the way. 'I'll come with. This place is like a maze. Besides, if I don't report for duty, Sophie will flip.'

Harry sweeps a hand in front of himself, bowing as we pass. 'M'ladies.'

'Such a moron,' Lily says, but as she leads me out of the kitchen, she's different. I struggle to figure out why but then I think of the way her gaze flicked between me and Harry. Why would she look like that?

Jealous.

That's insane. I'm a spectral, knot-haired mess who hasn't slept properly in a week. She must be envious of anybody who takes Harry's attention away from her.

This is dangerous. I'm supposed to blend in, be inconspicuous, let people forget I exist. I've already messed up by being too friendly to Lily. If she ends up following me around all night – or worse, singling me out as some kind of goddamn love rival – I'm screwed.

I stop her in the corridor just outside the kitchen.

'You don't need to come with me. I'm sure I can find Sophie on my own.'

'Don't be silly–'

'Nina wants the trays out of the van, right? I don't want to get you in trouble.'

Lily bites her lip.

'Go,' I say. 'Thanks for the ride. And save me some champagne.'

'Okay. Good luck.' She disappears back into the kitchen.

'Yeah,' I say to the empty corridor. 'Thanks.'

Screw Sophie. She sounds like the queen of Bitchtown and I could really do without the drama. I'm in now. I can dump the pretence, find somewhere to hide, upstairs where people won't be milling about. There's got to be plenty of places to hole up in a place like this. I can watch the party from afar then make my move.

First I'll get the lay of the land. Good to know if I have to make a swift exit.

The door at the end of the corridor opens into a grand lobby that resembles a museum. An elegant staircase sweeps up against one dark-panelled wall and expensive items glimmer on polished tables. Vinter likes to make an impression.

Soft voices come from a room at the front of the house and I follow them to an impossibly large ballroom. Inside, tables are being assembled and covered in white sheets by waiters and waitresses who move hurriedly but quietly, as if they're working a funeral instead of a party. I'll head upstairs before anybody spots me.

I turn back into the hallway and find somebody watching me.

'Who's this?'

The way she speaks tells me this is Sophie. She's not what I expect. Thirties. Brown hair. Average height. A businesswoman.

But her eyes are a supernatural blue and as they pass over me I can't help shivering.

She waits for my answer with reptilian patience.

'Uh, Jaime,' I say.

'What are you doing here?'

Her tone isn't rude, but it's not friendly, either. Sophie's all about efficiency; even her posture's efficient as she stands in the centre of the hall. She hadn't accounted for me and it's thrown a spanner into the works.

'Seth at the agency sent me?' I say, firmly but letting it sound like a question.

The blue circles of her eyes become slivers.

'Seth? Which agency is he with?'

I frown. 'Oh, Franklin's. I– He just gave me the time and address.

He said you'd be expecting me. Though, to be honest, this isn't the first time this has happened.'

'You're not even wearing the right uniform.'

I knot my fingers together in a show of fretfulness that makes me want to smack myself in the face. 'I can call him if–'

But Sophie isn't looking at me any more. She's peering over my shoulder, her jaw setting. I turn and follow her gaze.

A man stands at the top of the stairs. He's only half dressed, his white shirt untucked and crumpled over his smart trousers. His dark blond hair is slicked back and his moustache is stiff with wax.

I recognise him instantly.

Magnus Vinter.

My heart rattles in my chest because he's staring right at me. Vinter is staring at me like he's seen a ghost.

His gaze never leaves my face as he descends. I stop breathing, squeezing my hands together. Why is he looking at me like that?

He murmurs something that must be Swedish as he stops before me, his gaze searching my face. 'Are you…'

'Herr Vinter?' Sophie ventures, her tone less clipped now she's addressing somebody who isn't an idiot.

Vinter's sea-green eyes flicker at me and I smile nervously. Anything to hide Rumer. Push her down by her shoulders and let Jaime clamber up. Not Rumer. Not Celene.

Jaime likes pop stars and fast cars and cheap bars.

He can't know. There's no way he knows I'm her daughter. Celene said she saw him just last month, but he can't know about me. That I'm hers. Besides, I look nothing like her.

Vinter blinks as if emerging from a daydream.

'I'm sorry, for a moment I thought–' His accent is soft, buried under years of English living. If I didn't know he wasn't from here, I probably wouldn't notice it at all.

Sophie's looking at him with a kind of patience that makes me think this isn't the first time she's seen Vinter behaving strangely.

'Is there something I can do for you, Mr Vinter?'

'No, no, Sophie.' Finally, his gaze breaks from me. 'What am I saying? Yes, there is. I wanted to check that the pink roses had arrived.

Mother insists on pink and she'd like to see them before they're placed out.'

'They arrived thirty minutes ago, Mr Vinter. I can fetch a selection now if you wish.'

Vinter still seems distracted. His gaze drifts back to me, as if he can't help it. 'What's your name?' he asks.

I clear my throat. 'Jaime.'

'You're new.'

I nod. 'Seth—'

'Are you from here? London, I mean?'

'Yes.'

I'm burning up under his stare, the way a camera negative sizzles and curls if it's left under a bright light.

He can't know. Unless…

I wonder how truthful Celene's been with me. She said she had connections with Vinter. Was it more than that? He's forty-two, which means he'd have been in his early twenties when my mother sold him the Crook Spear.

Was there something between them? Something more than business?

The spider in my mind shivers and I try to ignore it.

Jaime likes…

'Mr Vinter—' Sophie steps between us and lays her hand on his forearm. 'The roses are being kept in the greenhouse. I can take you now. I won't have another chance. There's still so much to do.'

She begins to lead him towards the lobby.

'I like the new uniforms,' Vinter says.

'What? Oh.' Sophie flicks an annoyed glance at me. 'Yes, not strictly official yet. Jaime, speak to Lily. She'll show you what needs doing if she ever shows up. Oh, Mr Vinter, you'll just love the roses…'

They disappear into one of the rooms off the hallway and I let my breath go in a rush.

What was I thinking coming here? I must be out of my mind. Booby traps are everywhere. Any second one could snap its teeth into my ankle and I'd be down for the count. And what use am I to Bolt dead?

Bolt.

He's the only reason I'm doing this. The only reason I've got myself into this mess. If I can't save him, what good am I to anybody?

I have to keep it together.

Get the Crook Spear, let that bullet do its worst, free Bolt.

Screw the waitress act. I'm in now. I find myself staring at the staircase Vinter came down. The gun's up there and I can't resist its call any longer. It's now or never.

I hurry up the stairs, trying to ignore the nag. I feel more on edge than usual, and not just because of what I'm up to.

Celene? Am I worried about her? More than anything, I'm concerned she won't make it to the party. She's instrumental to the plan and if she ends up bleeding out in the Dead Room, I may as well put the Crook Spear to my head and blow my brains out now.

This is where it gets real.

Either I find the Crook Spear or I cut my losses and go home. This is no different to what I do as a shadow. I'm working a case Julian left under the removable floor in the phone box. That's all.

A pit of yearning unexpectedly opens in my belly. Those were simpler times. All I had to do was follow people and not get caught. Easy when I was Shadow Rumer.

I'm not sure what kind of Rumer I've become.

George said I was different right before Ellis sliced his throat open. That was days ago now. My heart convulses at the memory of him slumped to the floor. So fragile, so kind.

You have to surround yourself with the people who see the good in you.

There won't be any good in me after tonight.

It's almost as if the world wanted to give me a breather for those two years I worked for Julian. A taste of the real world before I was wrenched down into the realm my mother inhabits. Inevitably. Unavoidably. Inescapably.

That life's been at my heels every day since I was born, but I've always managed to outrun it, dart into side passages, turn corners blindly in the hope it won't track me down.

Not any more.

I'm on the landing. Below, a waitress hurries down the hall balancing champagne glasses on a tray. She disappears towards the ballroom.

I creep down the landing. Through a tall window, I glimpse the lawns at the back of the house, immaculate and green. Empty flowerbeds. Tilled earth prepared for a winter snooze.

I could sleep for weeks, my body's so heavy. For a moment I feel the full bone-deep weight of my exhaustion. The past week has taken its toll and I'm not finished yet.

Drawing a curtain over the tiredness, I hurry on. There's no time.

I hear a voice and throw myself through the nearest door. It's a parlour like nothing I've ever seen, except perhaps in Mara's warehouse. Mara would approve of this, a vision of yellow and blue and silver. It's like something out of old movies. I half expect to find Marilyn Monroe draped across a sofa.

Somebody's on the landing outside. Peering through the keyhole I make out Vinter, fully dressed, poised at the top of the stairs. He's impressive, done up like that. He could have stepped out of the past. There's something regal and mysterious about him and maybe a little childish. Like a kid at a wedding.

A quivering voice needles through the door so loudly I think she's in the room with me. She speaks a different language. Swedish maybe. Then pink silk rustles past the keyhole and a grey-faced old woman joins Vinter at the stairs.

'English, mother. Nobody will understand you.'

'The pink is ugly,' she snips. 'My dress won't match the roses.'

'I'll have a word with Sophie.'

She spits what has to be a Swedish swear word. 'She has liar's eyes.'

Mrs Vinter's fine, sharp-angled limbs bend like wire, her hair a woolly scrub fixed with gleaming silver pins. Her son resembles her, though she wears her pride angrily, perpetually half sneering.

If she has it in for Sophie she can't be all bad.

'Play nice, mama.'

He helps her down the stairs, though her back is ramrod straight and she seems to hate his fussing.

A few moments earlier I might have stumbled into them on the landing. I'm relieved I didn't. I have a feeling Mrs Vinter would recognise another battleaxe if she saw one – she wouldn't buy my innocent waitress routine for a second.

When I'm sure they're gone, I move to the large set of doors on the other side of the parlour. All the rooms downstairs were connected by these grand doorways and I'm hoping it's the same up here.

I go into another parlour, this one with a few trinkets on the bookcases, but none of them guns. The next room is filled with taxidermied animals. A tiger mid-pounce. An eagle spreading monstrously large wings.

Still no gun.

I have to pretend I'm invisible.

My hand tightens into a fist.

Invisible.

That's what's wrong.

I was invisible for so long working for Julian I thought I'd slip into Vinter's without anybody noticing. I'd work quietly behind the scenes, then when the moment was right I'd slip away and nobody would be any the wiser because why would anybody pay any attention to pale, boring little me?

Except that hasn't happened. Harry the cook's chocolate brown eyes were all over me. Vinter spotted me from the top of the stairs. And Sophie appeared behind me without me even hearing her.

They all saw me.

I used to be able to follow people for hours without them ever noticing.

What's different?

Me.

I'm different.

That's what has been nagging at me all afternoon. Not worry over Celene or the thought that I won't be able to pull the plan off. It's the fact that I'm not invisible any more. The events of the past week have bent me out of shape somehow. Rendered me corporeal. I was a shadow for so long, I didn't think it was possible to be any other way.

But here I am, talking to people, smiling and doing a job. A real job.

I'm not the Rumer I used to be.

This isn't good.

The next room takes me to the front of the house. Dusk is settling and lamps have been lit along the drive. Cars glide towards the house. I go to the window and peer down, careful to tuck myself just behind the curtain. The guests are arriving. A woman wearing a cleavage-flashing dress kisses Mrs Vinter's hand at the door, then peels her lips back in a predatory smile at her son.

I wonder how many of the guests are here solely to convince Vinter to marry them. Men *and* women. I'm fairly certain the women will all go home disappointed.

I'm about to move on when a man emerges from one of the cars. He hobbles slightly as he approaches the entrance but I'd recognise that big frame anywhere.

'Julian.'

What's he doing here? I left him tied to a chair in the tower block. Rose must've rescued him, but Rose is working for Mara. Is Julian another of Mara's puppets? Is he here for the Crook Spear?

I lean in closer to the window. A faint bruise runs along his jaw, a shadow left by Bolt's fist. We beat him up pretty badly; though not as badly as Ellis the Nicotine Man. I wonder if Mara's retired my mother's old accomplice. I think of the way the hammer felt against his bones with a mixture of horror and excitement.

Just before Julian reaches the entrance, his gaze flickers up at me.

Quickly, I shrink back behind the curtain, my pulse racing. Did he see me? I'm pretty sure I moved in time but my palms have started sweating and I can't think straight. Is he here for me? Or maybe he's one of Vinter's suitors. I honestly wouldn't be surprised.

There's no way Julian would know I'd be here. Even I didn't know until yesterday. Unless Mara's guessed I've joined forces with my mother. I clench my fist, remembering the shard slicing into my palm as I held it over Mara's throat. If Celene had turned up two seconds later, I'd have succeeded in killing him and I wouldn't be here, searching a mansion for a mystical gun.

The gun.

As Julian is greeted at the door by the Vinters, I go to the landing. A hum of voices comes from the ground floor as the guests congregate. I wonder how long it'll be until Celene arrives. If she makes it. An image of her determined face flickers in my mind and I know she will.

I head down the landing, creeping swiftly towards the door on the other side. As I go, I peer through the banister rails at the lobby below, blood thundering in my ears. There's Julian, champagne glass already in one hand, the other hand in his pocket. He looks lonely. His head starts to turn but I'm already through the door, clicking it shut and leaning into it.

How did I ever do this? All that time I spent shadowing people and not once did it feel like this.

Because I didn't care.

The cases I worked weren't personal. There's so much more riding on this than with any of the cheating businessmen I trailed.

I turn and my chest swells.

Cabinets fill the room, each holding expensive-looking artefacts. I prowl between them, ignoring the ceramics, swords and jewels. The gun has to be here somewhere.

When I reach the back of the collection, I rock to a standstill. The cabinet in front of me is filled with guns. Ten of them, all pointing in the same direction, like a school of killer fish. One of them has to be the Crook Spear but I have no idea which. They're all different shapes and sizes.

I press close to the glass, scrutinising each one, remembering the drawing on the wall in cabin one. The sorceress holding the firearm. The image wasn't clear; the gun an indistinct blur of brushstrokes.

Little placards rest below each of the weapons. Every one is inscribed with a country of origin. France. Norway. Japan.

Morocco.

My pulse quickens. Only one of the guns is from Morocco. Red and gold designs swirl over the dark wood and the metal is tarnished with age. It's elegant but nowhere near as ornate as the others.

'Jackpot,' I whisper.

Hastily, I check the cabinet for an alarm. There isn't one.

'You're far too trusting, Vinter.'

Listening to the buzz of voices beneath my feet, I try to gauge if anybody will hear the glass smashing. It's impossible to tell and I don't have a choice anyway, so I turn, crook my elbow, and jab it at the pane. Hairline cracks spread through it and I jab again. It shatters loudly but the buzz of the party doesn't waver.

There's nothing but air between me and the Crook Spear.

Carefully I reach in and lift it from its holder.

I half expect the floorboards to tremble or a ghostly wind to stir.

It's surprisingly heavy as I turn it over in my hands. I inspect the chamber, which only contains two bullets.

Mara was right about something.

One bullet to kill, one to render somebody unkillable.

This is the gun my mother used to murder Mara's father. Now I'm going to use it to complete the circle. I can't help trembling. The gun looks so unremarkable but it's hiding a dark secret. It's cursed, too.

It doesn't react to me, though. I thought maybe it'd be like two magnets coming together. I'd feel some kind of pull or charge. My hair would go static and I'd experience mystical visions, glimpse the farthest reaches of the universe, watch the birth of stars and the death of gods. Instead, I just want to get this over with.

The spider in my mind is restless.

My heard jerks to one side.

A noise from the landing.

I throw myself at another door and make it through just as I hear the main door click open. Not daring to breathe, I listen as somebody quietly enters the room. It could be a guard doing the rounds. Or Julian. Or maybe Mara's arrived and he's gone straight for the goods. That seems unlikely. The party's only just started. You'd think he'd wait a polite amount of time before ransacking the place, unlike me.

Footsteps resound on the floorboards and I'm pretty certain whoever it is has just strolled up to the gun cabinet.

I swallow the lump in my throat, waiting for a shout as they discover the smashed glass, or an alarm being triggered. Instead, the footsteps approach the door I'm hiding behind.

Panic builds in my chest. There's no way I can explain why I'm up here. Or why I'm cradling an old gun in my good hand.

Somebody's right on the other side of the door and I know they're going to come through and find me.

I grab the handle just in time. Somebody tries to push it down and I grit my teeth as I squeeze it up, forcing it not to move. It digs into my bandaged palm and I'm immediately sweating, pain spearing my flesh. I wedge the Crook Spear under the handle.

If the intruder thinks the door's locked he'll give up. He has to.

The handle rattles and I don't think I can hold it for much longer. Then the pressure eases and footsteps ring over the floor. I release the handle, my hand cramping with pain, checking the Crook Spear. It doesn't look like it's been damaged.

'Rumer?'

My heart's in my throat as I whirl towards the voice.

Celene stands in a doorway across the room, little more than a shadowy cutout.

How many goddamn doors does this place have?

'What are you doing up here?' I hiss.

'I could ask you the same question.'

As I stare at her, I realise we're in a library. Books chequer the walls and a couple of leather sofas huddle in the darkness in the centre of the floor. The only light comes in through the door with my mother.

'I got confused,' I say, hiding the gun behind my thigh. 'I was looking for you and–'

'Give it up, Rumer.' Her voice is a low rumble and I try not to let it get to me. 'The gun isn't your concern. If you come with me now, you won't get hurt.'

CHAPTER FORTY-ONE

I drop the act. There's no point. Celene stands in the rectangle of light, a blade of darkness in a black suit, the blazer concealing her shoulder wound. When I left her in the Dead Room, she was bent over, half dead herself. Was it all an act? Now she's holding herself with the arrogance of a prize fighter ready to hurl herself into the ring.

'Is Mara here?' I ask, partly because I'm interested and partly because I need time to think about how I'm going to play this.

Celene steps into the library. 'He will be soon.'

Good. Then we can finally get this party started.

'You have the gun?' Her gaze drops to my hidden hand and I bring the Crook Spear into the light, saying nothing.

'I asked you to leave it,' Celene says.

'I have a tragic history of failing to follow orders.'

'This isn't a game, Rumer.'

'Of course it is, and you don't get to set the rules. Mara wants the gun, I want Bolt's freedom. What do *you* want?'

Celene stops behind the leather sofa on the other side of the library, gripping its back with both hands. Is she imagining crushing my throat? Is she restraining herself?

Come on, mother. Show me your true face.

'I've made my feelings clear,' she says softly, a note of danger in her voice. 'Mara has to be stopped. As soon as he's in our custody, I'm done with this life. I'm leaving it behind for good.'

I snort. 'Like it's that easy.'

'Rumer—'

'No! You're living in a fucking fantasy world if you think you can just move on. People don't change. You're a killer. You'll always be a killer.'

'Give me the gun.'

The spider in my mind thrashes as Celene comes out from behind the sofa.

'Stay out of my way or I'll put a bullet in you,' I growl.

'Give me the gun and Mara will leave you alone. I promise.'

'I don't need your protection. I've survived this far without it.' I raise the gun. 'I'm not kidding. Stop.'

Celene doesn't stop. Her expression's serene as ever, a blank page, as if I haven't got the Crook Spear pointed right at her. The part of me that's her, the shard between my ribs, vibrates, urges me to do it. Pull the trigger. There's one shot left before the Crook Spear loads up the magic bullet. Why not use it on my mother? There would be a kind of poetic justice in that.

She's halfway across the library when Bolt's voice speaks in my ear.

If you had to kill her, could you do it?

My mother speaks in my other ear; the things she said in the Dead Room.

I'll never escape my past, not until it chases me down and buries me in the dirt.

I'm her past. So is the gun in my grip. We're a cosmic force and I feel the curse fizzing inside me, frothing through every sinew, burning and blistering, hardening my skin into armour.

'Please, Rumer. Don't.'

The sound of my name on her lips sets furious sparks spitting in my chest.

The words snap out. 'You lost the right to order me around years ago.'

'I know, but Rumer, I don't think you realise... I'm the only one who understands you.'

'You don't. You can't.'

She's halfway across the room and the Crook Spear follows her. My hand isn't my own any more; it has a mind of its own.

'I do.' Her grey eyes are unblinking bullet holes. 'I know more about you than you could ever imagine, because we're the same. We have the same mind. It's the reason I knew you'd be up here stealing the gun, why I've been able to track you down every time you've disappeared.'

'Stop.'

'I'm you and you're me.' She's speaking so softly it's like she's murmuring an incantation. A spell to subdue me. After everything, she's still trying to control me. She's Eris, the Greek goddess of war and strife and, though we're a pair, inextricably linked, she has powers I'll never understand.

'The only part of me that's anything like you is the part that kills.'

'You've never killed anybody,' Celene murmurs. *Troll. Frances. George. Dominic.*

Their names pump through my veins, a never-ending torture, and she can't possibly understand.

'You made sure I could never have anything, anybody,' I say.

'I want you to be happy.'

'You want me to be alone! You made it so I'll always be alone. If anybody ever gets close to me...'

She's so close now they'd have trouble identifying her if I pulled the trigger. Then she's reaching out, laying a hand on the Crook Spear, and my jaw hurts I'm gritting my teeth so hard.

Time's up.

'Screw this,' I spit.

I wrench the gun away from her, then swing it, clocking her in the face. She falters, white hair concealing whatever damage I've caused. She glares at me and her expression is torn between anger and something else. Fear? Remorse?

'You don't want to do this,' she says.

I've never wanted to do anything more. I throw myself at her and we crash to the floor. The party's a dull murmur beneath us but I only see her crumpled beneath me. I pin her to the floor with my knees and I raise the gun, not knowing if I want to shoot her or hit her again. Before I can decide, she bats my hand away with surprising force and the gun spins across the floorboards, disappearing under a table.

'Rumer, listen—'

I can't listen to any more of her lies. Her words scratch under my skin, drawing blood as they take root and all I want is to shut her up. Make her feel just a little bit of what I've felt since she abandoned me. Left me to become whatever it is I've become.

Not a shadow. Not a woman.

A nothing.

My fist strikes her jaw and for once it's *my* fist. Not hers, not the fizzing, oozing blackness driving me. I want to hit her again and again and again, see her bleed.

I grab her shoulder, the injured one, and she bares her teeth, bucking beneath me. I try to hold her down, but then she pummels my gut and I can't breathe.

There she is. There's Celene Cross.

She shoves me off her and I fumble to my feet, but then my skull's crashing into wood and my mother's got me up against the bookcase, my good hand twisted behind my back.

'Rumer, stop.'

'Showing your true colours,' I pant.

'I don't want to hurt you.'

'Why stop now?'

I take the only route available – I drop to the floor, sliding free and kicking her legs out from under her. Celene lands awkwardly, only just stopping her head smashing into the floor. I'm on her in an instant, burying my fist in her face. She grunts and I catch the scream in my throat as hot pain blazes through my left hand.

She's crushing it, digging her fingers through the bandages, reopening the wound.

I go to punch her again but she catches my fist, shoving me off. I back off, nursing my injured hand, watching as she pries herself up off the floor.

We stand staring at each other, panting, clutching our injuries, and I can finally see her. The blank page has screwed up, revealing shadows and seams. The bullets of her eyes are dirty steel aimed right at me.

'Do you want Mara to get away?' she asks.

'I knew you were in there somewhere. Had to come out eventually.'

Is that what people really see when they look at me? This demented banshee? All hard edges and smothering darkness? A murderous scarecrow?

'Rumer. This isn't the place to talk about this. We *should* talk, but not here. Afterwards.'

'If you get out of this alive.'

'You can threaten me all—'

'You're the one who said it. Half the world wants you dead. More, probably. Only way you're getting out of this is in a body bag.'

It's like I've slapped her again. The wild light dims, her hackles lower.

'I've got to try.'

'Why?' I demand. 'What's Mara really got on you? What are you so afraid of losing?'

I flinch as she moves away from the bookcase, but she's not going for me or the gun, which is still under the table. She walks stiffly to the sofa and leans against it, checking her shoulder under her blazer.

'If I can't redeem myself, I might as well let you shoot me here,' she says.

A floorboard creaks behind me and I whirl around just as Vinter comes in from the landing. I seize the moment, throwing myself at the table and closing my fingers around the Crook Spear.

'What's going on?' Vinter asks, but I'm already across the room, tearing open the door and hurling myself into the collection.

'Rumer!' Celene yells, but I don't listen, rushing onto the landing. I edge over to the stairs and peer through the banister rails. Gowns and suits glide in tides like exotic creatures. I wonder how many spies Mara has here. Lily? Sophie? I can't afford to waste any more time.

If I walk down the main stairs, there's no question I'll be seen, and I want to avoid a run-in with Sophie. If she's even half as good at her job as she pretends, she'll have noticed one of her staff members is missing.

I hurry to the other side of the landing, going through the parlour and descending the servants' stairs. It's a short walk back to the atrium.

I enter the atrium and run straight into somebody.

'Rumer?'

Shit shit shit.

Julian's shocked expression must mirror my own. He's cradling a half-drunk glass of champagne and he seems to have aged a decade in a week. His face is lined and now I'm up close, the shadow on his jawline is even more obvious. Guilt worms momentarily through my abdomen, but then I remember he could be here for Mara and I tighten my grip on the Crook Spear, which I hide behind my back.

For a giant mansion, things are getting uncomfortably crowded.

'What are you doing here?' Julian asks.

'What am I–? What are *you* doing here?'

'Rose dragged me. Said it was the event of the decade or something. Prospective clients all over the place.'

Yeah, I'll bet.

'Seriously, Rumer. What are you doing here?'

'Working.'

His gaze travels the length of my body, taking in the black shirt and jeans, and the shock hardens into something more dangerous.

'You going to tie somebody else to a chair and beat them up?'

'Something like that. And you shouldn't be back here. The party's out front.'

We're the only two people in the atrium, but I've got a clear view of the hall, where guests mill about in various stages of inebriation. Drunk rich people. I can't think of anything worse.

Except maybe what I'm about to do.

'Not really my scene,' Julian says. He seems to remember he's angry. 'You just left me tied up there. What kind of person are you?'

'The kind you hired not to answer questions like that.'

'Consider your employment terminated,' he says.

'I'm glad one of us said it.'

His knuckles are white around the champagne glass.

'Look, Julian, I really don't have time–'

'She found you, didn't she?'

I frown. 'Who?'

'You know who.'

I don't answer him. I have no idea how much he knows. If he isn't with Mara, the less he knows, the better. It could be why he's still alive today.

'I remember when I first saw you.' The angry creases have smoothed out and he's looking at me differently. The way a teacher might look at a student, which is pretty ridiculous, considering the only thing I really know about him is his name. 'You were so raw, so removed, so sad. I don't mind admitting I felt sorry for you. I thought I could help. Give you an income, teach you a thing or two. But it wasn't enough. Troubled children turn into troubled adults.'

He holds my gaze, then knocks the champagne back in one gulp. He tosses the glass onto a cushioned chair and spins to face me with a determined light in his eyes.

'Come with me. Let's get out of here. Neither of us belongs in this sort of place.'

I can't believe what I'm hearing. Bolt and I pulped his face and now he thinks he's a hero. Not just any hero. *My* hero.

'I'm not going anywhere, Julian.'

He leans closer, his boozy breath wafting in my face. 'Pride before a fall, that's what they say. Pride will be your undoing, Rumer. Let me help you.'

He takes my arm.

'I don't need your help.' I shove his hand away.

'You're just a kid. You don't know what's best for you, but I do.'

His fingers dig into my arm and he drags me towards the atrium doors, which lead out into the garden. It's dark outside and nobody would see us if we decided to make an early exit.

I shove him off me. 'You're drunk.'

'And you're not drunk enough.'

'This is pathetic.'

'Please, Rumer. I don't want anything to happen to you.'

Sympathy stirs somewhere in my ribcage. Either Julian's become an Oscar-winning actor, or he really isn't working with Mara. He's just a pathetic loner who runs a detective agency on his daddy's money. He probably only got invited to Vinter's party because his parents are loaded. Julian thinks I'm sad? He should look in the mirror more often.

He opens the atrium door, shooting me a pleading stare.

A rush of air zips inside and Julian looks down at his chest. A wet crimson stain seeps through his shirt.

'Christ,' he murmurs, stumbling to his knees. He raises quivering red fingers to his eyes and I stare at him blankly as he collapses heavily to the atrium floor. Then, instinct kicking in, I grab the door.

Before I can pull it shut, another hand seizes the handle and a figure swishes inside.

'Rose,' I utter.

She smiles coldly, her gown rasping as she shuts the door behind her.

CHAPTER FORTY-TWO

I take a few steps back.

Rose stays by the door, her snake smile unwavering. The sight of her standing there in her violet gown and splashy earrings, pistol in hand, should make me angry, especially as she's just put a bullet in Julian. Instead, my pulse pounds. The spider quivers.

If Rose is here, so's Mara. Just in time.

'You finally found a job that suits you,' Rose says, eyeing my outfit.

'And you look like somebody who charges by the hour.'

The snake smile freezes.

'Rose.' Julian's voice is a rustling whisper that she ignores.

'Do you have it?' she asks me.

There's no point hiding the Crook Spear. The hand behind my back might as well have its own flashing neon sign. I point the gun at her.

Her glacial expression becomes even frostier, her eyes gleaming like diamonds at the Crook Spear.

'Come and get it,' I say.

To her credit, I see her considering it. She's practically licking her lips. I wonder what Mara has promised her. Money? Rose definitely seems like somebody who could be bought. She skipped out on Julian; who's to say she wouldn't skip out on Mara, too?

We're at a standstill. Rose has her pistol pointed at me and I have the Crook Spear trained on her. We squint at each other and I want nothing more than to put a bullet between her eyes, but that'd be a waste of the bullet. I need it for somebody else.

Shrieking laughter erupts at the atrium door and a couple stumble inside.

I share a look with Rose, then we both hide our weapons behind our backs and face the couple who've interrupted us.

'Oh dear, is that red wine?' the woman says, peering at Julian's slumped form. She's late middle aged and very drunk; so drunk that she can't tell the difference between red wine and blood.

The man by her side is considerably younger and more sober.

'That's not wine,' he says, eyeing Julian, then us.

'He had an accident,' I say. 'I was just going to fetch help.'

'He looks like he's been–'

'I'll go,' Rose says.

Like I'm going to let her flit off to Mara. Before she can take a single step, I grab the young guy's jacket and shove him at Rose.

'Please, let me,' I say as they collapse to the floor. 'Sorry, Julian.'

In a flash, I'm across the atrium floor and in the main hall, hearing Rose yelling 'Get off me!' as the older woman shrieks. Guess the booze wore off.

The hall is full of guests, everybody dressed up like it's the Queen's birthday.

'Is there any more champagne?'

A hand snatches my elbow and a red-eyed man peers blearily at me. *You sure you haven't drunk all the fucking champagne?*

'I'll be right back with a fresh bottle, sir,' I say through gritted teeth, shoving his hand away and pushing through the crowd.

'I say.'

A ripple of annoyance bristles through the guests in my wake, and when I throw a glance over my shoulder, I see Rose is attempting to carve a path after me. The guests shrink away from her, part shocked, part irritated as she slithers between them and, for once, Rose's face isn't all porcelain. It's blotched and angry, which I like, because it means she isn't a robot. She's capable of getting pissed off, which is something I can use to my advantage if I have to.

Reaching the lobby, I scan the guests for Mara or my mother, but they're not here.

'Where have you been?'

Sophie, my fake boss, storms over, her face pinched with anger.

I point the Crook Spear at her and her mouth droops, the anger instantly sliding into fear.

'Stay the fuck away from me,' I growl.

She squeaks, raising her hands. A murmur circles me as the guests spot the gun but I can't waste any more time. The crowd splits apart as I head for the ballroom.

'Somebody call the police,' Sophie says.

You do that, I think. *They'll never get here in time.*

The ballroom is full of revellers. A kaleidoscope of affluence so daz-zling I'm momentarily blinded. Recovering, I clamber onto one of the tables, eliciting a wave of shocked complaints as patrons grab their champagne glasses out of the way of my boots.

'MARA!' I shout, scanning the heads. A tide of confused faces rolls in my direction, mouths gaping, whispers hissing between fingers. I wonder how many of them will survive the night. How many of them will get burnt up in my atmosphere.

One face stands out from the crowd because it doesn't look shocked. Beautiful dark eyes flicker at me and painted lips thin into a smile.

The ballroom falls silent.

'Rumer,' Mara says softly. He's wearing a purple kimono, his nails painted black.

I raise the gun at him, but then I see who he's with.

My mother stands beside him.

Static fills my ears and my throat closes up. She said she wanted Mara dead. He was the target, but she looks relaxed, like she's hanging out with an old friend. Is this part of her plan? I thought they were sworn enemies. They'd kill each other on sight. Instead, they're giv-ing me the same half amused glare.

'Come down,' Celene says.

Rose is at Mara's side now, and all three of them stare up at me.

'Join us,' Mara says to me. 'You look like you could use a drink.'

I could use ten drinks, but I don't move. Celene's expression is unreadable again. Has she really forgiven him? I thought she wanted to cut off the snake's head.

'Rumer,' she says. 'Please, come down.'

'You bitch,' I spit. 'Were you working with him all along?'

'If you get down, I'll tell you everything.'

'Let me guess, even more lies. I can't trust anything you say.'

'Then listen to me.' Mara takes a step forward. 'I have never lied to you, Rumer. I have always told you the truth.'

'Or your version of it.'

'I have nothing to gain from lying to you. I wanted you to join me and I wouldn't expect to convince you with lies.'

My arms shake. The gun's growing heavy in my hands. I jump to the floor and approach them, guests shrinking away like I have the plague.

Mara said 'wanted'. He 'wanted' me to join him. Past tense. Has he changed his mind? If he's decided he doesn't want to recruit me, that puts a serious dent in my plan.

'You don't want me in your club now?' I ask.

'Your mother is a very convincing lady.' Mara drags on a cigarette, his smoky eye swirling.

'What have you done?' I murmur at Celene.

'I assured him we could reach an agreement. I'll work for Mara again. It's better this way.'

Better? She's going to kill again? I don't know what to think. What to believe. She was so convincing at the camp. *I don't do that any more,* she said, and she'd looked wounded when I suggested otherwise. Was it all an act? My belly's spitting livid red sparks and they're flurrying up into my chest, spreading a dangerous all-consuming heat.

'Perhaps we should retire to the smoking room.' Mara's so calm it's all I can do not to blow his head off.

'We're staying here,' I say, flicking a glance at Celene. Searching for some sign. Nothing. The gun grows heavier by the second but I don't lower it.

'Celene was just telling me a charming story about you and your friend,' Mara says.

'Where is he?'

'He's quite safe.'

'Like I believe you.'

'Rose?' Mara says. 'Tell her.'

Rose shoots me a glare. 'He says he can't wait to see you so he can knock your teeth out.'

Mara laughs. 'Now, now, ladies. Let's try to keep it civil.' He's aware he has an audience, the other guests watching, half scared, half riveted.

'Your man friend is quite safe,' he says. 'You can have him back if you just give me the gun. Though why you'd want secondhand goods is anybody's guess.'

I won't let him throw me off.

'You take me to him,' I say. 'I give you the gun when I see for myself he's unharmed.'

Mara contemplates me and I can't think how else this can possibly play out. We each have something the other wants. I have no intention of handing over the Crook Spear, not when I know what Mara thinks it's capable of, but for now I have to play along. Make Mara believe I'll do anything to get Bolt back. He's not far off.

Except... my mother's ruined things, I don't know if she's trying to protect me or get rid of me for good but I won't let her take my place. Mara needs to think I'm loyal to him. I need to prove I'm better than my mother.

'Take me to him and the gun's yours,' I say.

'Celene, I think you need to have a word with your daughter,' Mara says. He's enjoying this, playing us off against each other. His good eye sparkles and I want to grab a knife from the table and jab it into his skull to the hilt.

'Rumer–' Celene takes a step towards the table.

'No,' I say.

I look at Celene. My mother. I'm holding the gun she stole. She's the reason all of this is happening. I can't let her mess anything else up. If she really is working for Mara, there's nothing I can do. I have one bullet and it might as well be for her.

But she's making it so difficult. She's unblinking as she stares at me and I hate that she made me feel like this. Like I got to know her. Saw the person instead of the monster. As she stands by Mara's side, though, all I see is a monster. This is her power; her ability to make people do whatever she wants.

I think of Dominic hanging from the beam and I see her hands tying the noose. I think of Frances lying on the kitchen floor and I see my mother standing over her, a blade dripping red. I see George's throat being cut and it's my mother who lets his body drop.

My palms are so sweaty I worry I'll drop the gun. Tightening my grip on it, I aim it at my mother.

'You made me into this,' I say through gritted teeth.

'Rumer–' she begins.

'No. I've heard enough lies. I don't need to hear any more.' Her face was so skeletal when I first glimpsed it in the hotel room. She resembled an emaciated banshee. A phantom come to drag me to hell. And she had to get a final dig in before she killed me because then she played mother. Only for a few days. And for those few days I glimpsed what it might have been like if we'd been other people. A proper family. Or as close to one as I can imagine.

But I know her better than anybody because I am her.

'You haven't changed,' I spit. 'Whatever deal you've made with Mara, it's not enough–'

'Rumer–'

'I said shut up!' The gun trembles and for the first time she looks afraid.

'Girl, you don't want to do this.'

A hand touches my arm and I bury my elbow in the guest's face. She reels back, the sound of popping bone mixing with her scream.

The heat has spread through my entire body and my forehead's sticky with sweat. All I feel is anger and hatred, and it's all for her. All for the woman who made me. I can't ever trust her. She's dangerous. If I let her live, she'll join Mara and go back to her old tricks. More people will die. More Georges and Trolls. She'll start with Bolt.

'Rumer, please–' she says.

'SHUT UP!' My voice isn't my own.

If she speaks, she'll make it worse. This is why she's so afraid of me. She knows I'm the only one who can do it. The only one who sees through her. We'll never be a family. She never wanted that anyway.

'Rumer–' she starts.

I grit my teeth.

'Go to hell.'

She lunges at me and there's a cracking pop.

I've squeezed the trigger.

The bullet explodes from its chamber with such force that the gun bucks in my hand, almost striking me in the face. I get it under control as my mother's knees give.

CHAPTER FORTY-TWO

It went straight into her chest.

The gun that killed Mara's father has killed my mother.

My ears are full of screaming and thumping and the kaleidoscope of revellers spins to life, rushing and rotating around me.

Celene lies on the floor.

Blood stains her shirt, dribbles from her mouth, down her cheek. Pale eyes sightless and staring, her hair splayed in wintry strands.

Vinter rushes to her, bends to the floor. Bends over my mother's dying form. He tugs her up, her head bobbing lifelessly, ghostly white hair spilling into her face.

'Let's go.'

Mara's at my side, tugging me through the tide of screaming mouths. His masked assassins spill through the front doors, shoving guests aside, stopping any of them who are foolish enough to try to prevent me from leaving.

Then we're outside, the wind snatching at me, trying to tear off pieces, and all I know is that I'm gripping the Crook Spear like it's the only thing keeping me alive.

We're bundled into the back of an SUV, the doors slamming, and Mara's grinning face fills my vision.

CHAPTER FORTY-THREE

'You made the right choice.'

Mara's voice echoes and I'm stranded in time. The clock's silent. I'm frozen on the ballroom floor, watching the bullet punch through her chest, and then the Witch Assassin, the Red Widow, Celene, my mother, collapsing, not getting back up.

This is where I'm going to live for the rest of my life. In the moment I killed and meant to.

No more bad luck. No more wrong place, wrong time.

Now I'm a murderer.

Funny, I don't feel free. If the curse is broken, like Domhnall said it would be, there's no way of knowing. The skies didn't hurl frogs to the earth and the clouds didn't crash with thunder.

I wonder if I'll feel free when Bolt's been released. What will we do? With the curse broken, I don't have to worry about spending time with him any more. Could we become friends? For real this time?

My hand trembles around the Crook Spear. It sits in my lap but my hand's still clamped around it, like it's become a part of me. I'm a weapon. Something to approach with caution, never get too close.

I've lived day to day for so long I can't begin to understand what it might be like to have a future, so I shut down thoughts of Bolt and my mother and the curse and I squeeze the gun. It's not over yet.

The final bullet. The one that creates immortals.

'Rumer?'

'She's lost it.'

Rose's voice is a slap, snapping me to. She sits opposite me so we're facing each other, Mara by her side. Our knees almost meet and I shudder at the thought. Rose's expression is as glacial as ever but she can't hide the light in her eyes. I can't tell if it's fear or respect, two things I'd never accuse her of feeling towards me. I don't like it. Not even the fear; she's only afraid because she watched me shoot my mother in cold blood.

'You made your choice,' Mara says, beautiful even next to Rose. His dark hair spills over the shoulders of the purple kimono and the street lights flash periodically through the window, turning him into a flickering animation.

'She was nothing to me.' My voice is flat, emotionless. I hate that we're sitting like this, confronting each other across the back of the SUV so I can't escape their stares.

'She was your mother.'

'Was.'

Mara contemplates me. 'Tell me, who did you kill her for?'

'What do you mean?'

'Was it for the man I have locked up in a cell? For the way she abandoned you?' His dark eyes flash. 'For me? To prove your allegiance?'

I look down at the gun. 'It was the only way I could prove she doesn't control me.'

'You despise her so much yet she's responsible for who you are. So cold, so angry. You'll make for an even better asset than she ever was.'

He's complimenting me for being a murderer? And my mother for turning me into one?

'You hired her to kill your dad, didn't you?' I say.

Mara's smile slips. I've only just made the connection but I can tell by his reaction I'm right.

'It was the only way you could move up,' I say. 'By killing your father, even if that meant losing Celene. Everybody had to think she did it out of jealousy or anger, but she did it for you.'

Mara says nothing but Rose stiffens in her seat. She must not have known.

'You didn't count on Celene betraying you,' I continue, 'selling the gun to Vinter and running off with the money. You figured she'd leave the gun next to your dad's corpse, then disappear. She got you good.'

Mara's lips twist into a grimace and his cheeks flood with colour.

'Pretty careless of you, trusting her with this thing.' I raise the Crook Spear. 'She used the third bullet on your dad, were you planning on using the second on her? That would have left you with the last one, the magic bullet.' I point the gun at him. 'Well, you've got the last one now. Want to find out if the legend's true?'

'Don't be so stupid, Rumer–'

Mara cuts Rose off, grabbing her wrist as I point the Crook Spear at her.

'Maybe we should try it out on Rose instead?' I sneer. 'She's put in her hours for you. If anybody deserves a reward, it's her. Let's see if we can make her a god.'

'Rumer, that would be a mistake.' Mara's voice trembles and sweat beads his forehead.

I slide forward in my seat, slowly bringing the barrel of the Crook Spear to rest against Rose's forehead. I grin, enjoying this more than I've enjoyed anything in a long time. The look of terror on Rose's face. Mara's white knuckles around her wrist.

'What do you say, Rose? Ready to see stars?'

'Get the fuck away from me,' she hisses, though her eyes are saucering and she's crushed herself right back in the seat, as if she's trying to melt through it.

'You'll never see your man friend again,' Mara snaps.

'That card's been overplayed, I think.' I keep the gun resting against Rose's forehead, savouring every second of her unease. Then I slide back in my seat, shrugging.

'Guess we'll just have to wait until we get to yours.'

The look of contempt Mara shoots me only fuels the giddiness setting fire to my insides. Rose looks like she wants to punch me, or throw herself at me, scratch and kick until she draws blood, but she doesn't move. The effort makes her tremble.

Something I've learnt – sometimes it helps being the craziest person in the room.

'I think we're done talking,' I say. 'Driver, put the radio on.'

The driver's eyes flash in the rear-view mirror, first at me, then at Mara. Pale and drained-looking, Mara nods and dance music pumps into the back of the SUV.

'Alright!' I raise my bandaged hand, thrusting it in the air to the beat.

'I told you she's a psycho,' Rose mutters.

'Takes one to know one.' I wink at her. 'So where exactly are we going?'

Mara doesn't look well. I guess that's how a man looks when some-

thing he's fought for is about to get dashed against the rocks right
when it was almost his.

'The warehouse,' he says.

'Seems right,' I say.

CHAPTER FORTY-FOUR

The SUV rumbles down the dirt track and I try not to think about Skinny. The spot where the bullet popped in his skull, blood splattering the window, his limbs flailing as he crumpled into the mud. And me, pressing my foot so hard against the accelerator it's a miracle my boot didn't go through the floor. Tearing away. Leaving Skinny behind, just another name to add to the list.

And now I'm back.

I'm not in the back of a van this time, though, and there's no bag over my head. I'm returning willingly and I want to laugh at the insanity of it all.

Bolt.

His name beats through me. My jaw ticks. I'm so close. At the end of the track is the warehouse where he's being held captive. My free fist curls into a ball as I imagine what they've done to him. He won't have gone easily. He'll have torn chunks out of anybody who came near and they'll have had no choice but to do the same to him. Is he shackled somewhere? Hanging in pieces? Coughing blood?

I swallow the nausea down. Grit my teeth. Order the spider to stop shivering.

I couldn't risk coming here until there was a chance the curse was broken. Me appearing when Bolt was already beaten to shit wouldn't exactly improve his chances of survival.

All I can hope is that it's enough.

I put a bullet in her. She's gone and the curse with her. I hope.

The SUV eases to a stop outside the warehouse. Shadowy figures surround it immediately, phantom-like through the tinted windows. The doors open and Mara slides out. Rose eyes me as she follows him.

My boots hit the tarmac and for a moment I expect Mara's ninjas to seize me and wrench the Crook Spear out of my hands, but I'm just being paranoid. Mara really does want me working for him and he knows that'll never happen if he humiliates me.

'Come,' Mara says, sweeping towards the entrance.

The stink inside the warehouse isn't as bad as I remember. Maybe I've grown accustomed to the reek of death. Mara passes beneath dangling chains, heading for a door with a weathered sign. OFFICE. One of his ninjas goes in before him, then gives him the okay.

A red neon haze hangs inside Mara's lounge. The last time I was here, my hands were bound to a chair. This time, I stroll over the threshold, batting a butterfly out the way.

'I don't know about you, but I could use a drink.' Mara's at a cabinet lined with glass decanters. He pours a measure of cherry red liquor and offers it to me. I ignore it, anxiety burying hooks in my gut. Why is Mara delaying?

'Bolt. Where is he?'

'Your man friend? He's safe,' Mara says, still holding the glass out.

'Take me to him.'

A hacking laugh comes from the other side of the room and a chill runs through me. I squint at a form on the sofa. The guy's face is such a mess it takes me a moment to recognise him. Nicotine Man. Ellis. He survived the basement at George's, but just barely by the look of him.

I see Ellis slicing open George's throat and the red haze in the air boils, flooding my veins. I'm already halfway to the sofa before I'm even aware I'm moving.

'No, Rumer.'

Mara's voice rings through the din in my head. I stop just short of the sofa.

'At least give his bruises the chance to heal before you use him as a punchbag again.'

Ellis isn't laughing any more. His left eye has puffed up into a soft dumpling, but the other one, unblinking, shines with anger and fear.

'I can wait,' I say.

'Stupid cow,' Ellis spits, then he screams, clutching his face where I have clocked him with the Crook Spear.

'No! The gun!' Mara's voice is tight. 'Stop!'

It feels too good to hit him, even if a flash of George's dying face accompanies every blow. Eventually, I'm dragged away.

'Get off me,' I grunt, yanking my arms free of Mara's men, pressing

the Crook Spear to my thigh, rigid with anger. Even if I caved Ellis'
skull in it wouldn't be enough. I'd keep hitting him until he's nothing
but mulch.

I was wrong to go back to George and I was wrong to leave him
in the first place. Nobody can know what Ellis robbed me of. George
could have loved me. He could have been my family. When all this
was over I could have gone back to him.

'I'll take you to your friend,' Mara says, sounding breathless. 'I'll
take you to him. Just be careful with the Crook Spear.'

I nod and Mara whisks the kimono about him as he leaves the
lounge. I recognise where we're going as we cross the derelict main
building, Rose behind me. We pass through a crumbling doorway
and I spot the black square in the floor. The one they tipped me into.

Mara gestures towards it and, tentatively, I approach, making sure
Mara's men aren't about to repeat any of their dirty tricks. A few of
them stand against the walls, clutching firearms and batons. They stare
straight ahead and I'm pretty sure they won't jump me.

I edge over to the grate and peer through the gaps.

'Bolt?' My voice catches and Mara must notice it. He knows my
weakness. Rose sneers beside him but she's nothing to me.

There's no answer.

Through the grate, I can just make out the dull flowers on the dead
girl's dress. She's still there. Still grinning.

I speak louder. 'Bolt? It's Rumer.'

Something rustles in the dark of the pit. I think I hear a whisper,
followed by a cough.

'Rumer?' a voice croaks. It's so faint but my insides somersault. It's
definitely him.

'Bolt, are you okay?'

More rustling and a shape shuffles into view. I can barely see him
in the dark of the pit, but what I do see fills me with rage. He's filthy,
blood plastered over his face, his clothes torn.

But he's alive.

I turn to Mara. 'Let him go.'

'Once I have the gun, he'll be released.' He says it calmly but I can tell the anticipation is killing him. His gaze wavers like he's trying not to look at the Crook Spear and each second is agony.

I point the gun at the ceiling and make sure he can see my finger on the trigger.

'Only one bullet left,' I say. 'You really want me to waste it making that bit of ceiling immortal?'

'You waste that bullet and you'll throw everything away. If you really want to join me, you'll do as I ask.'

'We had a deal,' I say, not backing down. 'Get him out of that pit and I'll hand the gun over.'

'I—'

'Clock's ticking, Mara. Did my mother never tell you about me? About what happens to people around me? You need this bullet more than ever.'

From his expression, I can tell he's heard the rumours.

'Get him out of that pit, and you'll have everything you need to rule London.'

Sweat trickles down one side of his face and I know I've won. He can't take any more waiting. He just wants the gun and he doesn't care enough about me or Bolt to drag this out any longer.

'Bring him up,' he says finally.

Two of the ninjas against the wall hurry away.

I lower the gun.

'Curses,' Mara murmurs. The way he's looking at me now is unnerving, like he's realised he has something on me. He draws himself up to his full height.

'Difficult to predict,' he says softly. 'Curses. How much do you know about yours?'

My lips press together.

'That little? How interesting. You know the basics, I'm sure. What your mother did to you. It must have been torture growing up with that knowledge. That she chose herself over you.'

'Shut up.' I hate that I'm trembling, that anything he says has any impact on me.

'Nasty what she did to you, but then you know what she was capable of. A curse like that, it'd take something big to break it.'

CHAPTER FORTY-FOUR

'It's already broken,' I say.

Mara's eyes become slits. 'You shot her and you think you've broken the curse.' His expression makes my temples throb. 'If only it were that easy.'

'Poor baby,' Rose says.

'Quite.' Mara nods. 'You get cursed, that curse becomes as much a part of you as the blood in your veins. Fused with you forever.'

What's he saying? That killing Celene was for nothing?

'Rumer...'

Bolt stumbles through the door, barely supported by two of Mara's men. He begins to cross the floor towards me.

'Stay back,' I say.

Bolt freezes.

'The gun,' Mara says but my mind's whirring, attempting to make sense of what he's just told me. The curse may not be broken, and if it isn't I'm still dangerous. My gaze flicks over the room, seeing hazards everywhere. Any second, the floor could give or the ceiling could cave in or one of Mara's men could trip and put a bullet in Bolt's head.

Bolt. He's the one who matters. He's the one who deserves to live. I raise the Crook Spear and aim it at him.

CHAPTER FORTY-FIVE

The bullet grants immortality. It'll make Bolt Rumer-proof. I won't have to worry about him ever being affected by the curse. All I have to do is pull the trigger, let the bullet do its thing.

Mara's gone so grey he looks like he's about to drop dead.

'Rumer?' Bolt's voice shakes. 'What are you doing?'

'It's the only way,' I say. The gun trembles in my hand and I grip it harder, trying to steady it. I can't miss.

'Rumer, stop.' Mara's fists are clenched at his side.

'It'll make everything okay,' I say.

Bolt's eyes are wide. 'Get that fucking gun away from me!'

'Don't worry, it's going to be okay.'

'NO IT FUCKING ISN'T!'

'Rumer, we had a deal!' Mara shouts.

'Deal's off.' I clutch the gun in both hands. Bolt's looking at me like I've lost it but he doesn't understand.

'STOP!' Mara yells. His ninjas all aim their guns at me, but he waves his hands at them. 'Don't shoot her!'

'This is the only way.' I need to make Bolt understand.

'Don't shoot me!' Bolt shouts.

'Rumer,' Mara says, 'think about this. You owe me. We have a deal. The Crook Spear belongs to me. We'll find another way to fix you. I'll help you.'

'You can't fix me.' The curse has taken so many people, I can't let it take anybody else. Not Bolt, who's only ever tried to understand me, tried to help me. Because of me, his place was burnt down and he was thrown in Mara's pit. He's suffered enough.

'Bolt, just stand still,' I say.

'ARE YOU FUCKING KIDDING ME?'

'RUMER–' Mara's screaming now. 'RUMER, STOP.'

I look at Bolt, scared, and Mara, terrified, and Rose, her face flushed.

'Rumer, there's nothing wrong with you,' Bolt says. 'Which is sort of funny seeing as you're currently pointing a *fucking gun* at me. But you're not cursed–'

'You don't know–'

'There's no such thing.' Bolt's voice is weirdly steady. 'You make your own luck. You've had a bad run, but things can get better.'

Troll, lying broken in the scrapyard.

Frances, motionless on the kitchen floor.

My mother, a rag doll on the ballroom floor.

I can't watch Bolt die. And if I can't be with Bolt, if I can't have one friend, one person who believes in me, I don't want to be here any more. It's too much.

He'll forgive me when it's over. When he's strong and nothing can hurt him.

You have to surround yourself with the people who see the good in you.

Everybody's screaming so much I don't hear somebody coming up behind me. Pain flares in the back of my leg and I go down. I throw my hands out to catch myself and the Crook Spear spins across the floor, skidding to a halt halfway between me and Mara.

I grunt as a boot digs into my back. Gritting my teeth, I roll over and drag Ellis off his feet. His baton clatters to the floor and he scrabbles for it, but I get there first, burying it in his face. Blood sprays my face and he goes limp.

From the floor I watch Rose lurch for the Crook Spear, Mara right behind her. Before they can get to it, though, Bolt's bending down, reaching out.

A masked mercenary punches him and Bolt topples over. The mercenary goes for the Crook Spear. I cock the baton, then hurl it at him. It whizzes through the air and makes contact with a bone-splitting *crack*. The black-clad figure sags to the ground.

Scrabbling across the floor, I close my fingers around the Crook Spear and roll onto my back, raising it just in time, stopping Mara and Rose in their tracks. Behind them, Bolt grunts as he gets to his feet.

I point the gun at Mara.

'Rumer, it's over,' he pants.

I switch the gun between him and Bolt, my chest heaving, my mind a spinning muddle of curses and cures and death.

'Don't do it,' Bolt huffs as the gun comes to rest on him. He looks fit to drop. I don't know what to believe, but as I look at Bolt, I know I can't shoot him. I could never do that. My gaze flicks back to Mara and maybe it's the crazed expression on his face but I think I see him clearly for the first time.

A madman.

A killer.

I point the gun at him.

'Yes,' he hisses. 'Do it, Rumer.'

'Fuck you,' I spit as I squeeze the trigger.

The gun bucks in my hand and a hole bursts open in Mara's forehead.

CHAPTER FORTY-SIX

Mara collapses.

Beside him, Rose's face twists in shock. She crouches over the body, clasps Mara's shoulder and shakes him. A gurgling sigh escapes his throat, but then he lies still.

'You killed him,' Rose murmurs, but she doesn't look at me. Her gaze is fixed on the Reverend.

I realise I'm almost as shocked as she is. The magic bullet didn't do anything a normal bullet wouldn't. It smashed open his skull and now he's on the floor, a pool of blood widening around his body, and there's no way he's getting up.

No way he's a god.

The stories were bogus. It didn't matter how much Mara believed them, how much he wanted to become supreme leader of the known universe. The bullet did its thing and Mara responded in the way any-body would. By being made totally and utterly dead.

Turns out you can't believe everything you hear.

Mara's men look at each other like they don't know what to do. Cut off the monster's head and its tentacles get all confused.

I struggle to my feet and one of the ninjas goes for me. He gets in a good blow to my jaw but I'm so beaten up now I barely feel it. I hit him with the Crook Spear and he hits the floor face first.

I grit my teeth. 'We're getting out of here, and you're going to let us.'

The remaining ninjas look from me to Rose but she's wilted over the body and clearly making decisions is above their pay grade. They lower their weapons.

Grimacing, I shamble over to Bolt and put my arm around his waist, shouldering his weight. I'm not gonna lie, I'm tense all the way to the door, half expecting one of the ninjas to lodge a throwing star in one of our backs, but then we're through the door and outside and the fresh rain is cool on my skin.

'So much for a magic bullet,' I mutter, still clutching the Crook Spear in my free hand. I tuck it into the back of my jeans.

'I thought you were going to shoot me,' Bolt says.

'So did I.'

He shakes his head, half smiling. 'You're nuts.'

'Don't make me regret saving you.'

'Saving me? You almost shot me!'

'Almost. Let's just get out of here,' I say. Bolt leans against my shoulder and we hobble away from the warehouse, away from Mara and the pit, and I turn my face into the rain, thinking of butterflies and spears and my mother.

CHAPTER FORTY-SEVEN

The story made the papers. How Celene Cross, wanted murderer and known criminal, made a comeback at Vinter's party. How there had been rumours she wasn't really dead, that she was responsible for the murders of a number of mob bosses, but then a dark-haired girl shot her and paramedics on the scene confirmed her death at 9:43 that night.

My emotions are strangers lost in a crowd. They're too painful to chase after, so I stay away from them, only catching them in the corner of my eye when I'm tired or hungry.

I wanted to kill her, make her pay for what she'd done – not just to me, but to all those other people before. But I've killed a part of me, too. The part that knew I'd never hurt anybody on purpose. I have to live knowing I took a life. Two, if we're counting.

Bolt recovers quickly. They roughed him up, but a few good nights' sleep and greasy fry-ups get him back to his usual grumpy self. We stay in the Dead Room but I don't sleep much.

One of the reports about Vinter's ruined party included a line about a young lawyer who survived getting shot. I like to think they mean Julian but I'm not tempted to check up on him. That's a can of worms I'm happy to leave at the back of the cupboard.

On the fourth morning of staying in the Dead Room, I start tugging the newspaper clippings from the wall. My mother's face crumples and the headlines fade before my eyes. They don't stab the way they used to. I crouch down to scrape the brittle pieces of paper into a ball, crushing them together.

'Gonna burn them?'

Bolt's propped up against the wall. I thought he was asleep.

'Bit clichéd,' I say.

'We could make papier-mâché hats.'

'No glue.'

Bolt smiles. 'Sometimes rubbish is just rubbish.'

'Yep.'

I throw the scraps in one of the dustbins down the road, then I go back for Bolt. After prying some nails loose we leave by the front door and get into Bolt's van.

I don't look back as we drive away.

Sometimes rubbish is just rubbish.

CHAPTER FORTY-EIGHT

Autumn leaves crunch under my boots as I wander through the cemetery. If I look back, I'll see Bolt waiting by the gates, but I keep going, looking for the grave I've only ever visited once before.

The wind wrenches at my hair and I rake it back out of my face. I shove my hands into the pockets of my leather jacket and slouch past a tree that stretches skeletal claws towards the sky. Its roots disturb the gravestones around it so it seems something down there has been moving.

Past the tree, I find the grave I'm looking for. Black, dripping letters carved into stone.

CELENE CROSS
BURNS IN HELL

The last time I visited, I was fifteen. I found out it was here from a newspaper article. What else? It made me feel weird, though, so I never came back. Maybe I suspected, even then, that she wasn't really buried here. Whoever's in the ground, it's not her.

'They could've spent a little more on the headstone.'

The woman's voice is behind me.

A chill prickles the nape of my neck. At first I think I've imagined the voice, or that the woman in the grave is speaking to me, but then I screw up the courage to turn.

Her skin's stone grey and she's cut her hair. It's short and wavy. She's swaddled in a winter coat and a scarf. There's nobody else in the cemetery but, if there was, I doubt they'd recognise her. There's no mistaking the steel in her eyes, though, and I realise every muscle in my body has wound tight.

'Ghosts in a graveyard,' Celene murmurs, standing there, just standing there, hands by her sides, no weapons visible. 'Who'd have guessed?'

Not for the first time, I think I've lost my mind. It's finally cracked under the strain of the past week and my brain is spewing phantoms into the autumn air. But she looks solid. Dangerously solid, like she could grab me any second, sink her talons in, unwind my flesh in stringy ribbons.

'Should've known it would take more than a bullet to kill you.' I exhale at last, my voice shivering nerves.

'It almost did.' She's motionless; a hunter with sights on its prey. 'If Vinter hadn't stepped in, I'd be in there.' She nods at the grave but I don't follow her gaze. I'm watching for a flickering muscle, any sign she's about to lurch at me the way she did at Vinter's before I shot her. It's been a week since I killed her and she looks stronger than ever.

'Vinter?' I ask.

Celene's lips split into a parched half smile. 'A good hunter always expects the unexpected. I knew you wouldn't make it easy. Vinter got me out of there after Mara took you. He acted quickly. Saved my life.'

I'm so thrown, it takes me a moment to understand what she's saying. She knew I'd betray her. Am I that transparent or is she just that distrustful? Her own daughter shoots her and she's already got a plan just in case.

'You realise how fucked up that is,' I say.

'Look who's talking.'

'But the papers. They said you were dead.'

'You believe everything you read in the papers?'

Colour floods my cheeks and I scowl. She's right, though. How much of what I've read has turned out to be true? Celene isn't the savage killer the press wrote about – she's more dangerous even than that.

'The press have a price, like everybody,' Celene says. 'It wasn't cheap but luckily neither is Vinter.'

'You wanted to die.'

'Mara had to believe it.'

'You knew I'd shoot you.'

Celene stares at me. She played me, just like she's played everybody her whole life. Was there a small part of her that hoped I wouldn't do it? Did she have a plan B in the event that I couldn't pull the trigger?

The look on her face tells me she knew exactly what I was capable of, even if I didn't.

'You had to shoot me,' Celene says finally. 'I guessed you would get into the party, and I knew you had a good chance of grabbing the spear. It's what I'd have done. Your anger... Those few days at the camp... You hate me. It had to come out some way.'

She strolls towards the grave and I flinch and take a few steps back.

'Relax, Rumer,' she says. 'What's done is done. Luckily, you're a terrible shot. Missed the heart completely.'

'Mara wasn't so lucky,' I mutter.

Her hand's reaching for me before I know what's happening, but it doesn't snap around my throat. It presses into my shoulder and the steel in her eyes flashes.

'What's done is done,' she says again and something in my chest shudders over and over, threatening to spill tears.

My mother's dead again, but this time she came for me. She knew she'd never escape her past unless everybody thought she was dead. She tried it before, with the Thames job, but then she messed up by taking down every major criminal in London who'd ever crossed her. She had to die again.

I don't know what this means. Where we go from here. I wouldn't go back to that camp, even if it hadn't burnt down.

'Was it legit?' I ask, the question occurring to me suddenly. At her blank expression, I add, 'The camp. What you were doing there. Was it all for show or were you really trying to... you know... save the world.'

The corner of her lip tugs into a shape like a comma and I realise mine does the same thing when I smile. All those pictures on the wall of the Dead Room and not one of them showed her happy.

'Legit,' she says.

'But...' I stop. I don't know what I'm trying to say. 'People... I followed loads of them for Julian. Loads. Nobody ever changed. Not the way you did. You were...'

I don't need to say it. We both know what she was.

'Yeah.' She releases the word as a breath. We stare at each other for a moment that fills and stretches with unspoken things and I think she's not going to answer. Because she can't. There *is* no answer. But then she draws a breath and her gaze settles on me, those eyes so impossible to escape.

'People change,' she says. 'They go back and forth and round corners their whole lives. Sometimes they end up back where they started. Sometimes they discover something new. That's what...' She blinks. 'I found out I was going to have a child. It's like... I did something. I created something and it was mine and it was on me if it survived. If it lived. All that death, ending lives, and then somehow I had created it. I didn't know what to do about it.'

Seems to me she still doesn't.

'That's it?' I'm still cynical. I wonder if I'll ever understand her. 'You got pregnant?'

'It was the start of it.' Clearly she doesn't want to discuss her crisis of conscience and, honestly, I don't think I'd understand anything she said.

'What are you going to do now?' Celene asks.

'I'm getting out of the city for a while. Bolt has family up north. We're going to visit. He needs a break, too.'

'That sounds like a good idea.'

My belly flutters. 'What about you?'

'I'm dead, remember?'

'Right.'

We both stare at the grave and then I feel Celene's eyes on me. It seems like she's going to say something, but then she doesn't. The spider in my mind is still. I don't know if the curse was broken when I shot my mother. I don't know if I believe in curses any more.

'Guess I'll see you around,' I say.

She's already gone, but I know it won't be for long. As wild as I am, she's wilder. Like the wind. I turn and stare across the cemetery at Bolt. He raises a hand and I know I'm not invisible any more. I'll never be able to shadow again, but that's okay.

Acknowledgements

It takes a lot of people to spread a Rumer, and I'm eternally grateful to everybody who helped make this book happen. To the beta readers, the early reviewers and, most of all, the pledgers who got *Vicious Rumer* out into the world: thank you.

Special thanks to the editorial team at Unbound, including Kwaku and in particular Craig and Andrew for their fastidious and enthusiastic guidance in all things literary. You whittled this manuscript into something better than I could have ever imagined.

Rumer's early cheerleaders: Troy H. Gardner and Erin Callahan. You always kept the faith and helped me keep mine. And Rumer wouldn't be here if it hadn't been for Rosie Fletcher. You helped me take a germ of an idea and make it grow. You're a brilliant friend and one of the most talented people I know. Thank you.

Finally, obviously, my family. You've always at least feigned interest in my little writing projects (kidding). You've shared in my triumphs, been my avid first readers, and believed in me when I struggled to believe in myself.

Oh, and the women I've never met but who were instrumental in helping me find Rumer. Stevie Nicks. Fairuza Balk. Holly Hunter. Joan Jett. Rose McGowan. You're all Rumer, and I love you for that.

SPREAD THE RUMER!

Reviews give books life, especially if they're posted on big sites like Amazon and Goodreads. If you enjoyed *Vicious Rumer*, please leave a short review and/or a 5-star rating on your bookseller of choice. It really will help keep this Rumer going. Also, tell your friends/family/cat about the book, and if you post photos/reviews on social media, be sure to @JoshWinning and use the hashtags #RumerHasIt and #ViciousRumer. Thank you!

Patrons

Manisha Anand
Francine Anker
Hugh Armitage
Louise Brailey
Louise Brock
Katy Bulmer
Jay Burgesson
Stephen Carty
Tim Coleman
Samantha Collier
Joe Cooke
Lindi Craddock
Paul Cunliffe
Harriet Cunningham
Theresa Derwin
Misti Douglass
Amy Duncombe
Rosemary Evans
Mel Fallowfield
Aileen Fiona
Craig Ford
Giorgia Garavini
Mo Gavin
Sarah Gill
Melina Greenfield
Annabel Greenspan
Sophie Hall
Kevin Harley
Tom Hawker
Paul Hirons
Shari Hollander
Tanya Horeck

Kirsty Johns
Stephen Kelly
Dan Kieran
Zoe Knight
Robin Lee
Justin Lewis
Matthew Leyland
Barbara Long
Edward Long
Debra Lowe
Andrew Lowe
Laura Martindale
Joseph McCabe
Harve McHarve
John Mitchinson
Carlo Navato
Sarah Olsson
Elias Ottmar
Ellie Palmer
Tristan Parker
Katie Pennell
Justin Pollard
Ruth Reyes
Roxanne Ridge
Eva Romarate
Mieneke van der Salm
Al Scott
Sam Sheppard
Patrick Sproull
Sara Tomlinson
Yahaira Toribio
Dayle Towell
Tom Treherne
Anna Treherne
Sarah Tully
Claire Turner

Kathryn Twyford
Simon Vandereecken
Ben Veal
Catherine Walker
Alys Webb
Christine Westwood
Emma Willett
Teri Williams
Daniella Wills
Rachael Winningwallace
Lynsey Withers
Katie Khan Wood
Hannah Wright
Ching Yick